CONNECT WITH KIKI

Join my newsletter!
And stay up to date on my newest titles, giveaways and news!
Want a free—full length— wolf shifter Mpreg novel? Join my newsletter when you get Finding Finn!

———

Join the Pack! Awooooo!
Come hang out with your pack mates!
Visit Kiki's Den and join the pack! Enjoy exclusive access to behind the scenes excerpts, cover reveals and surprise giveaways!

OUTLAW

WOLVES OF ROYAL PAYNES

KIKI BURRELLI

EXPERIENCE THE WOLVES OF WORLD

Wolves of Walker County (Wolf Shifter Mpreg)

Truth

Hope

Faith

Love

Wolves of Royal Paynes (Wolf Shifter Mpreg)

Hero

Ruler

Lovers

Outlaw

1

DIESEL

"IT'S THE NEXT EXIT." Quinlan sat straight, peering through the cracked windshield of the beat-up pack truck.

"What is, kiddo?"

He crossed his arms and dropped his chin in a deep frown. "I'm not a kid, Diesel. Not anymore."

"Oh, you aren't, huh?"

Quin's floppy blond hair hung low over his eyes. One blue, the other the same shade as his pupil. His gaze was yin and yang.

Unhappy yin and yang.

My heart felt like it was lined with thumbtacks that tore holes into me with each beat. The sour taste of Quin's sadness never failed to send me into a tailspin, doing whatever I could to make him happy again. I took the exit, still unsure where he wanted to go. This close to pack lands, there wasn't anything out here but trees and more trees, not that I was above looking at a tree if that was what Quin wanted.

When he didn't offer any directions, I had to be the one to break the silence. "Where now, kid—Quinlan?"

His red lips still curved down, but he looked up long enough to say, "There, at the scorched stump."

Taken over as I was with making him happy, I didn't notice where he'd directed us until we were already there. "Kiddo, this is Suckaface Creek." *Teenaged shifters had been coming here to make out—and hope for more—for decades.*

Quin turned his dichromatic gaze on me, and it felt like he'd punched me in the face. That was desire *in his eyes. Not just in his eyes, but swirling in the air around him. Quin was aroused, and the taste of it made my tongue dry.* "I'm not a kid, Diesel, and I think we've both known that for a while."

"I don't need you telling me what I know, Quinlan." *I never spoke so roughly with him, but the rebellion in his tone brought out my alpha's dominance. Remorse came immediately.*

Before I could rush to apologize, Quinlan's wide eyes narrowed, and he shivered.

Alarms went off in my head, a little too fucking late to stop my dick from taking a sudden, inappropriate interest. "Quinlan—"

"You're my Alpha, right, Diesel?"

Damn right I was, which meant I was smart enough to spot a trap. "You know I am. I know I am. Where's this going, Quinlan?"

At least now maybe he'd tell me whatever it was that had made him so quiet around me recently. I'd noticed the change in him a couple of months ago. His smiles didn't come quite so easily, but his blushes did. I figured it had something to do with him continuing to grow up. Life was confusing enough when you weren't the only human living among wolves.

Puberty was a whole different experience when everyone around you could smell what you were going through, but so far, Quinlan had remained the same, my shadow, companion, friend, and ward.

"Rebecca said—"

"Rebecca? What happened to Mom?"

"She isn't my real mother. We aren't blood-related."

I frowned at the distance Quinlan put between himself and members of his pack family. Rebecca wasn't the woman who'd given birth to Quinlan—we didn't know who those people were—but she was the woman who had raised him. She was also the woman Quinlan had called Mother until right this moment.

I needed to scent Quinlan, bury my nose behind his ear and breathe deeply until I was confident this was all regular teenage rebellion and he was happy and didn't want for anything.

Except he did. He clearly did.

Quinlan turned to me and licked his lips.

The gesture brought my eyes to his mouth and my hand to the door. Shame warred with arousal. This was Quinlan. He was gentle and innocent, in need of protection, not an object of desire. "You aren't related by blood, no. Do you not consider her your mother?"

I'd have the best outcome if I steered the conversation away from the way my wolf responded to Quinlan's new attitude.

"Yes, Diesel," he groaned, sounding appropriately like an annoyed teenager. "She's my mother. But I can call her Rebecca. It's her name, isn't it? Just like I can call you Diesel. Or...Alpha."

Quin didn't know what that title did to a shifter when said from certain lips. He should. He'd lived among shifters since he'd been a small child, and now, he was still small, but not a child.

3

"Do you like that? When I call you Alpha?" Maybe I underestimated what he knew.

My fingers tightened over the steering wheel. Instead of doing something unforgivable, like reaching over and yanking Quinlan into my lap, I gripped the gearshift, throwing the truck into reverse. "I'm taking you home."

His eyes widened, and he pressed on his seatbelt, exploding from behind the restraint. "What? No! Why? You haven't even kissed me!"

"Kissed you? Quin—"

He lunged over the center console.

He didn't have the power of a shifter, not even an adolescent shifter. He wasn't particularly strong for a human, either. Pushing him away would've been easier than blowing a feather aside, and if I had, I could've gone my entire life without ever knowing what Quinlan's lips felt like against mine. Now, I'd never be able to forget his hot kiss, the way his lips shook along with the rest of him. He was nervous and excited and smelled like the forest after the first autumn rain.

He smelled like he was mine.

Not mine to watch over or dote on—though he was still that too.

He just wasn't only that. Not anymore. Not now that I knew the perfection of his kiss. He was so young and yet...

Fuck. Diesel, you're a fucking piece of shit.

It didn't matter what his kisses felt like. It only mattered that he was Quinlan. His innocence needed to be protected, not stolen. Especially not by someone like me. I was a hammer, and someone as precious as Quinlan required a far gentler touch.

When I brought my hands to Quinlan's shoulders, a moan breathed past his lips. There wasn't anything I wanted to do more than to swallow his sounds and taste his tongue, but what sort of a man would I be to take advantage of a mind so impressionable?

"But I'm out of school now. There's nothing keeping us apart. You don't have to stay away from me like that anymore. I've seen your eyes linger on my body. Only recently, and only because I'm watching. I'm telling you I know what that means. And that I want it. I want you."

Jesus, fuck! When had Quinlan gotten so mature? It felt like just last week I was promising him a wolf-back ride around the pack lands if he'd sit for his shots at the doctor. Now, he was kissing me with lips far too eager, saying things I wouldn't even let myself acknowledge.

"I'm not—" Right for you. That was what I needed to say, that Quinlan was too good for a wolf like me.

I was big, so people assumed I was strong. I was that too, but not strong enough to push away that blue and black gaze. Not when his eyes tilted like they did when he was hurt.

I pushed his body back, gently urging him to his side of the truck seat. "It's still too soon."

"Too soon?" Quinlan parroted softly. He frowned and bit his bottom lip. "But just that, right? It's just too soon? You do want me, right? Diesel?"

Fucking, fuck, fuck, fuck! Did I want him? Did a drunk want whiskey? "Fuck!"

Quinlan whimpered, and jerked his shoulders back.

I'd never raised my voice to him, and seeing his fear now wiped away my misgivings. Yes, he was still too young to do any of the things he'd taken me up here to do, but I wouldn't demean his intelligence pretending there wasn't anything between us. My wolf had always been drawn to Quinlan, and that connection wasn't one that had remained static. It grew, matured. "I'm sorry, Quin."

Finally, I let myself pull Quinlan into my lap. He came

easily, his body pliant and trusting despite the way I'd just scared him.

"Did you curse because you don't? You don't want me?" he whispered meekly against my chest.

"No, baby boy, I do want you. But even though you're done with school, it's still too soon. You just graduated. You need to experience more of the world first. Meet some —people."

His lips twisted into a scrunched circle. "You want me to date?"

My snarl shot out of my chest, forgoing the usual route through my mouth. Somehow, I managed to bite the words out. "If you want."

It wasn't fair to Quinlan to stop him from living and having the normal experiences a guy his age should have. Even if it would kill me—if I had to get drunk and have Knox and Faust chain me to a chair somewhere—I'd let Quinlan date...if he wanted to.

His wide, innocent eyes searched my face.

What did he see when he looked at me? What was he looking for? All I knew was that I desperately wanted to be enough. And just the fact that this boy made me desperate was a good reason to keep him at arm's length.

"Why would I date? I know who I want. I'll just wait." He slid back, confidently rebuckling his belt before tugging his shirt down and smoothing his fingers through his hair. Seconds passed, and he turned his head, waiting expectantly.

That was it? He'd brought me here with a mission, and now...

Quinlan's lopsided grin turned my stomach into goo. "I knew you might not kiss me back today. But you will, Diesel. You're mine. I've waited this long. I can wait a little longer."

"Diesel, take the next exit—"

"I fucking know, Knox," I snarled, blinking away the sudden memory. Quinlan was gone, taken from me. I wasn't in the old pack truck, but in the Hummer, and we weren't driving to a make-out spot but to the location of Pierce's mansion.

I looked over once more, like Quinlan would appear simply because I wanted him to. He wouldn't. He was dead, and the shriveled organ in my chest had died with him. It didn't matter that he was dead, though. I saw Quinlan *everywhere*.

My pack brother, Knox, sat next to me, his eyes flaring before narrowing to search my face. Whatever he saw there made his lips twist. Spinning around, he addressed the other occupants of the car. "ETA fifteen minutes. Check your gear." His words were little more than growls.

If it had just been the alpha team—Faust, the twins, Knox, and me—then the mood inside the Hummer would be different. I was eager to put an end to Pierce's traitorous life, but thanks to another cryptic—incomplete, but no less ominous—message from an archangel parent who couldn't be bothered to help their kid until the moment was dire, Sitka, Jazz, and Storri silently rode along with us. Their first mission as a group and we were up against not only a traitor, but one with a weapon of *horror* and *anguish*.

Yeah, that sounded like the *perfect* time for a *take your mate to work* day.

In any other situation, Jazz might've complained that Knox was making them check their gear again. We'd left *being prepared* and had sailed right into *paranoid* a few miles ago.

"Clear," Jazz reported.

"Clear," Sitka added.

"Do you think the others are okay at the house?" Storri asked.

Faust kissed his temple, and I swiftly looked back at the road. Living with my brothers as they found their mates was a little like trying to remember a song, but only ever recalling a few words at a time. "Remember the checklist?" Faust asked patiently.

Storri's cheeks burned, and he nodded, looking down at his body with slight amusement. "Clear."

They'd dressed a kitten up in a lion suit, but Storri was still a kitten. Still had no business waltzing into unfriendly territory where an unknown danger awaited us.

Most of the idiots who had sold their souls to Portal had done so for money or sex. Or money *and* sex. Pierce's contract only listed a mansion and a weapon. Most of the contracts we'd found were held by a demon named Zall-muth, but not Pierce's.

He'd sold his soul to a demon named Thalasso, and for some reason we had yet to uncover, when Pierce said *portal,* he didn't explode into ash like all the others had. There had to be something different about his contract terms, but the contracts we'd uncovered were only photocopies, not the real thing, and they didn't include the terms.

The simple fucking truth was that we had too many unanswered questions to be bringing in people who hadn't trained and weren't ready for combat.

Then again, Sitka had already taken Pierce's left hand. It was only polite to give him a chance to take the other. The nephilim had abilities that made them stronger, and they could turn into wolves and fight—or flee, if the situation called for it.

"Are we still positive this is even the right place?" Jazz asked.

We'd found the location of the mansion the same way we'd found the photocopied contracts. Buried deep at the bottom of a stack of boring accounting paperwork, there'd been a map attached that listed Portal's US-based investment properties. Once we had that, finding out which was given to Pierce was a process of elimination. We'd figured out what all the other properties were used for and had sent that information to Badger and his pack. They'd get started tracking down the contract holders in their immediate vicinity.

Knox reached to get a hold of Jazz's weapons belt and wiggled it to check it was buckled properly. "We aren't positive, but it's likely. It's alright to be afraid."

I snorted. This was a kinder, gentler Knox in the field.

Jazz tossed a balled-up piece of paper that turned into a bat. "I'm not afraid. I want to get Pierce as much as you guys. He hurt you, killed your pack, *his* pack. Tried to kill us, threw Sitka pregnant into a muddy hole. I've got enough righteous anger burning. I won't be afraid for weeks."

Anger was good. It would keep Jazz focused.

It wasn't that the mates weren't capable. Storri had singlehandedly taken out an army of men. But they hadn't trained, and they were *precious*. Not just as nephilim, but as mates. If one of them got hurt...or worse...

I didn't wish that moment on anyone, least of all my pack brothers.

"I need that right hand," Sitka growled. "I've been walking crooked for days."

The twins both chuckled, the sound equal parts unhappy and amused.

The archangels better have been right about needing to bring the mates. If they weren't, and everything blew up in our faces, I didn't care if I had to break into heaven. I'd do it to kick every angelic ass I found.

———

"Do you have a visual?" Knox's quiet question sounded in my ear, but it was Faust he spoke to. Knox and Jazz waited in a field on the west side of the mansion while Faust, Storri, and I holed up in front, staying to the shadows of the surrounding foliage as Faust used his infrared scanner. "I don't see any lights. No movement. Not in the front rooms."

"What does the heat signature say?" Knox asked.

Faust shook his head. "Inconclusive. There's something in there putting off heat, but I don't know what."

"Human? Demon?" Huntley asked. I couldn't see his location, on the east side of the building with Jagger and Sitka. "I'm not picking up anything from here. No heartbeat...no shuffling..."

"We can stalk around, take a reading from every angle—"

"No, that will take too much time. Storri, what do the animals say?"

Storri straightened from his crouch, blindly reaching for his mate. "Nothing. I can't...nothing is responding. It's like... they can't understand me. Or no one's listening."

Knox was silent long enough for me to know the type of uneasy expression that lined his face. "If he's in there and doesn't know we're out here, he will soon. Pierce has all the senses we have and something we don't—a home advantage. Regroup. We're not going in blind and separated."

As we waited for the others to join our position, I searched over the colonial-style estate. The place looked deserted and not just for the few days it had taken us to find the map. Dark green algae grew up twin white pillars separated only by clumps of moss that continued around to the side of the house where it forced the paint to peel. The front windows were all dark, curtains drawn. Spindly, sickly vines twisted up the building face, disappearing inside the structure. Huge plumes of spiderwebs filled the vacant spaces like the place had decorated itself for Halloween.

Knox motioned with his fist for us to make a line formation. "We clear it together. But stay with your team." In other words, mates were to stick to their alphas.

Knox brought Jazz closer to his side, and I surged ahead. As the only unmated among us, I took the lead. If this was a trap, I wanted to be the one in harm's way. It would matter the least if I didn't make it back. My pack would be sad, my brothers angry, but they'd move on. I wouldn't leave anyone behind to mourn their life away.

"Diesel—" Knox caught my arm just above the elbow. "You with us?"

For a long time, we'd been the same, driven by anger. It had been easier to be empty when they'd been empty too. Now, Knox and the others had their mates, and I was left, still empty. "Where else would I be?"

I shook off his hand and trudged forward, taking in the scents as we stalked through the shadows to the front door. Wasting any time sneaking around would just make all of this take longer, and though we'd just gotten here, I already wanted the mates out and back on their way to the hotel.

Pierce's scent was light at the doorway. He'd been here, but not in a while. So he hadn't come straight here after disappearing. As fucking disappointing as that was, I was relieved. Pierce had nearly been successful in taking the nephilim away, using our fear and need to protect against us. He played dirty, and he was smart. Give him the backing of a hellish organization and he became an actual threat. One that we shouldn't face while distracted.

The front door opened with a long squeak, and cold air hit my face, much cooler than the air outside. It carried a scent of must and rotten food, sour and sweet, but muted...old.

Inside was silent. No low hum of an air conditioner like I'd expected. There wasn't *any* fuzzy, electronic static as there would have been in a normal dwelling. Fridges, heating and cooling devices charging in outlets—they all made noise. But if the place had power, nothing was using it. I motioned over my shoulder for the others to follow, and we spread out in the large entrance. A chandelier hung overhead, immense, crystal, and, quite fucking frankly, garish.

Sitka must've agreed because he tsked and shook his head.

Tan drop cloths were draped over every piece of furniture, each covered in more dust than could've reasonably accumulated in a year.

The place wasn't in disrepair. The doublewide stairs leading to the second floor looked intact. The rugs were dirty but not worn. There was a musty smell, but no mold in the air. Time wasn't responsible for this. A leaky pipe wasn't either.

"Do your missions usually take you to places so...ghoulish?" Jazz whispered, his face turned up to the tall ceiling where webs hung like leaves.

Sitka danced through the spooky space, his dark eyes falling on the room around him unimpressed. "Not ghoulish. No ghosts. Nothing."

Only Sitka would sound irritated by that.

"We continue with the plan. Clear the building." Knox

surged forward, Jazz's hand clamped in his. "Even if he isn't here, he might've left something behind."

Hand holding wasn't encouraged in the field. Neither was the way Faust had his arm wrapped around Storri's waist, nor how the twins stood on either side of Sitka, mirroring his movements so he was never more than a foot away from either of them.

Every room on the first floor was exactly the same as the entrance: dark, taken over by insects, with several layers of dust and plates of moldy food that had dried, shriveled beyond recognition. The stairs to the second floor creaked appropriately. When we ascended to the top, I half-expected the sound of rattling chains and ghostly moaning to greet us.

"I don't get it. Why sell your soul for a mansion you let fall to shit?" Huntley remained in step with Sitka, moving where and how he moved.

"This way, we should go this way." Sitka drifted down the hallway to the right. Jazz and Storri trailed behind him.

The vines grew along the hallway walls like arrows directing which way to walk. My wolf howled, urging me to go first, stay in front. There wasn't room to push through with the other alphas clamoring to also be close to their mates.

A flurry of cockroaches scurried along the carpet, passing a red centipede that wiggled down into a crack in the floor. At the same time, the cockroach swarm parted, half taking to the wall. This far down the hallway, I saw spiders, rather than just their webs. A black widow dangled from a single thread in front of my face, spinning in a slow circle like a lazy acrobat.

"Do you feel that?" Jazz whispered.

"Yeah." Storri wasn't the person I expected to hear from next. His voice was soft and his tone questioning.

The hallway looked like it narrowed, but really, it was the walls closing in. The paint and wallpaper peeled off the walls, more and more of it the farther forward we walked. The webs thickened, heavy with insect carcasses and strings of dust bunnies, growing thicker and thicker, making the hallway look like an ever-narrowing tunnel. At the end, there was a single wooden door smeared with dried blood.

"Demon," Knox hissed.

A demon's blood glazed the door, but that wasn't the only scent present. The spicy, rotten egg scent was cut with something sweet. A scent that made the hairs on the back of my neck stand up. It was a *wrong* scent, one that shouldn't even exist, though I didn't know what it was. Just that I didn't want it in my nose or in this space.

"We need in," Huntley, Jagger, and Sitka all said at one time.

I eyed the door, my chest tightening with something that felt most like fear. What would I be afraid of? Other than the mates being harmed, there wasn't a thing that scared me. I didn't give a shit about spiders or creepy bloody doors. So then why was my heart pounding?

Knox hadn't looked once from the door until he blinked sharply and turned to face us. "Wedge formation, every other, an alpha in front and an alpha in back."

He took lead, which left me at the rear. The others arranged between us. In the back, no one could see how my palms were sweaty. I grabbed a clump of dust and rubbed it between my palms so the first thing I grabbed didn't slip out of my hand. And because I wasn't already distracted enough, I thought about how much my Quinlan would've hated a place like this. He'd slept with a nightlight throughout his teens, a fact I'd kept a secret by threat of maiming.

Faust's scanner couldn't get a solid reading, but there weren't any other signs of life inside. No breathing. No heartbeat. The room could be empty for all we knew, but, if we were operating under the laws of Weird Shit Happening, and it was pretty clear from the spider tunnels and the general haunted mansion decor that we were, then *something* was inside there.

Knox grabbed the doorknob and twisted experimentally.

The fucking thing wasn't even locked. It swung open under his hand. Knox held up a fist, telling us to hold. He stepped through the doorway and dropped to the ground.

Faust leapt forward, pushing Jazz back at the same time that Jazz howled and reached into his pocket, throwing a plume of dust. He used his ability to turn it into a sheet. The mirage should've blocked what was inside from seeing us long enough for Faust to dart in and grab Knox, but before he could get a good grip, a huge plume of black smoke, thick as water, poured out from the doorway, darting down the hallway-tunnel, where it crossed behind me and darted back down the other side. The end looped around my backside like a slingshot, propelling me forward, where I slammed into the twins. Sitka poofed away to keep from being crushed by the train of our bodies, but the only place he could see was forward, bringing him farther inside the room.

Dread clenched my throat tighter than a miser's hands on money as my team disappeared, one by one, inside. The black smoke finished slinging us forward and slammed the door shut before spinning back around to where Knox lay passed out on the ground. Jazz lunged forward, knife at the ready as he crouched over his unconscious alpha and peered into the darkness.

Sparks rained down over my head. An arm of smoke shot out, hitting my chest before it pushed me off the ground and pinned me against the wall with my feet dangling and unable to make purchase. I roared, gathering my legs beneath me before pushing off the wall to no success.

There was a sound like blowing air through a straw before another round of sparks illuminated the enclosed space. I tracked movement in the clouds, spotting the flash of something metallic as it swung out like a whip, coming in contact with Faust's face.

The whip reared back, and Faust spun. His cheek bled steadily as another smoky appendage thrust out, holding Faust to the ground and effectively incapacitating over half of our team in *seconds*. I searched the blob of mist in the front of the room. Despite losing portions to hold us down, it never shrank or weakened.

I couldn't get a look at whoever wielded the strange metal whip—the black plumes obscured the shape completely—but whoever it was did so with finesse.

The black blobs shot out once more, coming in contact with the twins' noses. Each alpha fell back, heads hitting the ground at the same time. Sitka snarled, flashing to their side before he whipped his head up at a terrified Storri. He stood in the middle of the chaos, eyes wide as the razor-sharp whip whistled toward him.

Still on the ground, Jazz lunged for his angelic brother, attempting to knock him off his feet before the whip finished its arc and sliced his throat.

I pushed off the wall until I heard a bone crack. Pain shot up my leg, but I hardly felt it. We'd been fucking idiots listening to that goddamn archangel. *A weapon of horror and anguish...* We brought the most important people in our world to a weapon of horror and anguish. We deserved this —Knox, Faust, the twins, and me—but the nephilim didn't.

They'd still die because of it, though.

Sitka shadow-hopped, using the flashlight on Storri's shoulder to land directly in front of him, where he wrapped his arms around his brother and braced himself for the whip's razor edge.

The shadow arm at my chest jerked as if in surprise, letting up just enough for me to slip to the ground. I bounded across the room before ever fully standing, but as I jumped to attempt to intercept the danger and take it into my own skin, I realized there was no need. The whip pulled back sharply, as though recalled with haste before the weapon dropped limply to the ground.

The black plumes didn't clear as much as they separated, revealing a short man with shaggy blond hair, one blue eye, and one black eye. The man wasn't looking at me, but at the nephilim. His face filled with confused, enraged wonder.

The black plumes shrank to about the size of a winter scarf and wrapped around the man's neck.

All the while I stared, incapable of blinking, of breathing, of doing *anything* that would take away the image in front of me. I'd seen him so many times, in so many places. He was there, eating at the table when we ate and in the operations room when we did research. He sat on my shoulder every second of every day and I had to blink, breathe—I had to be *sure*.

"Quinlan?"

He looked at me. *Quinlan* looked at me. His eyes focused on my face, and he tilted his head to the side. I wasn't dreaming. I'd never dream a Quinlan in clothes so filthy. Or in a place so horrible. This was real life. Somehow, my Quinlan was here.

He took a step toward me, the wonder from before turning into rage and fear. "You're not real," he spat.

That was his voice... but it wasn't. "Quin?"

His twilight eyes flashed open, and he lunged forward, fingers out like claws as the black plumes grew and hummed, making the room shake so hard debris fell from the ceiling. And in the middle of it all was Quinlan, screeching at me like I was the devil under his bed. "You're not real! You're not real! YOU'RE NOT REAL!"

Quinlan fell. He'd screamed himself unconscious.

2

DIESEL

QUINLAN FELL INTO MY ARMS, his weight nothing more than a suggestion of mass. I still fell to my knees.

From my peripheral vision, I watched the shadow arm holding down Faust shrink away, drawing closer to Quinlan's skin. Sliding between my hands and Quin's body, the shadow smoothed over him like a protective shell. He was still in my arms, but it was like his body was draped in a thick sheet. I snarled, my fingernails extending to claws. The only thing keeping me from slicing my way through was that I didn't know if cutting the smoke would hurt Quinlan.

Frustration locked my muscles in place. I had Quinlan in my arms, and I couldn't even touch him. This wasn't a dream; it was a nightmare.

"Is it him?"

"Are you sure it is?"

Huntley and Jagger loomed over me, Sitka wedged protectively between them despite the fact they were the ones to get knocked out by the...

"What is that stuff? Hit my face like a brick."

"Was *Quinlan* controlling it?"

Their questions were like flies pinging against my head. I wanted to bat them away, but that would mean loosening my hold on Quinlan, and even though I wasn't touching him, I was *holding* him. He was alive. In Pierce's fucked-up mansion.

The same Pierce who had acted devastated when he *found out* our former pack was dead, that Quinlan was dead. Pierce had sat right across from me, playing like he was tortured by the news. All the while he knew where Quin was. He had him here doing fuck knew what.

I growled, managing to funnel my roar into that single rumbling sound like shoving a tsunami's worth of water through a straw.

"C'mon," Knox said, groggily, but conscious. "We need to fucking regroup and..." He let his eyes land for the briefest second on Quinlan, hanging in my arms. "Figure out what the fuck is going on here."

"He was terrified." Jazz stared, unblinking at Quinlan as he spoke. "When he saw you. He was..."

"Frantic," Storri gasped.

"This is your Quinlan?" Sitka slipped out from between his mates and crouched down, lifting the metal whip from where Quin had dropped it on the ground. Sitka eyed the weapon. Now that it wasn't whipping through the air, I noticed the thing was homemade, held together with fraying tape around the handle. What once had been a long line of chain links had been whittled and sharpened into something that moved like water and cut without mercy. "He is a fighter."

No, that wasn't how my Quinlan was. He'd had no need to fight with me around to protect him.

"Pierce clearly isn't here, but I don't want to linger,"

Faust growled. The cut on his cheek was nothing more than a pink line. His arm draped heavily over Storri's shoulders. With the smoke holding him down, Faust had been powerless to help his mate when he'd been threatened. The alpha's arm shook, the moment clinging to him like grease to a paper bag.

Whatever the mission had been when we'd infiltrated the mansion ceased to matter. Quinlan didn't belong anywhere near this place, and imagining him waiting years to be rescued made me want to rip off my skin. Though the man we found, the one who hid behind smoke and wielded a razor whip, that man hadn't been waiting to be rescued. He'd been on the attack.

"We're leaving." Let Knox try and argue. Faust was right. Pierce wasn't here, and Quinlan needed medical care more than we needed to rip apart his shitty mansion.

He said nothing as I carried Quinlan's unconscious body from the room. I stepped over the threshold, cupping the side of his head so he wouldn't suddenly wake up and see the blood smeared across the door. He didn't wake up, and not even the way the mansion suddenly began to shake could rouse him.

"What the fuck?" Huntley attempted to pull Sitka closer, but his mate refused to leave Quinlan, so Huntley just stepped nearer instead.

Jagger punched a chunk of molding to the ground and away from his mates' heads. "Earthquake?"

I kept Quinlan's head against my chest and continued forward. I didn't care if a fucking tsunami slammed into the side of this place; I was getting my mate out.

The shaking escalated. Rolling seismic waves made running down the hallway more like running through a funhouse. Chunks of molding and plaster rained overhead. The pieces grew larger the closer we neared to the door.

"It's coming down," Knox warned, carry-dragging Jazz forward with an arm twined around his waist.

We ran as a pack back through the mansion, making better time than we had going the opposite direction. My nose burned. The scent surrounding us turned acidic, burning my lungs with each hazardous inhale.

Safety lay feet ahead. It wasn't like the earthquake would stop at the door, but outside, we'd have fresh air and wouldn't have tons of ceiling material and plaster dropping like meteors.

The twins made it there first, pulling Sitka out moments before the chain holding the chandelier in the entrance snapped, sending the once-opulent decorative light smashing to the marble floor. I stuck my shoulder up, hunching so my body acted as a barrier between Quinlan and the sharp shards. The other alphas responded similarly, protecting their mates.

Knox hung back and took the rear, making sure the rest of us were out before leaping from the crumbling structure with Jazz firmly in his arms.

"That was close." Faust wiped the dust from Storri's face before letting him slide down to his own feet. "Is anyone going to try to say that was a coincidence?"

I felt Knox's burning stare, but I didn't look from Quinlan's face to confirm its presence. That had been no coincidence. The timing was too perfect. Somehow, removing Quinlan from that room had set off a chain of events that ended with an earthquake powerful enough to bring a building down.

But only the building.

None of the trees surrounding looked affected. The branches weren't even shaking.

What, the fuck could do that?

Once released from their alphas' protective embraces, Sitka and the other nephilim hovered closely around Quinlan's head, troubled expressions etched over their features. They remained within touching distance the entire way back to the Hummer. Knox, the twins, and Faust formed a protective circle and kept guard as we sprinted quickly through the forest to where we'd stashed the car.

I slid wordlessly into the back row of seats, raising my eyebrows at Sitka, Jazz, and Storri as they attempted to all climb in beside me. Jazz ended up having to sit in the row ahead, but immediately turned around.

Sitka hovered his hand over the black layer of smoke covering Quinlan's body. "It...it feels like him. All him."

Like the smoke was a part of Quinlan's body? No. That couldn't be true. Whatever had happened to Quinlan to give him this ability, it was something new. He'd never presented as anything more than human.

Faust pulled the Hummer onto the highway. The tires couldn't roll fast enough. Knox hadn't mentioned ransacking the place, and the fact that they hadn't would chafe at him later, but I couldn't be the only person eager to put the rubble that used to be Pierce's mansion behind us.

"How many hours back is it?" Storri asked with no small amount of concern. He didn't seem at all bothered by the fact that Quinlan had nearly given him a second smile with his razor whip.

"At least five," Jazz murmured.

"He'll be so scared if he wakes up in the car," Storri murmured.

While the nephilim doted over my resurrected, unconscious mate, in the forward seats, the other alphas discussed the mansion and the weapon we hadn't found there.

"Unless...the weapon *is* Quinlan?" Knox suggested.

"He isn't a weapon," I growled.

"You were there," Knox bit back. "He took us out in seconds. The Quinlan I remember couldn't kill a spider."

He wasn't lying. Quinlan had trouble shooing flies if they were too big or buzzed too loudly.

"Pierce had him, Knox. Who knows what he fucking did to him? Whatever Quinlan did to us today, it was for his own protection—"

"I know that, and I'm not saying otherwise." Knox's words rumbled out in a growl. "We're taking him back. Doc will take a look at him and get him fixed right up. But—"

Of course Knox would want to jump right into connecting the dots. He hated a mystery, the unknown, and right now, everything surrounding Quinlan—how he was here, what he'd been subjected to—was all unknown. As weak as it made me, I needed things to stay that way, at least for as long as I was forced to ride in an enclosed, cramped space.

"No buts. *Fuck*...just...no." I didn't know what I was saying. I'd lost the ability to think in full, coherent thoughts the same moment the black smoke cleared and my dead mate stood on the other side. An hour ago, I'd been empty, acting on memory and instinct. Now, my once-vacant body brimmed with emotion, but the only one I could concentrate on was fear.

When Pierce had come back, seemingly from the dead, the possibility that Quinlan could also be alive planted like a weed in my mind—unwanted and impossible to eradicate. I hadn't shared the thought with anyone. Sharing would've only brought me pity, and I didn't want pity, just like I didn't want to leap directly into pondering all the horrible things that had happened to my mate while I'd been failing to protect him.

Knox let the subject drop, and we drove in a silence that was broken only when one of the nephilim would peek at Quinlan and sigh. The three of them had a bond the rest of us didn't. It sprang up immediately upon meeting and remained, changing only to strengthen. Already, they felt a connection with Quinlan.

"He was so scared," Jazz moaned.

"He'll be fine," I grunted, repositioning Quinlan so he draped more firmly across my chest. All he needed was a bath, rest, and food.

In the back of my mind, I was aware that a bath and food would do nothing to help the terror that had filled his gaze. Nor would it change the way he'd screamed, saying I wasn't real.

Why would he say that? What had Pierce told him?

Quinlan moaned, and I dropped my chin as his eyes fluttered open, all dream-filled and sleepy until our gazes met, and his eyelids wrenched open.

"Quin—"

The black smoke covering his body swelled out like a mushroom cloud, smashing through every window and sending the Hummer careening off the highway and into the grassy shoulder. Knox shouted to the others to brace themselves while I held on tightly to Quinlan, thankful the nephilim had known to buckle up while Faust brought the vehicle to a rocky stop.

"Don't touch me!" Quinlan looked to the broken window, and the smoke there thickened like a pole. He reached out for it, letting the smoke drag him from my arms the moment his fingers wrapped around it.

I crawled after him, clamoring through the same rectangular car window. While the space had been just right for Quinlan to squeeze through, I was more than twice the size of him. The pearled edges of the tempered glass dug into my side, but the pain was negligible in the face of my mate *fleeing* from me.

Opening the damn door would've taken a half second more, but Quinlan's fear and the terror in his voice stole my reason and filled my head with static. "Quinlan!"

He was sprinting over the uneven field toward a line of trees. His blond hair bobbed, his clothes hanging off him in tatters that could do nothing to protect him from the chilly nighttime air.

I didn't know what the others were doing; I didn't fucking care. Quinlan was running *from me*. I'd never seen him run a direction that wasn't toward me and my waiting arms. And yet, he booked it toward the trees trailed by twin tails of smoke.

I was close enough to touch him when one of the black blobs shot back, hitting me square in the chest and sending my body sailing. I hit the ground hard, growling while lunging immediately to my feet and surging forward. An overactive shadow wasn't going to keep me from my mate.

Sitka settled his hand on my wrist. His unexpected touch distracted me long enough for him to say, "He's afraid. Let us try."

Sitka's gaze remained on Quinlan's shrinking figure. He made a small, curious noise before he vanished, reappearing fifty feet forward in the middle of one of Quinlan's smoke tails.

Though the two of them now stood on the other side of the field, I heard Sitka's muffled words perfectly. "Settle, brother, settle. You don't need to run. You are safe with us."

Quinlan didn't know Sitka. He had no reason to believe this stranger, and yet he stopped running and swayed uncertainly on his feet.

"Are you real?" Quinlan didn't look up from the ground when he spoke. The only part of him that moved were his lips. He held the rest of his body stiffly like he was afraid of attracting attention. "You seem real. But things have seemed real before. Are you...real?" His voice rang with such devastating hopefulness, I *needed* to wrap my arms around him. My mate was here, in my sight. He was alive. He was hurting. As his alpha, I had no business breathing until I attended to that hurt.

Sitka didn't answer his question, not directly. "Were you someplace where you didn't feel real?"

Quinlan nodded timidly, like he thought Sitka would start laughing and tell him how stupid that was.

Sitka nodded slowly. "I've been to a place like that. Grew up there. But that place isn't *everywhere*. It can't be. Right?"

"Right?" The word sounded more like a question than an answer.

"This is real. I am real. And you are my brother. *That* is extremely real."

Storri and Jazz reached them, both panting as they lined up beside Sitka.

Jazz doubled over, his hands braced just above his knees. "If you are going to run again, could you point out the direction you're planning on now? Give me a head start?" He wheezed out a dramatic cough. "Wait just, like...at least a minute, man, maybe twenty. You're fast, and I can't swim like Sitka can."

Quinlan's shadows rippled ominously around him.

The four of them stood within sight, but the space

27

between us made me nervous. I stepped closer, and Quin's shadows puffed up like an animal trying to look bigger than they were in order to intimidate a predator. Quinlan wasn't even looking at me, but he felt me there. And it scared him.

"I don't want to run," he whispered. "I'm so tired." His face was pale, his cheeks sunken and bruised.

I'd always held the image of Quinlan as he'd been, all soft curves and rosy cheeks, refusing to imagine him as ash. But the person I looked at now was malnourished and at the end of an already fraying string.

"Then don't run." Jazz reached out his hand.

Knox, the twins, and Faust stood behind me, knowing without me telling them that they needed to stay back.

"Come with us," Storri urged. "We'll protect you."

"From them?" Quinlan challenged, and it took me an extra second to realize he was referring to us. He wanted to know if the mates could protect him from *us. From me.*

"From...?" Jazz's confusion would've been adorable if my heart wasn't splintering. "Don't you know them? Your pack? You are Quinlan, right?"

Quin hissed and shook his head. "I don't...I am Quinlan. But...I can't be sure...what I've seen." His head swiveled to where I stood with my pack brothers, and he shivered. "I've seen so many things. I don't know what is real."

His fear wrapped around him like a shroud. He draped forward, his shadows braced beneath him, holding him upright. A million miles from *exhausted*, Quinlan tottered on his bare feet. The ground was wet and obviously cold, and his toes had to be freezing, but he didn't seem to notice.

"The things you've seen, the things that aren't real, they have to do with them," Sitka stated rather than questioned, jerking his forehead at where I stood uselessly while my mate shivered in fear.

"Always," Quinlan gasped.

"We need a second car," Faust whispered. "He's terrified of us. Jazz can drive, and we'll follow."

I growled, partly because I didn't like Faust making decisions about *my* mate and partly because I should've thought of that first. Forcing Quinlan in this state would do nothing but push him farther away.

Faust assumed my growl meant I disagreed with him. "We can't sit here on the side of the road. We aren't far enough away."

Huntley's shoulder bumped into mine in a silent show of support. "Where do we get a car? I'll hotwire it in a flash, but we're on the side of the highway in the middle of nowhere."

He had a point.

"Is the Hummer still drivable?" Knox asked without taking his eyes off the small group fifty feet from us.

"She'll get us home," Faust grunted. "Gonna freeze our asses off in the process. How did he do that? Damn near sent the Hummer rolling."

Quinlan's eyes darted our way before he sidestepped, putting Sitka between himself and us. "They're whispering about me. How to hurt me."

Distrust that violent didn't come by accident or time. It was cultivated. Crafted. I needed to know what had happened to him more than I needed air. The urge to fix everything warred with my inability to take one step toward the man without sending him into a fear spiral.

"If they are talking about you, Quinlan, it's to figure out how to help you." Jazz leaned in, taking one of Quinlan's hands in his.

I held my breath, exhaling with relief when Quinlan

didn't pull away. If I couldn't be the one to soothe him, then at least a packmate was able to step up.

"Whatever you were shown, whatever you saw about them, it wasn't real. Were you ever shown me? Did you ever see me?" Jazz shook out his curly, crimson mane.

Quinlan's silence was answer enough.

"See, and I've been attached to my alpha's hip since I met him. So if you saw Knox and didn't see me, then it wasn't really him."

"Faust is my alpha," Storri added. "The same goes for me."

"Huntley and Jagger don't even like going to the bathroom without me there."

The twins snorted, but my attention was on Quin peeking over Sitka's shoulder, somehow managing to lift his gaze under all that doubt.

"How can I be sure?" he asked with a hesitant type of hope.

"Don't you feel it? Our bond?" Jazz wasn't bothered by Quinlan's question.

None of the nephilim had attempted to just soothe over Quinlan's terror. They faced it head-on with logic, convincing Quin not that he should forget the danger, but that there wasn't any.

Quinlan answered by squeezing Jazz's hand. Storri saw that and made a noise like a small forest animal before hugging Sitka, Quin, and Jazz in one big group hug. I expected Quin to fight the confining embrace. It had only been minutes since he'd been dead set on running into the wild unknown, but he didn't. He leaned into Storri's comfort like he used to lean into my embrace.

Then the four of them, with my Quin in the middle, trudged back to where the rest of us stood like idiots.

"He's ready," Jazz announced, his eyes flitting to my face briefly before zeroing in on Knox in a silent request for support.

I wasn't going to like this.

"Maybe just the three of us can sit with him in the back? And the rest of you should sit in the front rows...and I don't know. Maybe Diesel can sit in the front seat."

No fucking way was I going to allow Quinlan to remain so far from me for hours—

"You do what's best for your omega." Knox's look turned all knowing and annoying.

Even if I were blindfolded, I'd be able to see that what was best for my omega right now wasn't me. His shadows coiled tightly around him, more like looping tires than a scarf, and when he did look at me, it was briefly and with a fearful, untrusting glare.

I would have—*would*—do anything for this boy. Prone to anxiety attacks and hyperventilating, I'd spent many hours of my life simply watching Quinlan breathe and pacing his breaths with mine until he'd calmed down. I'd face any danger and submit myself to every kind of torture if it would help Quinlan, and yet here I was, torn apart because my mate wanted to sit a little bit away from me.

I growled and snatched the keys from Faust. "I'll drive."

———

WE MADE it back to the hotel without another incident, other than learning there was nothing online, not on the local geological boards, nor with the USGS, about the earthquake we'd experienced. No one recorded any strange readings in the area. It was as if it hadn't happened. But how could an earthquake be strong enough to bring a mansion down, and yet no one else in the world seemed to have noticed it?

That mystery was secondary to what Pierce had done to convince my mate that I was a danger to him. Throughout the drive, I felt his eyes on me, though when I looked up in the rearview, his damn shadows were always there, obscuring his face from me. I stayed silent as I drove. The two times I'd tried to say something to Knox, Quinlan had startled in the backseat and whimpered into Storri's neck.

When I could catch glimpses of his face, all I saw was terror and the smallest sliver of hope. It was the hope that kept my heart beating and my lungs breathing.

Dr. Tiffany met us at the hotel entrance and held the door open so Quinlan could be herded inside by his entourage. The doc looked reasonably confused by not only the shadow-clad man, but the way he continued to shoot death glares at me over his shoulder while the nephilim treated him like he was porcelain wrapped in crystal.

At least one thing was going right.

I lingered in the hallway during his exam, bath, and a small meal. Quinlan didn't speak a word to the doctor during his exam. He would answer some of her questions if one of the nephilim asked him instead, so she was able to get the information she needed. Dr. Tiff said she was surprised at how healthy Quin was, and I barely stopped myself from puffing up with pride. If Quin was healthy, that had nothing to do with me.

When he'd finished eating and they began discussing where Quinlan would sleep for the night, my shoulders seized, and a dark growl tore from me as I shoved the door open. *My omega sleeps with me.* That was what I wanted to roar, but witnessing Quin flinching from my growl stole my fury. "He should sleep between your rooms. He'll feel best surrounded by those he trusts."

I didn't wait for a reply, couldn't. Quinlan was alive. Quinlan was healthy.

Quinlan was terrified of me.

From an early age, I'd accepted that my life was shit. If I got something good, there was always shit attached to it somewhere. The only thing shit had never been able to touch had been my relationship with Quinlan. And it still hadn't, not on my end. I loved him as I always had. More fiercely now that I knew what life was like without him.

"Give him time," Knox barked on my way out the door. "The nephilim will help him, and when he's calm and knows he is safe, he'll be ready to talk."

Maybe that was true, but it didn't change the fact that right now, my mate didn't want anything to do with me.

I blinked away the ocean spray that clung to my lashes. In my efforts to give my mate the space he needed, I'd stumbled down the winding path to the beach. I couldn't say this was where I'd wanted to go, standing beside the jagged rocks. I knew it wasn't where I wanted to be.

I wanted to be with my mate. That was all I ever wanted. Even when I'd thought him dead.

But life wasn't fucking fair—I'd learned that years ago. My alpha nature demanded I act, but my hands were tied. Like Knox had said, only time would—God-fucking-willing —heal what had broken between us.

I clenched my fists, squaring off with the ocean like we were about to duel. Pierce had taken my mate from me and brainwashed him into hating me. Not just hating me, being *afraid* of me.

Whether we found and killed him or not, he'd already gotten what he'd wanted, and when I thought about *how*

Pierce had achieved his goal so thoroughly, I wanted to stab my brain with a seashell to keep from thinking at all.

The waves crashed against the rocks, churning white froth that broke apart and lifted into the wind. Dark clouds rolled in, blocking the sun before releasing rain in solid streams that soaked me in seconds. My fury frothed along with the water, but I was all build up and no release. No rocks to pound out my anger nor wind to send me floating toward the sky.

I tightened my fists until blood dripped from my palms. The pain wasn't enough to distract me, not nearly.

Thunder boomed overhead, echoing off the cliff face and up to the hotel.

"Couldn't have helped me the fuck out, huh?" I didn't know who I was screaming at. My chin pointed toward the black clouds. I snarled at the idea that someone, like Quinlan's archangel parent, was up there listening. I deserved the shit I got in my life, but Quin didn't. "He's part you, you know. Part angel. Do you not fucking care? Or is it only because he's mine?"

Lightning cracked horizontally across the sky.

"Yeah? That's your answer? Well *fuck you*. FUCK YOU!" I screamed until the words dissolved into no words at all. They'd melted together to create a single, tortured roar that drifted away on the ocean wind.

3

QUINLAN

THE BLANKET JAZZ gave me was soft with a scent that was immediately soothing. With my nose shoved deep in the blanket's folds, I inhaled and sighed, lying back into the pile of pillows as my wraiths settled on either side of me. I couldn't recall the smell, nor place it to a source, but it made my pounding heart pound a little less.

Of course, the moment I let my guard down, this would all dissolve away, and I'd realize again that I was still in that room, under Pierce's control, helpless and hopeless.

Don't trusssst. Only ussssss. My wraiths vibrated. I felt their words more than I heard them. *Trussssst nothing but ussss.*

I shoved the blanket away from my face and gathered my legs tightly against my front. The others had left a while ago, telling me to get some sleep. They assured me they'd stay nearby, and some sense inside me told me that they were close.

When Jazz had asked me if I felt our connection, I'd been relieved to hear it wasn't in my head.

Liessssss. Trickssss. No trusssst. Only ussss.

It wasn't real.

It was never real.

But real or not, the things I'd seen clung to me like scabs that never healed. They only ever broke open, bringing fresh pain to old wounds.

If this wasn't real, then I had no reason to linger. Why pretend I was safe? Why pretend I'd found men who called me brother and made me feel safe on a soul-deep level? I reached for my whip off the bedside table and squeezed the familiar, worn handle. It was nice that one of them had remembered to grab it.

Be ready. Sssstay ready, my wraiths warned. My constant companions had sprouted from my chest the moment I'd realized my nightmares had come true.

They were right, like always. Already, I'd let my guard down.

I'd never felt this way toward anyone—not even the man who'd sworn to protect me—but, like everything else, this emotion could be fabricated. After years of not being able to trust what I saw or felt, I'd believed nothing could shock me anymore. I wasn't the same boy I'd been in the beginning, clinging to each fabricated image with hope, only to have it dashed at the end. Crying all day every day had been exhausting. This was better.

Being empty was better.

I ignored the connection that allowed me to know without verifying that Jazz was in the room to my right, Sitka was down the hallway, and Storri was in the room directly to my left. That was a weird detail to make up, and I couldn't quite figure out Pierce's angle, but he would have one. I concentrated on the things I knew that were real. Me. I was real. However unfortunate that fact had become, it was still true. My wraiths were ever-changing in form, size, and consistency, but they were real. My whip was real. I tightened my grip on the handle.

Everything else was debatable.

Let'sssss go. The wraiths slithered to the door. They trusted less than I did, which made sense since they came from me and had known only torture and despair. The days I'd been left alone in my room to stew and wither were as bad as the nights Pierce spent forcing image after image into my mind. I'd figured out that he needed me asleep to manipulate me, but he could make me sleep without me ever being aware of it. I'd determined he had some kind of ventilation system installed in the room that allowed him to pump in a gas that was odorless, tasteless, and knocked me out in half a blink.

I took a stuttering step toward the door. Usually, my wraiths and I were of one mind. I'd eventually assumed we were the same being, but on this position, we were divided. I didn't want to stay here in this room, not exactly. But something kept me from following quickly out the door and into the night.

Jazz had opened the window in this room, saying the ocean breeze and wave sounds would be soothing. The sound drifting in at that moment was not soothing. It was a noise that belonged to a wild animal, something feral and hurt. The brutal roar wavered in from the window, sparking a reaction in me that was neither sane nor advised.

Nooooo. Come with ussss. The wraiths slid around me, their touch as comforting as always, but I wouldn't be swayed. That sound. There was *something* about that sound. I couldn't leave it. Not when it shook with so much sorrow.

There wasn't only sadness, though. Fury resonated as well.

I couldn't leave such an angry, sad creature. Even if it was fake.

———

When I woke up with the sun a few hours after deciding to stay, I was in the same room. The same clothes. The same surroundings.

The length of time of an illusion didn't really mean anything. I'd lived entire lifetimes that Pierce had conjured, only to wake up a young man again, captured and kept. It had been a while since Pierce had put me through something so horrible. My wraiths had started saying they didn't think he had the power anymore.

I'd assumed it was wishful thinking.

With my new sense, I ascertained that Jazz was no longer in his room. Maybe he'd gone to eat...or maybe he no longer existed.

I shot upright, lunging for the door. The wraiths got there before me, opening it silently before coming to a sudden halt.

I bounced into them, and they circled around my back to keep me from falling. *Danger.*

The man who starred in every one of my nightmares sat asleep on the floor. His large legs stretched straight in front of him, ending in a pair of muddy work boots.

Mud had dried into the carpet in the shape of his boot tread. I frowned. He should take his shoes off when he gets inside the house.

Quinlan, noooooo. The wraiths curled around my chest. I hadn't moved, but they'd likely sensed my intent. I smiled, thankful for their interruption. Again, I'd let my guard down in less time than it would take ice to melt on the sun.

I didn't care about this man's boots. I didn't care about how sore wearing them all day and night would make his feet or about the mess he made. That face...those *hands* had shown me so many horrors. Again and again, always changing, always malicious. Sometimes, he was sadistic from the beginning and enjoyed hurting the people I loved where I could watch. Other times, he acted kind for a while—almost like he loved me—only to snap and kill me again and again.

I had every reason to be terrified by this man. Any moment, he'd open his eyes and attack.

I needed to run, find one of my brothers, do *something* to protect myself, and yet I stood there.

My wraiths pressed at my back, trying to herd me out of the room and down the hallway. They'd never force me to do something I didn't want, though they sometimes got heavy with the suggestions.

I let them push me a couple steps forward so that I stood in the space between the man's muddy boots. I could touch him, if I wanted.

The question was, why would I want to? What was so different about this version of the man? I couldn't recall watching him sleep, not since the day Pierce had stolen me from my bed in the middle of the night and taken me from my pack. Maybe that was why. In sleep, everyone looked peaceful. It was a common joke for the parents of unruly children to say they were cutest when they were sleeping. This was a common phenomena, and the man behind those peaceful eyelids was still capable of unimaginable cruelty.

Though I couldn't imagine any cruelty coming from a mouth as soft as his. His bottom lip was slightly larger than his top, and when they pressed together, I suddenly wondered what it would feel like to touch them softly with my lips.

My toes shuffled forward, touching paper, and I took a closer look at the folders that covered the floor around him. He'd set a stack of pictures on the carpet between his legs like he'd been looking at them—or planning to—when he'd finally succumbed to sleep. I reached down for the stack, and my wraiths begrudgingly swooped down to bring them to my hands.

The first was a picture of a plot of land that had caught fire. Whatever had been there was ash. The edges of the picture were worn, like it had been looked at and held long enough to break down the glossy finish. There was something terribly familiar about the trees on the horizon. I shuffled that picture to the bottom of the stack, revealing the next. This one wasn't a picture of destruction, but of me. My hair was shorter than I wore it now and shiny. I stood beneath the massive arm of the man currently sleeping on the floor in front of me. He smirked at whoever took the picture while I beamed like I was exactly where I wanted to be.

This sleeping man hadn't *always* been my tormentor. Once, he'd been my shelter, and I'd loved him with every atom of my heart. He'd held me when I was upset and tended to me when I was sick. He was always there when I needed him. All I had to do was look up, and he'd find me.

When my love for him had transformed from platonic to romantic, I'd been the aggressor. Or, at least, I'd attempted to be the aggressor.

"I said we're waiting, Quinlan. That's all I'm going to say about it."

Diesel never used to use that stern voice with me. Now that he was, that deep, rumbling tone had the opposite effect on me than the one he intended.

His nostrils flared, and he let out a low, continuous

growl. "Finish getting ready and I'll drive you to the club," he snapped.

I couldn't call what I felt anger, though it was similar. It was closer to extreme impatience. Diesel had said we needed to wait, that I wasn't ready. But I did the things he asked. I lived a life with friends my own age. I acted as his representative when he was away, I had hobbies and interests that didn't include him. There was no reason for him to not be in my pants right now, and yet no matter how I flirted, Diesel's gaze burned, but he never acted on it.

He wanted me. I might not have had a shifter's keen sense of smell, but I had eyes. I knew a boner when I saw one.

"Why are you mumbling about boners?" Diesel asked.

Oh frick, I'd accidentally spoken my thoughts again. At least that time they'd only been a mumble.

Our eyes met, and there it was again, Diesel's desire plain on his face.

He couldn't even talk about boners without wanting me as much as I wanted him. There I stood, ready and willing.

Diesel clenched his hands into fists, but not before I spotted the dark, blunted edge of his claws.

My chest warmed with triumph. He wanted me; he'd finally take me. All this waiting was at an end—

He turned around, opened the door, and stomped outside.

He left me.

No...I narrowed my eyes at his retreating figure. He was running from me, maybe not physically, but mentally. "I'm ready now," I called out.

Diesel snarled. I'd chosen today's outfit with Diesel in mind. We were in the middle of a heat wave, so he couldn't say anything if I wore a pair of biker shorts that stretched to mid-thigh but clung to my body like a second skin. I paired the shorts with a tight, white ribbed tank top and had enjoyed a day of flustering my alpha.

"I'll just wear this. It's a hot and sweaty club anyway. All those bodies writhing together, rubbing all over me. No way to avoid getting their scent on me. I guess when they do that, they'll cover your scent, won't they? No matter. When you pick me up, you can fix it. It'll just be a few hours without your scent. I still think it's more important I stay cool. Don't want heat exhaustion."

Diesel's head hunched between his shoulders, probably so he could hide the vein in his neck that always pulsed when I pushed him.

"I could just stay home. I don't need a lot of bodies to writhe against. Just one." I licked my lips, and Diesel's face burned a bright red.

He stomped over the space he'd put between us and promptly shut the door.

My heart sang, and I would've jumped for joy if I didn't think it would just undo all the seducing I'd achieved so far.

"You made plans with your friends to go to the club. You're going to the club, Quinlan, after you change."

Were they my friends or his? I should have been the one to care about canceling on them, and honestly, Rick and Miles had recently added benefits to their relationship and would likely slink away to a corner and make out the moment we got in. Diesel shouldn't have been standing up for them anyway—he should be standing up for me! I was his mate. At least, that was what Rick had said.

My limbs shook as impatience turned into fury. If I wasn't his mate, then what was I doing saving myself for him?

"Be careful, Quinlan," Diesel warned, letting me know I'd once again spoken my thoughts.

I felt that soul-deep yearning to do exactly as he said exactly as he said it, but acting like that had done nothing but given me a perpetual case of blue balls. As Knox was fond of saying, it was time for Plan B. "No."

Diesel went still like a hunting predator that had caught sight of its prey. "No?"

"No. No, I'm not changing. And no, I'm not being careful! If you won't take me to the club dressed like this, then I'll find my own ride. I'm a mature, capable, reasonable adult after all!"

"Yeah, that's exactly what you sound like right now," he said drolly.

When I made for the door, Diesel's hand shot out and gripped my upper arm not so tight that it hurt, but tight enough that I felt his hand shake. "You aren't going anywhere, Quinlan," he growled.

My heart did backflips, and if my dick had been able, it would've joined in on the happy gymnastics. Yes, yes, yes, my soul chanted, glowing warm in my chest as Diesel leaned in, obliterating my personal space. He was going to kiss me, a real kiss, one that was an opening of events and not a closing. I'd finally find out what it was that my body ached for.

His hair fell forward, tickling my jaw as his gaze looked through my barriers to the essence of who I was.

"Quinlan," Diesel murmured, watching me lick my lips.

"Hm?"

"Call your friends. Tell them you aren't going to be able to go out tonight."

Oh shit, oh shit, this was happening. As always, Diesel's dominating behavior tickled every pleasure center that existed in my brain. "Why?"

Diesel exhaled. There was something off about the sound. It hadn't been a sexy gasp of anticipation, but a long-suffering sigh. A parental sort of sound. He straightened and locked the door before replying. "Because you're grounded."

The door to the room next to mine opened, wrenching me from my thoughts as Storri shuffled out with a baby on his hip. "Good morning, Quinlan." Storri's greeting would've been pleasant if it hadn't roused the sleeping man whose legs I stood between.

My wraiths came to my immediate aid, shoving him against the wall while simultaneously lifting me off the floor and back into the bedroom.

The thumping of Diesel's body hitting the wall scared the baby Storri held, making it cry, which prompted a low growl from inside Storri's room. Dog, the owner of the growl, stalked out on the defense. I remembered him from my time before the kidnapping. Somehow, he hadn't appeared in any of my nightmares, and I'd assumed him gone like everyone else. His square head turned toward my wraiths, and he sank low to the ground, his bristly hair stuck up in a tight ridge down his back.

Whooooo issssssss thissssss? They'd never sounded so excited. I landed softly on my feet in the doorway as my wraiths abandoned me, zooming toward Dog, shimmering from black to a glittery gray. They'd never done that before either.

The wraiths wound around Dog's midsection, making soft humming sounds that I didn't think Dog could hear. He didn't appreciate the sudden restraint, evident by the way he snapped at the air and scrambled out of the wraiths' grasps.

His wiggling maneuvers were no match for the wraiths. Like being hunted by water, they split, flowed, and reformed in whatever way required to stay wherever Dog was. Overwhelmed, Dog made a break for it, racing down the hallway as the wraiths made chase, bouncing off the walls like pinballs, causing just about the amount of damage expected from such an activity. Leaving cracking plaster and broken picture frames in their wake, the chase continued down the hallway.

I ignored everything else and took off after my wraiths. Seeing them fly around the corner made my gut lurch. I was hot all over; sweat gathered rapidly at my forehead and palms.

How long had it been since I'd run unassisted? It was the difference between jumping in water and jumping on dry land. My body moved the same, exerted the same energy, but I felt as if I was walking in slow motion, not running so hard I panted. I wasn't sure how I had my wraiths or what they were, exactly, but they protected me, kept me safe. If I hadn't had my wraiths, I would've been left unprotected every time I slept, or every time Pierce *made* me sleep.

I didn't control them so much as they seemed to prefer taking care of me. Except now, they were careening down a large set of stairs, bouncing off the wall by the front door and breaking the window in the process. The shattering glass didn't slow them in the slightest, and they rolled forward like the sudden waters of a flash flood. Dog, clearly still bewildered by what was chasing him in the first place, had a one-track mind. He spun around, not seeming to care where he went as long as it was away.

The chaotic group disappeared into a room with a doublewide doorway. More shattering and splintering sounded from within, and I didn't have long to imagine the destruction before I saw it with my own eyes. The room must've been a dining room, perfectly functional and organized. Now, the table lay on its side as well as most of the chairs. Many of those were splintered beyond use. Flowers lay scattered around the floor, along with sharp shards of crystal.

The chase continued through another doorway, where Jazz's high-pitched scream joined the existing crashing sounds.

I wasn't the first through the doorway. At Jazz's scream, Diesel surged forward. I followed on his heels, blinking rapidly as I wiped a white powder that clung in the air off my face, sticking to the tears streaming down my cheeks. I gasped on a sob, licking my lips.

Flour.

4

DIESEL

Once I was sure Jazz had only been startled and not harmed, I searched the room for Quinlan. He stood surprisingly close to my side. At this distance I had to look down to see him.

Terror rolled off him in waves, turning his scent bitter. His shoulders bobbed jerkily with his breaths. I knew immediately what was happening. In his early years, Quinlan's panic attacks had been frequent. They'd spread out as he got older and more established in the pack. On the day of the explosion, he'd gone more than a year without one.

Before, I'd hold him, rocking him gently as he matched his breaths with mine. I couldn't do that now. My arms didn't bring him comfort. Though it hadn't been fear that I'd first smelled when I woke up with my mate standing over me. A fleeting emotion expressed only with the intent that I never know, wasn't consent.

Knox barreled in behind me, going straight for his mate.

Dog snarled, snapping at the approaching shadows. The way they moved didn't feel threatening, but Dog didn't seem to care. He snapped at the air, surging forward in an attack that sent a jug of milk on its side.

Quinlan sucked in a short breath and, pressing his lips tightly together, whistled sharply.

The wraiths responded immediately, condensing and slithering toward Quinlan like snakes. They wound around his arms, a living shawl that doubled as protective armor.

Though they rested gently around Quin's shoulders, the man didn't look the least bit soothed. His breaths came more quickly, and the red on his cheeks spread down his neck in nervous splotches.

"What the hell is happening here?" Knox barely restrained his bellow.

Jazz shushed him, gesturing to Quinlan, gasping for air.

Storri rushed to Dog's side and dropped to one knee. "Are you okay?"

Dog must've said he was because Storri worriedly searched the disheveled space. A carton of eggs lay face down on the ground with the lid open. Thick egg white oozed out from under the cardboard, mixing with the broken shells. It looked like Jazz had been in the middle of making pancakes, and every ingredient and utensil he'd planned on using lay discarded like it had all been tossed around the room.

"Why do I feel...?" Storri spotted Quinlan and stood slowly. He didn't rush to his nephilim brother, but approached cautiously. "You are safe, Quinlan. Breathe. You have to breathe, or you will lose consciousness."

Quinlan gasped but nodded. His pupils dilated, making his gaze dark.

"If you can, look at me, Quinlan. Look at my eyes. Watch me. You are safe. You are among your brothers. This is *real*." Storri's voice broke. Honestly, he'd lasted longer than I'd ever imagined possible before crying. He swallowed a loud breath, clinging to Faust's hand, his alpha having appeared silently beside him.

He wiped his cheeks with a tissue from Faust, continuing his slow approach so as not to startle Quinlan.

Quinlan's shadows squeezed around his arms like a hug. They were helping, as were Storri's words. Neither comforted Quinlan quickly enough to avoid him passing out. His breaths weren't coming any faster, but they were sharper, every inhale so desperate each one sounded like the last gasp of a dying man.

I didn't turn toward him. I didn't look at him. Neither was necessary for me to match my breaths with his, keeping pace until our shoulders rose in tandem. For the next several seconds, I concentrated on just breathing as he breathed. When I was certain that we were synched, I slowed my breathing, inhaling a fraction later.

When Quinlan's next breath also came a little later, my chest tightened with an emotion I couldn't place. Familiar in the same way as an old photo album uncovered after decades in an attic.

We breathed in sync for several more seconds before I slowed again, continuing until we were both breathing normally.

The entire time, Storri spoke in low tones. He stepped close enough to hold Quinlan's hand, and when he didn't pull away, Storri embraced him in gentle arms. Slowly, his breathing slowed; his skin cooled and cleared.

It was Storri physically comforting Quinlan, but my breaths he mimicked. I realized this was likely a basic survival reflex and not anything he realized he was doing, but just knowing something deep in him responded to me in any way made me and my wolf want to howl for joy.

"That's very good. You're doing so well," Storri crooned.

Jazz stepped forward, joining their embrace. "Don't even worry about all the broken stuff. I've been trying to find a way to convince Knox to do some redecorating. Problem solved." He flicked his index finger in the air as if checking off an item on a to-do list.

Quinlan let out a shaky breath that sounded like the echo of a chuckle and warmed the bones in my chest. He let out a loud exhale, longer than all the rest. "I'm sorry. They've never acted that way before." His eyes searched the shadows clinging to him as though he was searching for injuries.

"I believe it. Angus always waits to have his loudest outbursts when there are the most people around." Jazz led them to the table, and I hurried to turn the chairs upright. Isaiah lifted the chairs on the other side.

The entire pack was there, either cramped inside the kitchen or peering curiously in from the meeting room, like Siobhan and Jamie.

"What do you call them?" Jazz indicated the shadows with his forehead.

"They're my wraiths," Quinlan responded with some bewilderment, like the concept of his shadows having individual names had never occurred to him.

The shadows swelled and rolled as if they knew they were being spoken about. One angled around Quinlan's back to peer at Dog, who let out a low growl and stepped behind Storri. At realizing he'd used Storri as a protective shield, Dog snarled and switched their places, to Faust's amusement.

"They're clearly attached to you." Jazz smiled.

Quinlan smiled fondly, sending a bullet of jealousy

tearing through my heart. All his fond smiles used to belong to me. "They are my protectors."

"What do they protect you from?"

Quinlan's shoulders jerked back, and his wraiths turned into angry maracas. He didn't turn his mismatched eyes to look at me.

First, he claimed I wasn't real; now he was set on pretending I wasn't there. But he hadn't been pretending upstairs. I held onto that thought as Jazz repeated my question.

With his gaze stubbornly turned from me, Quinlan hugged himself before answering in a dark whisper. "Pierce."

Hearing that name, Knox couldn't hold back his growl either.

Dr. Tiff hadn't asked Quinlan very many questions about how he'd been taken or his daily life while held captive during her exam. She'd been more concerned with his physical wellbeing in that moment. He hadn't been malnourished or dehydrated, no major injuries or wounds other than sleep exhaustion. Quinlan's physical state was better than the doc had been expecting, but that did not mean he was unharmed. Something had happened to him. He didn't need marks on his body for me to know he'd been hurt.

The part I couldn't understand was why Quinlan looked at me like I'd been the person who hurt him. I'd sworn to protect him, had guarded him for most of his life. Was that it? Were my broken promises to keep him safe what made him so angry?

"If you want to talk about it now, we're here to listen. I know it's early, but it looks like everyone's up." Jazz cleared off the small, circular table. When Jazz had joined us, we'd often eaten in the kitchen, but now the table wasn't near large enough. Transitioning into the other room might spook Quinlan, though, and Jazz seemed to realize that as he motioned for the coffee, sugar, and cream to be brought to the table. Knox and Sitka grabbed what was needed. Sitka sat at the table with Storri, Siobhan, Quinlan, and Jazz, while Knox retreated to stand shoulder to shoulder with me against the wall.

"There isn't a lot to tell." Quinlan accepted the mug of black coffee from Jazz with a small frown that formed a tiny wrinkle at the bridge of his nose. "I haven't had coffee in..."

If he hadn't had any while captive, then the last time Quinlan had coffee was with me the morning before we left for our mission. It tended to make him jittery, so he only ever drank it when he knew I'd be around to help him if his anxiety reared up. His gaze flitted my way, confirming my hunch.

He stuck his chin out. "A long time," he finished stubbornly.

"Well, some days it flows like water, so you'll get used to the sight."

With his wraiths wrapped around his neck again, Quinlan doctored his coffee, adding several spoonfuls of sugar and a generous portion of cream. Him drinking coffee wasn't ideal so soon after a near panic attack, but he looked so pleased I couldn't bring myself to say anything about it.

It was still a mystery why Pierce had made sure Quinlan had food and water for all those years but not coffee, unless he also knew about Quin's panic attacks. Obviously, Pierce was more invested in Quin than he'd let on. I'd only ever thought the two had a pack bond from Alpha to pack member.

Quinlan took his first sip, and there wasn't a force on the

earth that could've made me look away from the momentary joy that one sip brought him. Any pleasure I might've derived from that expression faded with the words that came out of his mouth.

"I don't remember much. It was night. I'd been sleeping. Then I was tied up in the back seat of Pierce's car. He told me..." Quinlan's voice shook, and he looked up, but not at me. At Knox. "I hoped he was lying. It was the only thing he didn't make me *see*."

What the hell did that mean?

"About what?" Jazz asked, but the pain in Quinlan's voice was a clear indicator of what he was talking about.

"Our old pack is gone, Quinlan. They died in an explosion that we believed also killed you. Pierce faked his death on our mission, and I believe he then teleported to our old home. He set the bomb off, but not before drugging you, tying you up, and loading you in his car." That was Knox, giving out the information straight as an arrow. On most days, I respected that in him, but this was Quinlan. The same boy who'd made me put on a funeral for a bird that had run into my kitchen window and died.

However, the shaggy-haired man in front of me didn't flinch at the confirmation. "So he could tell a truth," he scoffed. "Surprise, surprise." His wraiths rattled like snakes about to strike.

"Do you really think it was Pierce who set off the hellfire bomb?" Isaiah asked, nodding briefly at Quinlan. They were meeting for the first time, but somewhere between the wraiths chasing Dog through the mansion like hellhounds— no offense, Dog— and keeping Quinlan from passing out in a crowded kitchen, we'd skipped right over introductions.

"I believe it is what he signed his contract for." Knox hadn't shared that guess with any of us yet, but it seemed like the only logical conclusion. Pierce wasn't the strategist in our team; that was Knox's role then, as it was now.

I watched Quinlan lift his mug to his lips a second time. His lips were turned down, and his eyebrows were flat, the very picture of unbothered, cool, bored, even. But before the ceramic could touch his lips, his hand trembled, shaking the mug so minutely, the only person who noticed it was me, and because I refused to stop looking at him.

"What do you mean by what he made you see? We at least know he made you see the alphas doing horrible things. But what else?"

"Sitka, that's...a personal...question?" Jazz started strong, but his confidence rapidly gave way to uncertainty. "I don't know." He threw his hands up, and Sitka bumped their shoulders together.

"It is and isn't. It isn't personal in that I care if people know, but it is in that it happened to me. Only me, I guess. Was it horrible of me to hope at one point that my pack-mates were also there in that place with me? It felt nice imagining our rooms side by side."

"That isn't horrible," Storri replied nearly before Quinlan had finished speaking. "I understand." His eyelids wrenched up, his eyes wide. "I don't mean I want you all tortured if I am tortured!"

Quinlan reached over the table, and the wraith on his right slid down his arm, beating Quinlan to the back of Storri's hand. The wraith patted Storri's hand three times before sliding back.

"You don't have to tell them to do things?" Sitka asked with an adorable amount of jealousy.

At the same moment, Jazz pulled Storri's elbow, bringing their faces together. "What did that feel like? I've been dying to know."

"Cold," Storri said like he wasn't at all happy about that fact.

Faust shuffled closer to his mate's backside.

"I don't usually have to speak. They normally just know." He paused to roll his eyes at the wraith that had patted Storri's hand.

"They talk too?" Sitka asked with a tone that was just as much a whine as an inquiry.

My wolf preened, proud of our mate until we both remembered it was the wraiths that Sitka was jealous of.

"They do." Quinlan's pride rang so clear, it sounded nearly paternal.

"Yeah, well, you can't move things around for me," Sitka snapped at the ceiling.

Jazz's cheeks blazed an unfortunate shade of red, the same way they always did when one of Sitka's ghosts was definitely in the room with us. Really, he didn't enjoy the concept of the hotel being full of ghosts in general. The nephilim weren't a group of identical people who had no trouble getting along, but a group with a bond that transcended their differences. That Quinlan had fallen so smoothly into place was the only thing bringing me peace at the moment.

"Sitka can talk to ghosts," Huntley explained to a very confused Quinlan. He hesitated, nearly taking a step away from Quinlan before he asked, a fraction belligerently, "Do we get to talk to you now?"

The moment Quinlan's lips turned up into a smirk was the moment I knew what hell felt like. Another man. Another alpha had made my mate do something that I knew to be impossible for me. He'd made him smile.

"You can," Quinlan said softly. "Just you."

Jesus-fucking-Christ, thank you. At least *both* twins weren't in his good graces before I was even dealt a hand.

"He showed me what he called truths. In the beginning, anyway. He told me that the other Alphas had gone crazy for power. That you were attacking the pack, killing them. He said he'd barely had time to rescue me. He told me about the people each of you killed, described the murders in detail, every horrible, awful thing he witnessed you do. All except Huntley." Quinlan's flat lips twitched into a smirk.

"What did he say about me?" Huntley's outrage rang loud and clear.

"He said you mostly cried in the car and could only do what the others told you to do. Then later, when he got more creative... He..." Quinlan sighed, looking at a loss as to how to put the thoughts to words. "Put it this way, if the others were the horror, you were the comedic relief."

"*What?*"

Sitka patted his forearm consolingly. "There, there, Alpha. I believe you could be horrible if you wanted to."

Jagger snorted a moment before Huntley let his annoyance drop and did the same.

He stood close enough to touch my mate. I eyed his arms, hanging loose at his sides. "Fine," Huntley grunted. "I accept that. At least being the wimp of the group means I get to talk to you, Q." Huntley's gaze found mine.

If this motherfucker plans on hugging my mate—

Huntley smirked but made no more moves forward. He settled his hand on Sitka's shoulder instead. "I am very glad you aren't dead."

"I wasn't." Quinlan let the words drop like stones from a ten-story building. "But...I think I am now. Yes," he snapped at the wraith on his left. "*If* this is real, I will be glad."

"It's real." I wrenched my eyes away so that when he looked at me, my face was downcast. I knew my voice was the last he wanted to hear, but I *needed* him to know he was safe now.

My own list of things I needed to know grew steadily, foremost on that list *how* Pierce had made Quinlan see things.

"He's right," Jazz added softly when it was clear Quinlan would pretend he hadn't heard me speak. "Whatever you saw after Pierce took you, it wasn't real. None of it happened. Those truths were bullshit. Absolute *bullshit*." His voice rang in the room by the end, his passion getting the best of him. "These men were the ones who lost their families that night. And they thought that included you. I'm really glad it doesn't."

Never in a thousand years would I have guessed that I'd ever have another omega defending me against my mate. I felt Quinlan's burning gaze on me the moment before I found his eyes, staring unblinking at my face. They weren't only different in color, but in emotion as well. One held anger, the other fear.

For the first time in both our lives, I felt like I was staring at a stranger.

5

QUINLAN

"Not so fast."

The wraiths hovered at my bedroom door, sliding around the door frame like captive lions searching for a weak spot in their cage.

"If you could leave Dog alone, maybe I could trust you on your own."

The wraiths flashed like twin strobe lights, though neither spoke.

We'd had disagreements in the past, but I'd never truly denied them anything. I didn't believe they did what I wanted or obeyed my command because they had to, but because they wanted to. And since chasing Dog through the hotel a few days ago, the only thing the wraiths wanted to do was be where Dog was.

The wraiths had a crush, and while the thought gave me warm—slightly confused—feelings, the wraiths crushed *hard*. Sometimes, they *just* crushed. Mirrors, pictures, furniture that wasn't bolted down, they were indiscriminate in the items their destruction ruined in order to get to their target. They'd always been enthusiastic little balls of I-don't-know-what.

Unless we were counting now, when they refused to do more than flash at me and poke at the door. "So I get the silent treatment then? Fine." I flopped down on the bed and eyed the chair and desk sitting in the corner. Huntley had carried it in the day before, saying it was so I could write or draw if I wanted. The way he'd spoken, like he'd just thought of the idea and brought the desk of his own accord, stank of deceit. I hadn't always been able to scent a lie, but after so long hearing only lies, I'd gotten good at it.

Jazz was supposed to stop by any second for a picnic. It hadn't taken me long to realize that what Jazz had said was true. Pierce had shown me Knox murdering children, but he hadn't really. He'd shown me Faust ripping my pack-mother's throat out, but that wasn't really Faust. I'd witnessed Diesel perform every atrocity one human could to another, and none of that was real, but knowing didn't block the memories.

Could they be called memories if they never really happened?

The wraiths pulsed before floating to me and sliding around my waist. In the distance came a low rumbling. A motorcycle, and not just one.

A pack.

This was a new pack, but led by the same Alphas, and I knew *they* didn't have a pack of motorcycle-riding friends.

What if they weren't friends at all, but enemies? What if they came to hurt them?

I flung the door open, thankful for my wraith, who grabbed it before the door could slam into Jazz's face.

Jazz jerked back. Thankfully, he didn't have Angus with him. "Whoa, hey there!"

"I'm sorry!" I held on to the door as if it would swing back and try again. "I heard motorcycles."

"Yeah, it's Badger's pack. Well, no, I don't think you would know Badger. He came after you die—shit! Sorry! They met Badger after it *seemed* like you had died." Jazz went to shove his hand through his curls but stubbed his fingers against the bill of his hat instead. "Ow! Dang! I forgot I put that on. *For Knox,*" he said like the words were the most tiresome words ever spoken in all of time.

"Mate?" Knox called up the hallway from the first floor.

Jazz rolled his eyes. "I'm fine. Just hurt myself on this *hat you made me wear.*"

"He hurt himself on a hat?" Diesel said, his voice coming from the same direction as Knox.

I forced my lips to remain in a straight, unamused line.

"Fork you, buddy!" Jazz called back.

"Fork you?" I couldn't believe the alphas I'd once known would have a problem with anyone swearing.

"I'm trying not to cuss for the baby," he explained.

"Why?"

Jazz threw his hands up in the air, "I don't know? I wish someone would've told me that half the time of being a new parent is thinking up ways other parents would judge you! I can't have Gus's first word be shit. Or, more likely, asshole."

It was lucky I wasn't still trying not to smile because I would've lost the war. "Let me guess, pet name for Knox? It suits him."

"At this point, we could probably get away with calling it his legal name."

The Knox I'd known hadn't been so unlike the Knox I'd witnessed since he bust into my cage. The former Knox hadn't been quite so certain nor so steady. He'd been a force, relentless, demanding and blunt, but with a restless edge.

This Knox wasn't restless, but confident, and I believed that had a lot to do with the person standing in front of me.

"That is the nicest thing anyone has ever said about me." Jazz's eyes filled with tears, and he hugged around my shoulders, taking special care not to bump into the wraiths.

One thing about—mostly—solitary captivity was that I never had to worry about accidentally speaking my thoughts. Whenever Pierce had visited me, my wraiths wrapped around my body like a protective film that blocked his sight as well as sounds. Still, he never gave up on trying.

"It's the truth." I shook off the dread that thoughts of Pierce always brought me. They'd said I was safe here and that Pierce couldn't get in.

Agaaaain yooou believe?

I didn't know what made it worse, the derision or the fact that taunting me was what got them to talk again. This wasn't like last time. I wasn't placing my body, mind, and soul in a single man; I was merely relying on the pack's Alphas to protect. Just as every pack member should.

And youuuu call us sllllllliiiiippery.

"Shut up."

"I...wasn't talking?" Jazz cocked his head to the side, quick like a songbird. "And really, for me, that is, like, a miracle."

"Good afternoon, brothers!" Sitka said after popping up in the shadow of the door in the hallway.

Jazz gripped his chest, making a big show of being startled. "I'd say to get you a bell, but that wouldn't help at all." He smiled widely as he spoke, emphasizing how he was only joking.

I nodded my hello. Several days had passed since my arrival, letting me see more of how the nephilim interacted. I liked how, at different times and from each of them, the jokes sometimes got a little barbed. It made them seem more real. When I'd truly seen Storri, the moment before my whip nearly did the unthinkable, I'd been so sure he wasn't real. Something that made me feel *that good* couldn't be real. But then I realized Pierce never showed me anything that made me feel good. Not once. So he had to be real.

Jazz looped his arm in mine but I was reluctant to continue. "Aren't we waiting for Storri?"

Jazz smiled like he understood. "He's outside getting the critters to tell him the least peed-on spot. We don't normally picnic so close to the hotel since Dr. Dark Doolittle has an animal magnetism that the little critters can't resist."

The wraiths pulsed, eager for a chance to see Dog.

During our walks the days previous, I'd enjoyed the view from the yard and further to the ocean where it stretched for endless miles, but not so much I wanted to potentially eat in urine. "Where do you usually picnic?"

"Um, well, we don't picnic all the time..." Jazz said breezily. "But, we've gone a few places. On the beach, over at the river, you know, boring places."

Those places sounded awesome. Or at the least, not so blatantly pee-covered. "Why not the beach? It's nice."

Downstairs, someone coughed, but it sounded suspiciously pointed.

"Get a drink of water!" Jazz hollered over my head toward the unseen cougher. "We promised Diesel we would keep you within sight of the hotel, and seriously, I think it's a good idea. Quite frankly, really strange, crazy dramatic things happen to us all the time, and you just got here. I'd rather not have you killed or kidnapped in your introductory phase. That's strictly stage two stuff."

I wanted to be angry at Diesel for trying to control where I went, but who could be angry looking at that adorable guilty face? I saw why Knox probably had such a hard time at first.

"Hey!" Jazz slapped my arm, prompting Sitka to smoothly slide between us like our referee.

"Let's join the others and eat. Then people will be in better moods."

For as sweet and caring as Sitka was, he could throw a jab when he wanted, and most times, you didn't see it coming.

I loved that about him.

Outside, Storri and Dog waited with Hallie, Siobhan, Jamie, and all the children. Sitka poofed to his son's side, lifting him from Jamie's arms and nuzzling his face to his baby's neck.

Gus spotted his dad and raised his arms, chubby hands clenched into ineffectual fists as he let out needy little grunts when Jazz didn't pick him up right away.

My wince lasted less than half of a second. Here, there wasn't anyone studying my face every moment so my pain went, thankfully, unnoticed. I didn't even know why I hurt. I didn't want a kid. With everything I'd seen, everything that I knew could happen to a person, how could I bring a life into that?

Looking over my shoulder, I spotted the row of motorcycles. Shiny, imposing bikes that probably had names with many initials. Diesel had fancied himself a biker at one time. I remembered a particular span of a few weeks involving Diesel, a leather jacket, and *fringe* that I'd sworn to never bring up again in mixed company.

My lips felt light with the memory.

He prooooomised a lot.

If my wraiths were only going to talk when they had something mean to say, then I'd rather they keep it to themselves. The wraiths split, one rubbing my shoulders comfortingly while the other clenched around my hands in their version of an apology. They worried about me, with good reason. The entire time my wraiths had known me I'd been in captivity. I'd needed their worry, their protection.

Sitting among the other nephilim, I felt like nothing could hurt me, but that wasn't true. Jazz had said as much. Dramatic, crazy, and strange had been his words. None of those screamed safety.

Jazz bumped into my shoulder. "They're just inside, probably staring at us like dorks through the meeting room window."

I turned my head away, bumping into my wraith in my haste. "I wasn't worried. I was just looking at the bikes."

Jazz didn't look like he believed me, but he played along. "Are you interested in riding? I'm sure Storri could get Faust to make you one. And then we can take it out when Storri sneaks away from the hotel with Dog to do dangerous things like he does when he doesn't think we're watching."

Storri's cheeks were red, but his lips turned in a soft smile.

"So they've still got that overbearing, uber-protective, my-way-or-the-highway attitude?"

Jazz inhaled like a warrior facing a battlefield. "Buckle up. I believe it's gotten worse. Losing everyone...*almost* everyone...it did something to each of them. They dealt with it in their own ways. Still deal with it, actually."

My ribs ached at the thought. No matter what I'd seen since that horrible night, every day before that had shown me a pack of Alphas willing to do whatever was necessary to care for and protect their pack. Losing them, losing *everyone*...

I didn't mind that Jazz continued to make the same

mistake. In a way, the Quinlan of that pack *had* died. Wholly unprepared for the real world and all its horrors, that innocent, naive, pure boy was gone forever.

Just like my pack family.

And my mother.

Rebecca reminded me a lot of Hallie. We hadn't spoken face to face much, but she was a nurturer through and through. She also demanded the same level of respect as Rebecca had—though Rebecca never had any trouble getting it from me. I'd been an obedient child, and later, when I had gotten sassy, it hadn't been with Rebecca. Only Diesel.

I gave my entire life over to that man and as a result was grossly unprepared for how horrible the world actually was. Maybe if I'd known there was evil—if he'd explained to me the nature of cruelty—maybe then landing in Pierce's clutches wouldn't have come as such a shock. I wouldn't have been so ill-equipped.

"I need to go somewhere." The moment the thought had formed, it rushed from my mouth.

The others were sitting scattered on a huge blanket that Sitka had laid out under Storri's instruction. The stares pointed my way varied from hurt to confused.

"Not right now," I rushed to clarify. "But, if I did need to go somewhere, how do I make that happen?" In the old pack, traveling off pack lands would've been as easy as asking a pack member to drive me. Or it would have been that easy if anyone but Diesel had ever taken me anywhere.

"Um..." Jazz looked to the others, giving me my answer.

I decided to spare him the discomfort. "I have to ask Diesel, don't I?"

Jazz winced away from my tone, making me feel like a jerk.

I'd have to talk to the man at some point. I knew this Diesel was the real Diesel, and the other Diesels were Pierce's twisted recreations, but when I got around him, a tornado of emotions swirled inside me. There were the old feelings of joy and attraction—as much as I wanted to deny those feelings were still there—mixed with new feelings of fear and revulsion at the things I'd seen him do. And covering all of that was a betrayal so thick I could wear it as a winter coat.

I didn't know how to be around him, what to feel. Everyone surely wanted the old Quinlan back, me just as I had been, but that person didn't exist. "I'm going to ask. I'll be right back."

There was no use dragging out the task. If I waited too long, I'd only lose my nerve.

I kept my steps even but strong toward the hotel entrance. The door swung open before I could touch the handle. Jazz had been right, of course. The guys hadn't just been watching through the window, but apparently they'd been listening in as well.

Which meant Diesel, staring down at me with that searching gaze that soured my stomach, knew exactly what I was here to ask.

"So? Can I?"

My wraiths narrowed into thick black ropes that wound up my arms. Diesel's gaze tightened as it flicked to them. "Can you what?" he asked without looking back up at my eyes. He kept staring at the wraiths in their endless movement.

He'd been listening in. He already knew what I wanted to ask. I rolled my eyes.

A sharp growl cracked from inside his chest. The sound shot through my gut, making a sharp turn toward my dick.

Pierce had never had Diesel make that sound. Probably because Pierce *didn't know* how to make that sound.

My throat convulsed as I attempted to swallow down my arousal. I knew he could smell it. I'd used that little fact shamelessly when I was younger. Somehow, Diesel knowing that he'd aroused me without hardly trying felt like a failure on my part. Like I was giving in, bowing beneath him.

"I. Want. To. Go. To. The. Old. Pack. Lands." I spoke as fast as cold syrup poured, carving each word out of my mouth like I thought Diesel was either hard of hearing or extremely dimwitted.

"That *isn't* a question," he snarled.

Now I was glad Diesel had met me at the door. If I'd had to go in, meet with him in a narrow, enclosed space, like the corridor, this contact would've been too much. As it was, I was still outside, where my wraiths and the open air around me kept me from feeling too pinned down by this man. He shouldn't have been able to do this to me anymore. I wasn't the same person.

I bit down hard on my lower lip. "Fine, I'll ask Knox."

"Goddamnit, Quinlan!" Diesel cried out, wrenching my arm—technically, the wraiths that had covered my arm—back from my forward trajectory.

I huffed and ripped my arm free. "I'm not jumping through your fucking hoops, Diesel. If you will take me, take me. If not, then say no so I can ask the next person."

While I spoke, Diesel's frown deepened until I was sure there was a mirror image of it poking out on the backside of his head.

Knox cleared his throat, leaning against the banister as he watched our conversation. Diesel must've been distracted if he hadn't noticed Knox's approach. Or maybe he was just getting older. I snorted. The old impulse to save the thought for when I wanted to try to make Diesel ravish me next returned on a wispy wind that was gone just as quickly.

"Nothing here is your business," Diesel grunted.

Knox just smiled.

"I don't like this, Quin. I don't know why you want to go back there. There isn't anything left, ba—Quinlan. It's just ash. Everyone, everything."

My heart ripped apart like the Yellow Pages in the hands of a bodybuilder. My stomach jolted, and I hunched forward slightly, like I'd actually been hit. Rebecca couldn't be ash. She'd had too much life, a light that had shone so brightly it was impossible to imagine the world without it. But, if Diesel had returned to pack lands, finding me gone and Rebecca alive, she'd be here. Diesel would've taken care of her.

Tears, hot and urgent, pressed against my eyes, and I desperately blinked them away. If we were roleplaying the Diesel and Quinlan of before, this was when Diesel would've wrapped me in his strong arms and rubbed my back until I calmed down enough to talk about it. That was before, not now.

I swallowed down a cocktail of tears and sorrow, wiped my face clean of the nonexistent tears, and met Diesel's gaze with my hardest look. "I want to go."

Diesel stared me down, his face never changing unless you looked at his eyes. Those two orbs flashed with emotion, desire, anger, worry. His lips twisted into a scowl. "Fuck!"

———

DIESEL's same expletive repeated four more times—three if you counted Huntley and Jagger as one. As soon as I'd told the other nephilim Diesel would take me, they wanted to go too. I got the feeling they had always been curious. They'd possibly wanted to go before but, for whatever reason, hadn't asked. I understood for me it was a little different. The pack lands were the last home I'd known.

And it was gone.

Diesel had been telling the truth. I'd spotted the destruction the moment I'd expected to see a familiar ridge of trees. They'd been my favorite to climb as a child.

When he'd said ash, I'd imagined a campfire. In there would be soot and charcoal, but still some semblance of what it had once been.

The trees were gone, but not only the trees. The grass, bushes, *hill*...what could destroy a hill?

Diesel continued forward. The closer we got to the central spaces, where most of the people lived, the more there was left behind, but even that was being kind. The charcoal pieces were just larger here. He stopped the car, and I tried to picture where we would've been pre-hellfire. Maybe in the rec hall? The theater?

"The preschool," Diesel replied, and I couldn't be sure if I'd spoken out loud or if Diesel could read my thoughts. If there was any place in the world where he could, it would've been here.

I let his answer settle in my gut, committing this feeling to memory. One man had stolen so many lives. He couldn't be left with his. I'd come for closure, but all I wanted now was revenge.

6

———

DIESEL

I LOATHED the anger that settled on Quinlan's features.

It wasn't that I didn't understand. He'd already lasted longer than I had before exploding. At least we'd been able to come to the awful realization gradually. Quinlan had to take it in all at once, knowing without a doubt that everyone was dead.

I parked, rushing to unbuckle and get to the other side of the vehicle where Quinlan's boots stood among the ash. I'd expected his wraiths to drape near him, and in this place, I'd been counting on that fact. I didn't like Quinlan so exposed to the aftermath. I didn't want him anywhere near this fucking place, but letting Knox indulge my mate when I refused to just wasn't going to happen.

"Rebecca's house is this way." I headed south. Having mentally mapped the barren landscape years ago, I could walk the ash in the same paths I'd walked with Quinlan.

He followed in my wake, and I did my best not to check with every step that he was still back there.

I paused at where the front door would've been.

"This is it?" His voice shook, drawing his wraiths near at last.

If I couldn't hold him and ease his trembles, I could gain comfort that his wraiths were.

The other nephilim hung apart, each staying near to their alpha. It didn't matter how many times we returned to this place; it was always like walking into a hellish, alien landscape.

"I don't know what I expected," Quinlan whispered, eyes cast down and roaming the ground. "I think I thought there'd be *something* here. How could there be nothing?"

"How could there be nothing left?"

I'd never known a single tear could bring me to my knees until I watched one roll down Quinlan's cheek. He bent forward, resting his forehead against his clasped hands and redirecting the tears so they fell straight down.

Only the two of us and Rebecca remained in the fields, Rebecca's mother's pyre long since burned and collected.

At least he wasn't choking on those racking sobs like he did when we returned to the field. He knew the remains would be gathered, distributed, or scattered as the shifter had requested. But when we returned to the field and Quinlan spotted the empty spot, he'd dropped to his knees.

I folded my legs under me, sinking into the muddy ground beside my crying boy. Quinlan crawled into my lap, wrapping each of his limbs around whatever part of me he could manage. "She isn't gone, baby. She's just...redistributed." *My baby boy deserved so much more than me. I kept trying to tell him that.*

Quinlan snorted into my shoulder. "You made me get snot on you."

I scented him, rubbing my forehead against his temple. "I love your snot."

"So you don't love me? Just my snot?" He sniffed several times while speaking, stopping to take small, shuddering breaths.

"No way. I love you unconditionally, so anything you do, I love."

Quinlan looked back over his shoulder at the dark, empty spot on the ground. His bottom lip trembled, and I nearly lost to the urge to just rip him from this place that was causing him so much misery. "I love you unconditionally too, Diesel. Just as long as you always hold me just like this, whenever I need."

I would, obviously, but I smirked anyway. "Quin, that is a condition."

He frowned, making his bottom lip go all red and plump. "Oh, be quiet and just hold me."

Quinlan wiped his face. The rub of his sleeve against his face made a sound as unpleasant as sandpaper in my ears.

Fuck, I needed my arms around him. I didn't have the tools to deal with this any other way. I'd comforted Quin with my body, presence, and words, but now, none of those things were a comfort to him. I was an empty tool bag.

"He needs to die, Diesel," Quinlan growled darkly. The Quin I knew hadn't known how to make a noise like that.

His words set off a chain reaction of thoughts. My own desire for revenge, letting anger fuel me to avoid my grief. I got the irony. "I know what you're feeling because I've felt it. About you. And if someone tried to tell me to accept, forgive, let it go, I'd have told them to fuck off—"

"But you're still going to ask me to?" His voice was angry, and his face betrayed nothing, but his scent told me *everything*. The tendrils of desire were the lightest they'd ever been, but they were still there, brought out by my nearness.

"You're fucking right I will." I understood Quinlan's anger, but there was one key difference: I was the only alpha among us. "This is for the pack Alphas to handle. We'll get your vengeance."

Quinlan's nostrils flared, and his short nose lifted into the air. "Nope, I don't plan on sitting around waiting for the world to right itself. I've been restrained for too long. Finally, I can act. I'm going to."

"No. You aren't."

Quinlan stood straight. His plump lips parted with indignation. "I made a mistake asking you to bring me here."

Finally, Quinlan was seeing reason. He didn't need to be here. There was literally no need. He should've stuck to letting just me come here, letting me bear the brunt of the sorrow that leached into your skin whether you invited it or not.

"It gave you the illusion that you decide what I do."

My snarl brought the wraiths zooming, flattening between me and Quinlan like a shield.

Quinlan swiped an irritated hand through them, parting the smoke to continue glaring at me.

No one could poke at my buttons better than Quinlan. It had been so long, I'd forgotten how white-hot and furious he could make me. Was he saying he no longer considered himself my omega?

A crow cawed, flying overhead in the murky sky.

Technically, Quin hadn't ever been my omega. An actual plan that involved me dropping to my knees and groveling until he forgave me for not claiming him sooner.

So yes, I'd *planned on* claiming Quinlan. That fact had been widely known but didn't change how my plan was still just only that, a plan. In the eyes—and noses—of other shifters, Quinlan was unclaimed.

"Unacceptable," I growled, stomping forward.

I watched Quinlan's eyes widen before my sight was blocked by a pack of omegas.

"And that's a timeout on that," Jazz said with his arms crossed.

As much as my wolf howled for me to grab Quinlan, put him in my arms where he belonged, and fuck him against the hood of the Hummer—*showing* him who he belonged to—the man side of me knew that was the quickest way to lose Quinlan forever.

I spun around, plodding through Rebecca's garden. She'd grown the sweetest tomatoes I'd ever tasted in this rectangle of land. Jazz and the others huddled around Quinlan, their heads together. If I wanted, I could listen in on what they said, but with the way Quin had been looking at me, I wouldn't like what I heard.

I joined the twins at the Hummer while Quin and the others walked around the general area of Rebecca's home and garden. Sitka held one hand and Storri the other as Jazz asked Quin to describe what certain spots had once looked like.

Huntley nodded in welcome, his eyes tight, not liking being here. "Listening to you two fight..."

Jagger finished the sentence. "...it was like old times."

My jaw popped. "We never fought like that."

"Diesel!" Quinlan yelled out my name, and for a split second, I didn't recognize that the excited voice had come from my mate.

I was by his side in a second. Despite his tone, I searched him first for injury and then potential dangers. "Are you okay?"

The others surrounded, doing the same thing I'd done but to their own mates.

Quinlan made a small, lost sound. He wrenched his eyes from mine. "I didn't mean to—saying your name...was habit," he mumbled.

I saw what had sparked Quinlan's excitement next. They still stood in the loose circle they'd formed when they'd stopped to chat. The ground beneath their feet was the rectangle of space where Rebecca used to stake the tomato cages. In the ground at the center of their circle was a juvenile tomato plant.

I'd just walked through this space and knew that plant hadn't been there a minute ago. For five years, nothing could grow in any of the land that the hellfire had touched, and now a plant sprouted in minutes? It didn't take a master of deductive reasoning to figure out the likely cause.

"This land was tainted with hellfire," I said, staring at the fledgling plant. "You four are the opposite of that."

Knox lifted his arm, and Jazz slid beneath it. "I think we did that. Hold on! Does this trick work everywhere? Hallie was so smarmy after she won best pumpkin."

"Your plants died before they flowered," Sitka reminded him.

"Yeah, and now we can do our 'stand in a circle' thing, hold hands, and grow us some gourds. Oh yeah!"

Storri frowned, and they turned as a group back to the vehicles. "I don't think you can use your angelic gift to make your packmate jealous."

"Pshaw. Why not?"

The bantering continued, fading the farther they walked.

Just the three of us remained.

Quin's wraiths draped over his nape, hanging long in front of his body. "She grew the best tomatoes." He didn't look at me, but I knew I was who he spoke to.

"There's a garden at the hotel. You can use what she taught you."

Quinlan didn't smile at me, not technically. That honor belonged to the tomato plant he'd crouched in front of, gently rubbing the leaves between his fingers. "She used to say this was her favorite smell."

He stood, wordlessly walking back to the Hummer.

He hadn't smiled at me, but *I made him smile.*

My eyes dropped to the plant, and my gut dropped. Several of the leaves had withered, not the brown of a neglected plant, but black and rotting. The entire plant hadn't died—most was still a vibrant green—just every leaf Quinlan had touched.

7

QUINLAN

Sɪᴛᴋᴀ's ᴅᴀɢɢᴇʀ pierced the strawberry before both blade and fruit slammed against a tree trunk. The strawberry exploded on impact, splattering and then running down the trunk in red drips that looked far more menacing than they were.

"Impressive!" I said, bringing my hands together in a slow clap.

My nephilim brother stood on the other side of the lawn, smirking in that way that should've been arrogant and annoying, but on Sitka, it was just endearing. "I can probably do farther. And smaller." He shrugged like the cocky spider he was.

He bent down to the container of remaining strawberries.

Jazz and Storri sat with the children on a blanket on the opposite side of the lawn, watching the showdown. Technically, only Jazz and Storri watched, while the babies preferred staring up at the clouds, at the fabric books scattered around, or at each other. Jazz was still disappointed that we hadn't been able to grow anything like we had on the scorched pack lands. The best we could figure was that the place had been destroyed with hellfire and when we'd held hands, it was enough combined angel power to counteract the destruction.

We'd finished eating a while ago, and after reading to the children—with character voices, since Storri insisted that was the important part—me and Sitka got to talking weapons. He insisted a knife was superior because of the flexibility, and I disagreed. There wasn't anything more flexible than my whip, and I was about to show him. My wraiths brought me my friend, the weight a familiar feeling that had brought me the closest I'd come to happy during my captivity. The wraiths zoomed away to hang like vines on the branches surrounding us.

I gripped the handle, cascading my fingers down the familiar object. I'd never forget the look on Pierce's face when he'd seen what I'd made. I'd told him that I had a present for him and that he needed to come inside to see it. Despite that being the only time I'd ever asked Pierce to come into my room, he bolted inside, panting in front of me like a puppy. I would've succeeded in killing him that day if I hadn't lost my nerve. At that time, I didn't know what he was capable of or what he'd already *done*. If given another chance, I wouldn't let myself hesitate again.

I met Sitka's gaze. "Straight up and then swim a bit back, just in case." I had complete control over every single link in my whip, but I didn't want to take any chances. The guys were more than far enough away on the blanket.

Sitka nodded and palmed the strawberry in front of his chest. At my cue, he launched it straight up in the air, swimming to a shadow a few feet away immediately after.

I tracked the strawberry's journey, flicking my whip back as it started its descent. Each chain link slid smoothly and soundlessly over the other, rippling like a wave that split the strawberry in two. I flicked my wrist, diverting the whip's trajectory and snapping it to the side, cutting the two halves once more horizontally.

The chain dropped, and I jerked the handle once more, spiraling the whip in a circle beside me. Sitka swam back, his eyes full of tears.

My gut dropped. "What's wrong?"

"That...was...the most beautiful thing I've ever seen."

"Hey!" Jagger hollered from the hotel entrance. He stepped out, followed by Huntley, the doctor, and Diesel. "Your baby can hear you! And more importantly, I can hear you!" He turned to Huntley, gesturing dramatically. "Are you listening to this?"

"I hear it," Huntley replied somberly.

Sitka rolled his eyes but swam back to the blanket to scoop Onyx into his arms. The twins split off from Diesel and the doctor and headed for their mate.

Seeing Diesel aiming for me prompted my wraiths to return to my shoulders. He watched their progress and frowned. Diesel didn't like my wraiths because they made me feel powerful enough to go after Pierce. It was pretty clear he didn't like seeing my strength. He kept waiting for the old Quinlan to come back, the one who hadn't even known how helpless he was because his life was bliss.

"You had an appointment with the doc. Did you forget?"

How could I have forgotten? He'd only told me the night before and reminded me this morning. I hadn't planned on skipping it, but we'd started playing real life Fruit Ninja and I'd forgotten. That was what I should've explained to Diesel, but that wasn't what spewed from my mouth. "I don't even know why I have to. I don't feel sick." I met Dr. Tiff's eyes. She wasn't happy with me, and for that I really was sorry. I hadn't explicitly meant to stand her up, but the annoyed edge with which Diesel spoke to me stole any ability I had to be reasonable. "Dr. Tiff, I'm very sorry for missing my appointment today. But, you said already I was fine, right? So maybe I don't even need one. That would be best. Less of a chance of me forgetting that way."

Diesel glowered, his eyebrows meeting the deep line of his forehead. "This isn't that kind of appointment."

Dr. Tiff cleared her throat and stepped between Diesel and me. "I know that I told you in your first checkup that we would need to do a more thorough version at some point. By now, it is way overdue. If you don't want to have it in the infirmary, we can do it in your room or anywhere, really."

I still didn't want to go. I didn't want to talk about my time in captivity. I didn't want to highlight just how changed I'd become. But I couldn't refuse the doctor. She didn't deserve my attitude. "The infirmary is fine."

———

THE THIN PAPER crinkled under my butt. I had my own clothes on, the same jeans I'd worn all day, yet I still felt like my ass was bare and sweating into the paper.

I jerked my chin at Diesel, standing against the wall on my right. "Does he have to be here?"

Dr. Tiff looked up from her clipboard, where she'd been going over her notes. Her gaze tightened a fraction when she realized my question, and immediately, I regretted it. I hadn't asked because I'd been uncomfortable; I'd asked to be a dick. "No. He doesn't. It's up to you, Quinlan. If you would like this to be a private appointment, it will be."

Her reply, even and nonjudgmental, made my cheeks burn. "No, it's fine," I mumbled.

"Okay, then I think we can get started and get you back to your day." She went through the regular steps like my weight—I'd lost a few pounds, but the doc wasn't worried since I had more room to move now. She listened to my deep breaths and checked my blood pressure. When she had enough to compare to the measurements she took last time, she grabbed a chair and sat down in the space in front of me.

With my feet hanging off the edge of the bed, I felt like a kid as I peered down at her.

"I'd like to talk to you a bit more now about what you experienced while Pierce held you captive. He was here at the hotel for weeks, healing from some truly serious injuries. During that time, how did you care for yourself? Eat?"

That question didn't seem so much about me as it was a fish for information about Pierce. There was a spark in the doctor's clever gaze that said she held a grudge and perhaps took it hard that she hadn't noticed something was amiss with the man since she'd spent the most time with him. I didn't mind the not-so-pointed question and exhaled before leaning back and answering. "My room had a fridge and a hot plate. There was a small bathroom area, no proper door."

It sounded as though a rib in Diesel's chest had snapped. His gaze burned, but he said nothing.

My heart twisted at the pain this was causing him. I'd made a mistake not ordering him out, but not for me, for him.

Though who was I kidding? We could've ordered Diesel out, and the asshole would've stood on the other side of the door listening in and not for a moment feel any shame about it.

"By then, Pierce didn't visit often. Not like in the beginning, when it was day after day, hour after hour. The nightmares had slowed down until they came only sporadically, so I hardly noticed he was gone until my wraiths mentioned it. That was just a few days before the guys showed up."

"Tell me about the wraiths and their abilities. Did you ever ask them to help you escape?"

It was only my respect for the woman that kept me from shooting her with a dry stare. "Yes. Many times. I couldn't get out. Not because the door was locked, but there was something stopping me. Like an invisible shield."

She sat a little straighter and narrowed her eyes. Her gaze went distant like she was lost in her thoughts. "Didn't you say there was blood on the door, Diesel? Demon and angel? Could that have something to do with why Quinlan couldn't leave?"

Diesel grunted, the only indication either of us would receive that said he would ask the rest of the team what they thought.

Dr. Tiff pursed her lips together, so slightly I wouldn't have noticed had I not already been looking at her mouth. My heart pounded, and Diesel leaned forward, clearly listening in on that too. I knew what the doctor was going to ask, where this conversation was going.

"Did he ever attempt to starve you?"

Oh good. We were starting in the shallow end. My wraiths slid between my head and the back of the bed, acting like a pillow. "No, he never starved me. He always asked me what I wanted to eat, and if I answered, which I didn't often, he would actually go and get it."

Another bone cracked in Diesel's chest.

The doc's annoyed gaze flicked from Diesel and back to her clipboard. "Did he ever subject you to any kind of sensory torture; loud, sustained sounds, extreme heat or cold?"

I'd gone through a great many tortures in that room, but none to my physical body. Pierce had promised never to hurt me the moment I woke up and demanded to be let free. If we defined that as not inflicting harm on my body, then he'd kept that promise to this day.

"He took care of you?" Dr. Tiff's head tilted, her body the shape of a question mark.

Damn, I hadn't meant to say any of that out loud.

Diesel's heart must've been exploding from his chest for all the deep rumbling, snapping growls that came from it.

"Diesel, I see the merit of you being here, but if you can't refrain from adding your own commentary, then I will have to ask you to leave." Dr. Tiff's cheeks burned, two bright red circles.

I couldn't help my smirk at seeing the grizzly bear of a man dropping his head, his hair covering his thoroughly chastised face.

"He provided what I needed to meet my basic needs," I corrected her, telling myself immediately after that my heart didn't feel light from the way Diesel's lips had twitched up in the corners. I would *never* say that Pierce took care of me.

"He made you see things, though. And he made you sleep. What do you mean by that?"

Diesel's lips weren't pressed together, but his face was by no means relaxed.

"Gas. I don't know what kind. I'm pretty sure he pumped it in through the vents in the ceiling."

Dr. Tiff's expression darkened. "How often did he knock you out?"

"Varied. In the beginning, it was daily. That slowed down once he saw it wasn't having the desired effect."

"And what was that? The effect he desired?"

The muscles in my face clenched as though searching for a way to contract that allowed them to speak without Diesel hearing. I was a little shit to him, I knew, but I'd never inflict this kind of misery. "He wanted me to choose him."

There was a loud cracking sound, and I looked to find Diesel had snapped a wood shelf in pieces under his tight grip.

Dr. Tiff shot him a sharp look. "Diesel—"

I couldn't have him taken from me, not now, when he so clearly needed to be by my side. Or, more specifically, at the side of the Quinlan he wanted me to be. That hurt like a still-glowing iron poker, making my skin sizzle. "Technically, that wasn't commentary," I muttered under my breath, knowing both shifters in the room would have no problem hearing me.

"You're repairing or replacing that." Dr. Tiff leveled Diesel with a stern glare. She tightened her ponytail before looking to me, indicating I keep going.

"That was his goal all along. The reason for everything. Why he showed me his truths. He was always the hero of the story, if there was a hero."

Dr. Tiff sat straighter, pressing pen to paper. "Did he rape you?"

My heart pounded. I wasn't afraid of my answer; I simply hated that we were talking about this. How would this help anything? All these questions would do was magnify just how far removed I was from who I'd been. "No."

Dr. Tiff frowned along with Diesel. "It's important that you tell the truth."

Fucking shifters and their internal lie detectors. I was anxious and likely giving off all the signs that I was being dishonest. I wished we could move on and get to the part where we were done.

Diesel leaned away from the wall. "Quin, if you need a minute—"

"I don't need a minute!"

Fuck, his voice was so understanding. Soft and pacifying. It grated on my nerves like old bones grinding without the protection of cartilage. "He didn't rape me. That's the truth. He never even touched me, not once. That first day, he swore he'd wait until I wanted it, and then later, my wraiths protected me, even when I was unconscious. They couldn't keep me from passing out, but they covered my body like a second skin whenever I slept."

Dr. Tiff's face transformed, softening in a way she hadn't before while looking at the wraiths. "They took care of you."

My mouth stretched into a smile. "Yes."

"Well," Dr. Tiff chirped. "This feels like a good place to take a break. There's no reason for us to have to go through the interview all at once, and I don't think it would be a good idea to anyway. I'm due upstairs to check on the girls in a bit. Are you all right if I go, Quinlan? I have no problem canceling if you need company or a chance to talk more. I know these questions can dredge up forgotten emotions."

One of the wraiths unwound from my arm and ghosted over Dr. Tiff's forearm. *Goooood. Goooood.*

"They like you."

"I...will...spend some time deciding how I feel about that."

I smirked, and the wraiths vibrated, their version of a laugh.

After gathering her things, Dr. Tiff gave us both a long, questioning look, but she never opened her mouth to ask one. Instead, she smiled and headed for the door. "I have more than enough time to walk you back."

I very nearly took her up on her offer. I wasn't afraid of being alone with Diesel but knew this conversation was far from over. Diesel wasn't satisfied with a single word answer; he needed to know *everything*. My stomach felt like it was ripped out of my body, and I opened my lips to say yes, I'd love to walk with her when Diesel grunted again.

Fucking Neanderthal couldn't use his words, but he didn't need to anyway. I knew what that grunt meant. At least, I used to know.

"No thank you."

Her eyes didn't linger on my face like I might've expected. She seemed the type of person who would go above and beyond to make sure I was really comfortable with a situation. Her attention remained on my wraiths as they slid up and down my arms. She huffed, but her worries must've been satisfied by what she saw in them because she waved over her shoulder.

I looked at the door for as long as was reasonably possible before letting my head drop. There was an interesting crack beneath my left foot shaped like a butt, and I was thankful for it. I could sit and stare at that butt crack for —*ha, butt crack.*

"*Why* are you laughing?" Next to the word *exasperated* was a picture of Diesel.

The wet blanket descending heavily against my chest lifted. As quickly as that, Diesel brought me from the edge. "It's personal."

"Then there's no reason I can't know."

He was a bullheaded, arrogant, smothering, jackass of a man.

He smirked. "Thanks. I'll take that as a compliment."

Only Diesel would hear *smothering* and think it was a good thing. There had been a time when I'd considered it a good thing. Back when Diesel had been my world and I'd been ignorant to everything else. "That crack is shaped like a butt." I jerked my forehead while pointing my toe at it.

Diesel leaned forward, craning his neck to see that part of the floor.

"Huh. You're right." He pushed off the wall, stepping nearer to get a closer look. He stared at the butt crack for longer than the crack deserved. It wasn't *that* interesting, but then, Diesel did have a thing for butts.

The heat radiating from his body soaked into my skin like water into a desert on the first day of the rainy season. I refused to close my eyes and let them flutter. Somehow, Diesel always burned hotter than anyone I'd met. It called to me like a tropical beach, waves lapping against the sand, as if gently insisting I jump in and let the heat cover me. I'd been cold for so long; I'd convinced myself it was how I liked it.

There was no lying when the proof stood directly beside me, staring at a crack in the ground like it was the most precious thing. "It isn't that funny," I snapped, feeling something too much like jealousy shoot up my spine.

Diesel sighed, and feeling his breath kiss my skin was a stupid reason to groan, so I wouldn't. Barely. "I know that was hard..." His face softened, turning gentle and *under-standing*. I much preferred him scowling at me, giving me a trademark Diesel glower. That was at least sexy in a visceral, no-feelings way. This version of him now, it didn't promise a rough fuck, but a gentle lovemaking, and though I didn't really know what either of those things felt like, I knew my heart could only handle one of them.

"You know?" My words flung from my mouth like stones from a slingshot. "How do you know? Did that happen to you? Were you kidnapped and held hostage?"

He jerked back, his eyes closing briefly. Long enough for me to feel like shit. "No, I wasn't. Quinlan, I just wanted to say I'm proud of you. No matter what you do, or have to say, I'm proud of you."

No. No, no, no, no. I couldn't let this happen again. I had to find a way to stop the wave of pleasure that his words sent rolling. I wasn't the same kid I'd been before. Diesel had been right all along—I'd been a kid then. I was an adult now, and I would not let myself drop back into the same bad habits. Like letting Diesel's praise run my life. "Who says I want your pride? Why do you think I care?" I jumped from the bed, forcing Diesel back as I put more space between our bodies.

Too bad I'd put myself in the position *farthest* from the door.

"Fine, Quin. Fuck! I'm not proud of you. You're a little shit. How about that?"

Hearing him call me that didn't hurt in the slightest, I felt relieved. Finally, he was saying something, calling me out—fighting back. "Honest. For once."

"What the fuck does that mean, Quinlan?" Diesel's voice dipped low, the question sounding so much like a threat, my wraiths expanded to cover more of my body.

"You let me believe this world was sunshine and roses when really it's a broken sixty-watt bulb and *weeds*."

Diesel straightened, lifting his face to show off the

haughty line of his nose. "You're mad at me because I protected you? Too fucking bad. That's what I'll always do."

No one could infuriate me like Diesel. Before I quite knew what I was doing, I stomped back and pushed Diesel's chest as hard as I could.

The asshole didn't budge. I couldn't feel helpless, like there was nothing I could do to change this situation. I had to fling *something* at him that he'd feel. "No, I'm *mad at you* because you sheltered me. Coddled me, body and mind. Maybe if you hadn't, if I'd known more about the dangers, maybe then you wouldn't have to be proud of me in the first place because I never would've been taken."

If I'd known the evils of the world, perhaps then I would've at least locked my windows and doors that night. Who knew how that could've changed things? If I'd taken the slightest attempts at protecting myself, instead of relying on a man who hadn't even been on the same continent, maybe our pack wouldn't be dead right now. "He didn't torture me. Didn't touch me. I am as *pristine* and *unsullied* as ever, but I am *not* the same person. That Quinlan died along with the rest of the pack."

I somehow managed not to let my voice crack. Pushing Diesel from me was harder than I would've thought a month ago. At first, flashes of what I'd seen him do were *all* I could see when I looked at him, but at some point, I didn't see the fabricated Diesels anymore. Just him. Even if it hurt, Diesel deserved to know this. Maybe then he'd finally see the dream he'd clung to so tightly just wasn't possible. My tale had gone from fairy to cautionary. The life Diesel could have with me now was nothing like the life we would've had. The life he still expected. Why else would he look at me exactly as he used to?

"Okay?" Diesel threw his hands in the air, the very picture of frustration.

My wraiths dropped from my limbs, slinking toward the window. They weren't normally cowards, but Diesel brought out strange emotions in us all.

"Why is that such a big fucking deal? None of us are the same person, Quin. If you're alive, you change. You grow. That only stops when you die."

"I don't mean it like that! I mean it like... inside. In here." Putting space between us, I backed to the wall and tapped my chest, my eyes swimming with tears. "This is where I am changed, Diesel. In my heart."

His body froze as though the man had suddenly become a sculpture of himself. He didn't blink or breathe. I wouldn't have been surprised if he'd forced his heart to stop as well. He opened his mouth with the slow progression of a rusty drawbridge. "Your heart has changed?"

"No, Diesel, not like that." I rushed to speak because it was beginning to feel like I could detect his emotions, and the only thing that filled my senses was anguish. "But it's *broken*, and even if I somehow manage to put it together, it won't be the same shape. That's impossible."

Diesel managed to start his heart back up.

I didn't look at him, but I felt him drawing near. That damn heat.

"I'll help you put it together, Quin. And whatever shape it ends up will be perfect."

If I didn't yearn with every cell in my body to believe him, sink into his embrace, and let him fix me, I wouldn't have gotten so angry. I pushed him again, but this time, I knew he wouldn't budge. "Stop calling me perfect, Diesel. Please. We both know it isn't true."

Diesel snagged my wrist, pulling my arm toward him

with a growl. His lips were on mine before I finished drawing in a gasp of air. He covered me, from head to toe. I was never so aware of how much bigger he was than when he kissed me. Taller, wider, more muscled, he could do what he wanted to me, and I'd be unable to stop it.

His palms gripped my thighs tightly while he lifted me to sit on the window ledge. His grip never loosened, not when he pulled my thighs wide open, nor when his body thrust between my legs like a wedge through a block of wood. He filled the triangle between my thighs like he owned it and everything surrounding. My knees were his, my thighs, my cock...

Fuck, his dick pressed hotly against my core. Thick, wide, and throbbing, finally, something that hadn't changed. The hours I'd spent picturing his massive dick probably qualified me to get certified in Dick Picturing. For a while, I'd convinced myself he was wider than he was long, but that couldn't be true. Compared to my own, he was a giant.

I moaned, reaching for his waist. I found his belt buckle, but instead of leaning into the motion and helping me get closer, Diesel stepped back, growls coming from his chest as he took away his lips, belt buckle, and gigantic dick. He looked at me with an expression full of so much love, it was all I could do not to turn away. "This isn't how we imagined it five years ago, Quin, but that doesn't matter because you're here with me. You're alive. Yes, the world is a shithole, and no, I didn't ever want you to see that."

My resolve couldn't crumble; it had never been fully formed in the first place.

"We can live in this shithole together. Our pack gets stronger every day. The world can get cold, but I'll be there to warm you."

How did he know the exact words to begin mending my heart together?

"I'll be there to keep you warm, Quinlan, *always.*"

I felt like a spear, set loose into the air and flying free before slamming into the ground with a vicious twang.

Diesel noticed the change in me, and our eyes met, but not until after mine darted to the door. Our stare-off lasted a moment before I moved first, ducking under his arms with the help of my wraiths. "Quin!" Diesel yelled when I got to the door.

I spun around, all fury and hurt. I'd fallen for the same exact lines. The *same exact* promises. Our gazes collided, and my anger grew too large for me to handle. "Not. Always."

8

DIESEL

OF COURSE, if something wasn't covered with shit already, I could always cover it myself.

I didn't blame Quinlan for running after what I'd said. He'd spent half of the last decade being cold. I knew he had because all that time I'd been cold.

Even if I didn't blame him, I couldn't hold back my instinct that demanded that I give chase. This was the second time my mate was running from me.

But the other nephilim, likely sensing his distress, were there to greet him at the foot of the stairs. They enveloped him in their arms, turning to glare at me in unison as my boots pounded down the hallway behind him.

"Diesel, a minute?" Knox peeled his body away from the shadows, appearing by my side like one of Sitka's ghosts.

The nephilim scurried Quinlan out the front door while Knox headed for the stairs, making it clear with the angle of his body that I was to follow.

I didn't always do what Knox said, and this felt like one of those moments.

"Come to the operations room. I want to show you something."

I looked back out of instinct, in the direction I last saw Quinlan travel.

"He's still Quin, Diesel. Scared and confused, but still Quin. He'll come around. You just have to be patient."

"I. Am. Patient." My teeth should've crumbled out of my mouth for how hard I clenched them.

Knox snorted. "I can see that."

Knox turned, taking the first step up when the hotel walls echoed with the sound of the alarm blaring, followed immediately by screaming that filled the staircase, coming from outside. I wrenched the door open, taking a single bounding step to get there, as Knox shifted and darted out. Footsteps pounded loudly from the second floor, but I didn't wait to see who it was coming.

I found Quinlan cowered behind the Hummer with the other nephilim. Jazz clung to Angus and Onyx as Sitka covered as much of them as he could with his body. Quinlan covered the rest.

Towering over fifty feet high in the middle of the yard on the other side of the vehicle stood a wall of water, shaped roughly like a man, save for two large horns that sprouted from its head like trees with no branches. Featureless, the demon constantly churned, looking like an ocean storm come to life—a type of monster sailors used to whisper about when the stars were out. It swung a massive, liquid fist toward the Hummer, sending it rolling down the drive and into the crumbling fountain, leaving the nephilim unprotected.

The wraiths stretched, spreading like a hanging sheet that billowed inward as the water beast sent a ball of seawater that would've drowned them all in seconds. There was too much water for the wraiths to keep back, though, and they snapped apart, rattling loudly as both wraiths swelled in defense. But while the wraiths were lightning-fast shapeshifters, the water creature beat them when it came to raw power.

They were able to hold on long enough for me and Knox to bound forward. He hoisted Jazz and the children toward the hotel entrance—and I assumed the panic room in the basement—while I hauled Sitka under one arm and Quin under the other.

The twins, Doc, and Faust appeared in the door for a fraction of a second before another water bomb soared over our heads and blasted through the hotel entrance. Their bodies disappeared, swept back by the flash flood. A second water bomb hit the ground behind us, rushing forward in a wave that knocked me off my feet. Before I could establish which way was up, another wave ripped the air from my lungs, flinging my limbs around like a rag doll. Sitka and Quinlan slid from under my arms. My fingers grasped at nothing but water until I fell abruptly against the sodden lawn on my hands and knees. I scrambled to my feet, coughing up enough seawater to fill the fountain—if it wasn't currently cracked beyond repair.

I ran forward, knowing already that I wouldn't get to my mate in time. He lay sprawled out on the lawn more than twenty feet away. The water giant loomed overhead. I couldn't see Sitka and assumed he'd poofed away.

The water demon opened his hand, palm down, sending a solid stream of ocean over Quinlan's head.

The air leeched from my lungs, leaving me as breathless as Quinlan.

When I reached the endless spout, no more than two seconds later, I leaped forward—and bounced right back. It felt like my body hit a cement wall, and I would've been forced several feet away if I hadn't shifted and dug my claws into the dirt.

I hadn't been pushed away, but I still couldn't break through the rush of water, and it had been far too long since Quin was trapped beneath. I lunged forward again. My muzzle slammed into the water wall, cracking as the bone snapped. Blood poured from my nose, but I didn't give a fuck about that.

Not when it looked like the water demon was weakening, shrinking by the bucket, soaking into the dirt and pouring over the edge of the cliff. I looked back toward the driveway, spotting a young man with sandy brown hair and bright blue eyes. He held his hands palms out and stretched in opposite directions, a look of complete concentration on his face.

I turned back to Quinlan and dove, shifting once more when I breached the wall. The force of the water nearly brought me to my knees, but I grabbed Quinlan and rolled. My shoulders dug into the ground, and I clutched him tightly, rolling once more to push off the ground and get into position to begin CPR.

I froze with my hands clamped together, prepared to begin chest compressions. Quinlan's entire body was covered with a black, smoky bubble. I poked my index finger against it, and the wraiths popped open. Quinlan blinked rapidly, turning his head toward me, the smallest smile turning his—

A tsunami of water pushed me off my feet. I'd kept my eyes open long enough to see that Quinlan hadn't also been swept away, but then I dropped over the edge of the cliff, and I couldn't see his face. It looked like he'd been screaming.

I half shifted, dragging my claws through the rock wall sliding by in front of me. The friction ground at my claws, snapping several down the middle before I managed to snag a root. I closed my fingers over it, gripping while waiting for the root to snap in two, which would send my body plummeting to the rocky shoreline below.

It didn't. At least, not before I peered up the cliff at the line of faces looking down at me from over a hundred feet away.

"He's here! Tell Quinlan he's fine."

Fine was an overstatement.

Knox's announcement was met with a shuddering gasp that sounded too much like the beginning of a sob. I climbed upward, arms shaking as I fought to keep hold of the wet cliff face while also plotting the fastest route up.

"Hi! I'm Kansas, Wyatt's omega," a cheery voice said up top while I climbed. I figured it was the sandy-brown-haired man I'd spotted.

"How did you do that?" Knox asked sharply.

He got an equally sharp growl in reply, I assumed from Wyatt.

"I-I can suck a person's energy—well, not just a person, actually. I recently learned that. And, thankfully, I also recently learned how to draw and release without giving it back or consuming it, which, thank God, because that was some nasty energy. Like old dirt. Borrowed. But *powerful.*"

Borrowed?

My arms ached, the way made treacherous by slippery roots and handholds. I dug my feet into the wall beneath me and pushed to the top, gripping two handfuls of grass and mud. The twins were closest and reached their hands down, but I was too focused on getting back to Quin to accept the help.

First in my line of sight, hovering close behind Kansas's shoulder, was Nash's twin, Wyatt. I didn't know why they were here, but I was fucking glad.

I found Quinlan, my gaze dropping to the pulse in his neck, pounding like a tiny piston under the skin, his breath making his shoulders bounce as quickly as a hummingbird's heart. My boy needed me.

"Quin."

9

QUINLAN

Though the demon creature was gone, I still felt like I was underwater gasping for air that I didn't even want while I pictured Diesel's body broken and lifeless. I'd rather be lifeless too.

With my wraiths around, I'd grown bold, cocky. Nothing happened to me that I didn't want—except I *really* didn't want Diesel to go over that edge. Beneath all that power, the wraiths still had to choose. I knew they would choose me.

Aliiiive. Heeeee's alive.

"He's here! Tell Quinlan he's fine."

The world snapped back into sharp focus, flooding my senses with too much stimuli. My skin tingled like insects crawled the surface of my body. I wanted to cry but knew if I did, I wouldn't be able to stop. I'd sob my internal organs right out my mouth like a frog vomiting out its own stomach to expel toxins.

"Quin."

His voice was the sweetest sound. Rough and raspy, it slid over my body like a lion's tongue, bringing pleasure *and* pain. I couldn't speak. I wasn't able to ask him if he was okay or why he was such a fucking idiot in the first place to put himself in that position *for me?* Didn't he know, if his death didn't kill me, knowing he lost it to save me would?

The wraiths glided from me to Diesel, looping behind his lower back. Traitors.

They urged him forward. He needed no urging and was already striding toward me like him holding me was a foregone conclusion. When he was close enough I could see into his eyes, and the life that still burned there, I could finally speak. "Don't do that again!"

I whirled around, stomping back toward the hotel.

Halfway there, I glanced up, stumbling over my steps. It looked like that one stone from that one Indiana Jones movie had rolled right down the middle.

It didn't make a difference to where I was going. I still had no fucking clue. I couldn't go back to my room. The space created by those four walls had started feeling colder with each passing day. But now I had everyone's eyes on me, thanks to my panic attack and the following awful display of ingratitude.

The longer I imagined their eyes burning into me, the more I felt like I was burning. Not from fire, but ice. My teeth chattered while sweat poured down my forehead. My body shook, lessened only by the way my chest heaved for air—air that I couldn't find. Knowing I was having a panic attack didn't mean I could do anything about it. After a certain point, it was just easier to jump in headfirst and ride it out than it was to try to tear out of your own skin. I prepared to do just that when a new sensation hit me, one that warmed my frozen places.

A hand squeezed my neck. Not *a hand*. Diesel's. He gripped my nape with his fingers on one side and his thumb the other, squeezing just tightly enough. My body remembered the feeling. Before, the way he held me had never failed to make me drop, stealing any negative emotion and replacing it with warm, safe Diesel.

"You're safe, baby boy," Diesel murmured in my ear. "That's it, breathe. Good, my *good* boy."

The bubble of warmth formed in my heart and grew, expanding to cover the rest of me with happy zings of pleasure. My breaths still made noise when I sucked them in and blew out, but I knew I was coming down. And I didn't even have to jump.

The space around us was dark. He'd carried me into the hotel. The damage looked concentrated at the entrance, and the trajectory had, thankfully, veered to the right, obliterating the hallway and corner of the sitting room, but leaving the stairs intact. There was less damage than I expected, but I'd forgotten they'd reinforced this space with hellfire stone.

When Diesel ascended the last step and turned down the hallway to our rooms, I let out a final, slightly shaky breath, pressing my nose flat against his pectoral. His chest was warm and firm, making me feel fragile but safe. I peeled my face back and looked up his body, to his thick, corded neck, and then his relieved face. "That's the second time you brought me back."

His mouth went slack, and his eyebrows briefly rounded, like he'd been sure I hadn't noticed the way he'd brought me back from the brink when my wraiths had destroyed the hotel.

He dropped me, sitting on his bed. My head swiveled around. I wasn't sure what I was searching for until I didn't find it.

Me. Pictures of me.

Silly, candid photos of the two of us had forever lined

his room and mine. Every so often, or when he moved from pack house to pack house, he always agreed to let me decorate his bedroom, and I'd never wanted to give him a single chance to forget me.

But here, I wasn't anywhere. My picture wasn't anywhere, and though I *knew* it was a selfish reason to be upset, my spine still stiffened. I lifted my arms, waiting for my wraiths to wind back around me, but they never came. They weren't even in the room.

Nothing was stopping Diesel from continuing to ravish me until my desire took over and I eventually gave in—except my consent. That was how he was so much different than Pierce and why Pierce hadn't ever been able to create a version of Diesel that had truly seemed like him. I didn't need my wraiths to be safe with Diesel. I just was.

But not always!

That was a petty thought to spring up, but it was enough to let me put a stop to the way I leaned toward him like a dog at the end of its leash. As much as his touch made me feel like it was *then*, it wasn't.

Diesel, noticing the change in my body, leaned back, making it clear he wouldn't crowd in, and rubbed a heavy hand down his face. He made an irritated noise before stomping into his bathroom. The faucet ran for a few seconds before he returned. His face was still dripping, but he'd pulled his hair back. He pulled the chair out from his desk and sat down, crossing his right ankle over his left knee, the very picture of calm. "I *feel* as though you are experiencing some conflicted feelings. Do you... want to talk about it?"

I smiled. He sounded like he was reciting a line from a couple's therapy brochure. Feelings were Diesel's kryptonite. Recognizing them and talking about them. Hence the way it had taken heavy hints to get Diesel to see we weren't just bonded, but mates. I should've recognized that I still felt too raw to control what came out of my mouth, but the fact that he'd initiated this, despite how uncomfortable it clearly made him, compelled me to be honest.

"I miss you. But not you? Or is it you? I don't know, anymore. You aren't the same. I'm not the same. The projections I saw of you were just that. I know you didn't really do any of that stuff. But I don't know what to do now with that information."

My nervous energy pushed me to my feet, and I paced the width of Diesel's room, continuing to try to explain only once I'd done a few repetitions to work off the edge. "I see you every day. But I still *miss* you. And I don't know why. And it makes me feel like there's this darkness hanging over me, something bad—I mean, a monster made of water is a pretty dark thing. But I don't think it was that. It feels like... I'm still there, in that room. Like this is his best nightmare yet, and I'm waiting for it all to go bad."

I spun to face him, panting more than I should've for moving so little.

Diesel grinned.

I didn't all the way trust it.

"I know how to fix that," he said, both as a sultry promise and a boast.

I must've fallen into a bad porno because the only response I could summon was a wide-eyed, "You do?" *Why* did I have to lose my cynicism with this man? Fate couldn't let me keep that much to protect myself?

He stalked closer, gently pulling me by the hand until I stood tucked between his body and the dresser. "From today on, you're sleeping here, in my room, *with me*. In *our* room, Quinlan."

My gut did a tight backflip and just kept spinning. Could I survive constant contact with this man with whom I had no boundaries? My body tightened, coiling warmly with anticipation and *need*. I waited for my wraiths to come and keep me from having to face anything I didn't want to, but my skin remained bare, naked, without them acting as my armor. I harnessed the flash of fear that elicited and used it to fuel my sudden burst out from under Diesel's arm. Being so much smaller had its advantages.

"No way! I'm not staying in here with you! We've never even...we've never..." I spun, turning away from the door to confront him.

He stood exactly as he had, moving only to face me. "Fucked?"

My stupid whimper escaped too quickly for me to muffle it. *Fucked*. There'd been a time when I'd said coarse words to get a reaction out of him. Now a single word from his lips made my entire body throb. Getting fucked by Diesel had once been my only goal in life. Right now, it still felt like my only goal.

Could it really happen that easily? Spending what felt like an eternity waiting, only for it all to come to an end in a single moment, while people downstairs were surely wondering what the hell we were doing still up here?

"That's your plan, isn't it? So you can get...your hands all over me!" Apparently, I'd gone from porno movie to virginal school marm.

For a second time, Diesel stalked my way, and I was just as helpless to move. He felt like standing next to a roaring bonfire, hot and *crackling* with lust. My eyes dropped to his waist because, like my wraiths, they were also traitors. I bit my lip in time to stop me from making any noises in the face of the thick bulge that stretched the front of Diesel's pants—like two cans of pop stacked one over the other.

I allowed my gulp. Technically, it wasn't a sound.

Though he stood close enough to touch, Diesel's body didn't press against mine at any point. "The next time I touch you, baby boy, it will be because you *begged* for it."

Sweet Jesus, how am I still standing?

"In your dreams." I'd meant my reply to be sharp, but there hadn't been enough air to produce anything more than a whisper.

Diesel nodded, accepting my reply like a gauntlet. "Sit on *our* bed and don't move. I'll be right back."

"Where are you going?" *And why are my hands clasped under my chin like a goddamn maiden?* I yanked them apart and shoved my fists into the mattress.

Diesel smirked. The twinkle in his eye said he knew of the battle going on in my head between my logic and my instincts. "Don't you worry your pretty little face about it."

That damn man. I was going to beg, all right, and when he got close enough, I'd kick him in the balls. I couldn't kick him in the balls if I wasn't still in his room, though, so as much as I didn't want to, I'd have to stay.

Unless he took too long.

Ten minutes later, Diesel kicked in the door, a huge duffel bag slung over his shoulder while he carried three boxes. When he set the boxes down, I recognized my book and the whetstone I kept in the nightstand beside my bed.

My lips popped open. "You can't... I didn't say yes."

Diesel emptied the duffel, carefully moving folded stacks of my clothes from the bag to an open dresser drawer. He didn't even need to push the other items already inside out of the way. The space was already there, waiting for my shirts.

And even if that filled my heart with bubbles, the kind found only in sugary soda water, I couldn't back down now. He expected me to *beg*. "Fine. Unpack my clothes. I'll just make you pack them back up before the day ends."

Diesel grunted, sparing me the briefest glance before he looked down at the carpet, spotting a pair of my underwear like he hadn't left it there intentionally. He stretched down to get it, bending at the waist in the opposite direction and giving me a full view of his firm ass.

I could crack a glowstick on that ass.

Maybe Jazz had a glowstick I could borrow.

"In case you were worried," Diesel said, his voice pleased and entirely too knowing that he'd caught me staring with dirty things in my mind.

While also drooling.

I wiped my mouth, and the room turned tropical, the muggy heat making me sweat. "In case I was worried— what?" I snapped, which only made Diesel smile wider.

"The worst injury from the attack, other than you almost drowning and me falling off a cliff—again—was a broken elbow that is already healing. For how much Huntley is complaining, you'd think his arm was ripped off. Kansas scanned the area. There aren't any other threats around for the moment. The Walkers came here with a message from the council and to get briefed on the Portal situation. They'll wait."

Wait?

My confusion must've shone clear on my face because Diesel's lips curled again. "Change out of your damp clothes and then *stay*. Only a few more loads."

"Until you turn right back around and move it all out?" I countered, but he was already down the hallway.

I didn't actually have that much stuff. He was strong

enough; he could probably haul it all in one. Those *glorious* rippling muscles weren't just for show.

He came back much more quickly the second time. I'd only just pulled down my dry shirt when he kicked the door open, returning in half the time of the trip before. He carried less than he had the first time and did so without a stitch on from the waist up.

"*Why* do you have your shirt off?"

His naked chest had *always* been a thing of beauty but, like fine wine, Diesel had *aged well*. Coarse strands of silver mixed among the light dusting of dark hair across his pectorals and down his happy trail. Would they taste differently than the black ones?

Somehow, he was also broader, and I was pretty sure I spotted an extra pack on those abs. Maybe that wasn't humanly possible, but Diesel wasn't human. He was a shifter. An alpha. Such a fucking *alpha*. I wanted to climb him like a tree and ride him like it was windy.

"It's hot work moving your stuff where it belongs."

So we were both just going to ignore the obvious fact that he wasn't sweating. Okay. Cool.

"Don't worry, baby," Diesel said, catching me once again ogling parts of his body. "Only one more load and then if you have anything to ask me, I'll be here to hear it."

Yes, Diesel was arrogant. That wasn't the issue at hand.

My wraiths made me feel safe. They were amazing cuddlers and always knew how to soothe and relax me, but Diesel made me want to rip my clothes off, howl at the moon, and hump his face. Or he could hump mine. I'd need a whole lot of time figuring out how to get my mouth around that beast, but I'd give it my best shot.

But damn it, why did he have to be so cocky? He

expected me to beg. Like he didn't want into my pants just as badly?

This wasn't anything like how our dynamic used to be. I'd hardly ever given him a reason to be truly angry with me. For the most part, I'd done what Diesel said when he told me to do it. In return, he'd been gentle and compassionate.

Those things were still inside him, but he was also rough in his responses. *Hard.*

But, like he'd said, if you're alive, you changed, and at least *this* change in our relationship—the one I was failing at pretending didn't exist—made me weak at the knees.

When he returned with the rest of my stuff, he didn't immediately begin putting the items away like the times before. He set the boxes down, as well as the rest of the jackets Sitka had made for me, and shut the door. The lock clicked into place, making me flinch. I wouldn't beg from this man. He was *mine.* I'd take what I wanted.

"So—" he said, but there wasn't time for him to finish.

I launched forward, leaping in the air and wrapping my arms and legs around Diesel's body like a monkey. He caught me easily and held me with just as much ease. "Fuck me, *now,*" I demanded, making sure it sounded like an actual demand. Before he could reply, I clamped my lips over his. The angle was a little odd, me coming from above, but I liked how I could easily nibble his bottom lip. He'd changed, but I had too. Maybe the old Quinlan would've gladly begged, but I took what I wanted now.

Diesel growled, kissing me back. Once he took over, the angle felt even better. He pulled away, much sooner than I would've liked. "No." He kissed my nose.

I barely felt the kiss. He was *rejecting* me? A surge of freezing cold humiliation soaked me to the bone. Was this the part where Pierce's fantasy dream turned into a nightmare?

Diesel pushed his face against my neck and inhaled for several seconds.

He didn't want to have sex with me, but he wanted to sniff me?

"Sweet omega, I'm covered in dust and sweat. I need to wash."

That wasn't a flat-out rejection—and he'd called me his omega—so maybe I could show my face in this hemisphere again. "Okay."

I pushed against his chest, planning on hiding somewhere suitable, like in the closet or under the bed. Diesel slid his hands lower to more firmly cup my ass before carrying me with him into the bathroom, where he shut the door.

He continued to carry me as he moved quickly around the room, starting the water, rummaging through a drawer for a bottle of bath bubbles. The thick liquid poured from the bottle in a single stream that quickly filled the bathtub with white foam. The tub was as large as three tubs pressed together. Diesel was a big man, both in size and attitude, but there was more than enough room in that tub for him *and* another body.

Jealousy sliced my midsection like a hot knife.

"Why?" Diesel grunted, his arm's tightening as he sensed my distress.

"Big tub for just you," I muttered.

His thick, shapely eyebrows curved into a V. "That's the point."

I didn't hear his words, not really. The sounds broke apart, coming together to form the ring of a boxing bell. "If you think I am getting into a tub where you have...*messed around* with some other...some other...hussy, then you have another thing coming, mister."

Diesel beamed. As infuriating as it was, his smile still made my breath tremble. "I put this tub in after we found you, as well as all of the smelly stuff."

My lips twitched, threatening to smile. The smelly stuff must've been the bubble bath and lotion bottles on the counter. I knew he didn't use that stuff; he didn't smell like anything but himself.

"I haven't touched a single *hussy*, Quinlan. You're my mate. *My fucking mate.* Why would I ever want to touch anyone else?"

I licked my lips, both to wet the dry skin and to ease their trembling. "But...I was dead. You thought I was dead."

"So?" He lifted me to sit on the edge of the tub and knelt between my legs. Even in that position he was taller, but only by a little. He grabbed the hem of my shirt, fingering the fabric as though he was looking at the gates to nirvana. "There's no one else for me, Quinlan. No one. No matter what. That was never the question." As he spoke, he let his fingertips glide under my shirt, bringing goosebumps in his wake.

"Then what was the question?" I gasped.

The look he gave me was *potent*. We weren't playing. And we weren't waiting, not any more. "Is this your favorite shirt?"

I shook my head.

Diesel tore the shirt from my chest like it was made of wet paper. He brushed the flapping sides off my shoulders, tossing it to the side. He didn't ask before gripping the crotch of my pants and tearing a large hole where the seams met. He lifted my hips from the tub with one hand, steadying me with his other splayed between my shoulder blades.

I caught myself on the other side of the tub, reclining so far back, if he dropped my hips, I'd be unable to stop myself from plopping into the water. He gripped my hips tightly, making it clear I didn't have to worry about that possibility.

Diesel brought the apex of my thighs to his face. His nose buried between my cock and balls—still clothed by my boxer briefs—and *inhaled,* breathing me in like a drowning man breaking the surface.

I could only whimper as my alpha scented me in the most primal of ways. My cock was hard, leaking precum at an embarrassing rate. Diesel growled at the dark spot on my briefs, where my dick strained against the fabric. He pressed his face forward and nuzzled the cum stain.

"Mine," he grunted, immediately fulfilling the beginning of about half the fantasies I'd ever had of him. How many times had I stroked myself to completion, imagining him growling that one word? Diesel made a low, unhappy whine. "Need you to smell like me. Only me."

He ripped open my underwear. I was surprised they'd lasted that long. When there was nothing on my body to separate his tongue from my skin, he closed his eyes and lapped a single line from my balls and up the line of my rigid cock. He repeated the motion, licking over and over, changing the angle so that when he was finished, his tongue had swiped over every inch of my core.

I moaned, unable to care about who might hear me. The motion didn't feel explicitly sexual—any *more* sexual anyway, than his tongue on my balls already was. It felt more like a cleansing as he laved away the world, replacing it all with only him. His scent. Diesel lifted my hands from the edge of the tub as though I was as heavy as a feather. I curled into him, not bothering to cling to him. He had me without my help.

"Diesel..." I whispered as he lowered me into the hot water. My heart spun. Leaving his arms was the last thing I wanted. "...am I awake? Is this really happening?"

"Yes, baby boy, *yes*." He stripped in a blink of an eye, sensing how much I needed back in his arms. He lifted my dripping body from the water, bringing my back to his chest before dipping beneath the steaming water. He squeezed his arms, nestling my ass against his humongous cock. "You're awake. This is real. I have you in my arms, and I will fight until I am dead to keep you here."

He leaned forward, pushing my front closer to the water to grab the loofah and a bar of soap that smelled like oranges. He leaned back, settling against the end of the tub, and I went with him, sinking deeper into the water.

My eyes drooped. The warm water, and Diesel's presence, made my body lax—boneless.

Diesel worked the soap against the loofah, rubbing up a thick lather. He spread the white foam up my left arm, working the loofah between my fingers and moving up to my armpit.

I laughed, wiggling to get away.

I froze at Diesel's sharp growl.

"I'm sorry, baby boy. I tickled you and made you laugh, but if you don't stop wiggling, I'm not going to be able to keep this nice for you."

It was then that I noticed, while my body relaxed into goo, his was tight. I didn't need it nice or kind. I just needed to finally discover what it felt like to hang off his dick like a flag on a flagpole.

"When did you get such a dirty mind, baby?" Diesel sounded more impressed than judging.

Clearly, I'd spoken my thoughts again. My cheek pressed against his chest. "I've always had it. Why do you think we got along so well?"

We both knew that wasn't entirely true. In my early years, I'd been a model student, son, and pack member. It wasn't until I hit puberty and my loins called for one man that I started misbehaving and letting my mind run wild with possibilities. One thing not having sex with the man of your dreams gave you was a lot of really horny hours imagining what you would do if you ever had sex with the man of your dreams.

"I assumed it was because you're mine."

I elbowed him, but there was no fire in it. My elbow just slid over his wet, soapy skin.

Diesel continued washing me, bringing the loofah over every inch of my skin, no matter how personal or private. When he lifted me and set the loofah on a course for my butt crack, I wiggled and yelped.

"Hey! Personal spaces!"

Diesel growled, and if I didn't know for a fact this man would never hurt me, I'd have been afraid of the dark sound. "All your spaces are mine."

I really shouldn't let that possessive behavior continue, but who the heck was I kidding? All of Diesel's places were mine too, personal or not. "Okay, but are you going to start *doing* anything to me? This is a real great bath and all." I rotated my hips down against his erection. Though wiggling had been my idea, I gasped from the thrill skittering up my spine as the move brought Diesel's length prodding against my rim.

"Sit *still*, baby boy." Like before, his whisper was as much a warning as a command. "I'm going to stretch this sweet hole open." He jerked his hips ever so slightly, enough to elicit another gasp. "But first I want you clean. Both of us. I don't want anything in our room except the smell and taste of you and me. Understand?"

Yes, but only barely. I understood him wanting to rinse away the world, but not how he was able to continue hesitating despite the fact I was there, wanting and so very willing. I'd built up this moment so much in my head. There wasn't a chance it would live up to my expectations, but I didn't care. I remained as patiently as I could, letting Diesel manhandle my arms and legs, turning me over so he could do a *thorough* cleaning of my backside that left me moaning and needy.

When Diesel finally bent forward to pull the plug, I leaped from the tub, surprising him with my speed, agility, and overall slipperiness. He stood, sending rivers of water down his muscular thighs. His cock jutted out from his body, as proud and bigheaded as the alpha.

With eyes like saucers, I stared at my mate—my Diesel. I'd always known he packed heat, but had never gotten a clear look at the weapon of mass destruction he carried in his pants. A thing of beauty, the seventh, eighth, and ninth wonder of the world. I didn't know how I wasn't *already* pregnant just from having stood near *that* for so long.

And it was all mine.

My hand whipped forward of its own volition, taking a firm hold of Diesel's erection and tugging, not like I would for a handjob, but to pull him from the tub and back into the room to the bed.

Diesel grinned, yanking out of my grip before we reached our destination. "My cock isn't a leash, boy."

He easily lifted me off my feet, but before I could wrap my arms and legs around him, he repositioned me so that he carried me bridal-style against his chest. His gaze softened, and he cupped my cheek, smiling softly.

This was the Diesel that was always mine, had always been mine. The version of Diesel that he showed to his pack was him too, but he'd only ever let his guard down around me. I frowned at the sudden thought that without me around, he'd had no one to relax around, to let the walls crumble enough they could see the man within.

Diesel's lips curled softly as he caressed my eyebrows with his thumb. He tapped my curved lips with his claw. "What's wrong?"

"Nothing. Not anymore." I curled into him. "I'm sorry, Diesel, for the time you spent thinking I was dead. That had to have felt very lonely."

Diesel's eyes darkened with the memory of those days. His chest rumbled in what was likely supposed to be a growl, but it came out a whimper. "You're here now, Quin. That's all that matters. I wanted you to have the life you deserved so much, I thought I was protecting you from me." He kissed my nose and liked it so much, he pressed gentle kisses to my cheeks, chin, and eyelids.

My skin felt alive and tingling. I blinked away the happy tears and looked at Diesel with new clarity. He was so strong and determined. There wasn't an obstacle he wouldn't fight his way through to get to me. And yet he still couldn't seem to see *his* worth. "Why would I need protection from my alpha?"

He set me down on the bed, and I scrambled to my knees, lunging like an arrow let loose from an archer's bow. My mouth found my bullseye, but I only managed to swipe my tongue over his thick head before he lifted me up by the shoulders. "I can't make up for lost time, but I can say *no more.* I've waited long enough to taste you," he rasped, spinning me around like a toy.

As quick as turning a doorknob, I suddenly hung upside down. My wet hair dripped onto the comforter as Diesel wasted no time licking my ass like he'd buried treasure there and it was time to collect. With his lips, tongue, and teeth, he toyed with my pucker. His soft but rigid tongue pressed into my tight ring, and I would've flopped to the floor from pleasure if Diesel hadn't been holding me suspended, upside down, where he raised my ass to his mouth.

"Diesel! Holy fuck, that...that's your tongue?" Tight and mostly untouched, my pucker wasn't used to being toyed with, and even Diesel's tongue felt like more than I could bear.

He didn't reply with words, only a low rumbling purr that made me smile, not because of how I felt, but because of how he sounded. Happy and content.

While I was happy at his satisfaction, I wasn't content, not when Diesel brought me so much pleasure. With the way I hung from his hands, I didn't have much leverage, but my head was already in position, so I let it hang upside down and opened my lips, cleaning Diesel's dripping tip.

He snarled, pausing what he was doing for a fraction of a second. I liked that I'd distracted him that way. Emboldened, I tongued the slit at the head, searching for more of his earthy, wild flavor. Diesel roared, humping my face and mindlessly shoving more of his thick, veiny dick into my mouth.

He didn't hold my head in place, leaving me to decide how much of him I could swallow. I took him as best I could, but he was just too large, and it wasn't long before I sputtered for breath, having only been able to get the head of him in my mouth. Meanwhile, Diesel had no problem licking me open. He used his tongue like a finger, contracting it before flattening it wide. He easily slipped a finger inside my heat, already relaxed from his ministrations. My heart pounded. This was it. My alpha was finally going to make me his.

"Nothing can take you away from me. Not after I claim you. This sweet hole will know what it's like to be stretched by its alpha, and I'll never let it close. I'm going to keep you open for me, ready for my dick. Would you like that, sweet omega?"

Like that? I'd kill a nun to get that.

"I *need* that, Diesel." I wasn't just giving him sexy-time platitudes either. Every inch of me ached for him, and the ache only grew. It had quieted a little with Diesel's tongue in my ass, and attempting to give him a blowjob distracted me well enough, but now that Diesel simply stared at me like I was the sparkling night sky, I *throbbed*.

He spun me around without warning. I yelped, but he quickly righted me and sat down on the bed in an upright position with his back against the headboard. "I won't lose control, Quin. I won't let this hurt...too much."

Of course I trusted my mate, but I couldn't see how this wouldn't hurt. I was ready...but nervous. Maybe if I hadn't been so woefully unprepared. I hadn't just saved my virginity for this man—I'd saved my entire body. Yes, I'd spent a few hot, sweaty nights, exploring my body. But I only ever was able to work in a finger before it became too much.

Diesel's dick was more than a finger. It was also too much, but in a way that made me determined to take it. With my alpha's hands on my waist, guiding me, I slowly worked my way down his cock.

We'd only just started, and already I felt stretched to my

limit. With the help of gravity and Diesel's gentle urgings, I let my body do what it was made to, accepting my alpha on a primal level.

"You're not going to be able to take it all, baby. Not the first time. We don't have the time right now, and I won't be rushed. We'll stretch you slowly, train your body to accept me, and when it does, I'll never. Stop. Fucking. You." Diesel emphasized his meaning with sharp thrusts that didn't take him any deeper but lit my nerve endings on fire instead. "I'm sorry, baby boy. I should've waited until we had time enough for me to kiss you for hours."

"No!" While I had a lot of questions, a lifetime of sexual curiosity to fulfill, I knew without a doubt that the one thing I didn't want to do was wait any longer. When you waited, you opened the possibility of something bad happening. I couldn't know if something horrible would attack us all tomorrow too, but at least I'd die knowing what it felt like to accept my mate. "No more waiting! I don't want gentle if it means waiting. I don't want *anything* more than this, alpha. Make me hurt. Please."

He grunted low in his chest, looking like he needed an extra second to make his mouth work. "As you wish. I'm going to fuck you until you can't walk without remembering what it felt like to dangle on my dick."

His filthy words stoked my core into a blazing inferno, while his dick lit the rest of me on fire. This feeling. This. *Feeling.* Held by my alpha, cherished as he branded me from the inside out—creating a space in me that was only his.

"Look at me, omega," Diesel growled out his demand. "I will see your pleasure. All of it."

I hadn't realized my eyes were closed, and when I opened them, I wondered if my body hadn't been trying to protect me from the full impact of this moment. A deep, burning desire darkened Diesel's gaze. I couldn't look away if I wanted to. He held me captive.

His expression alone was nearly enough to send me over the edge, but before I could fall, something pulled me back, letting my orgasm dance in the distance without ever approaching. I'd waited so long for this exact moment, and while it had all turned out nothing like how I'd imagined, I felt alive for the first time. Like every taste and sound was magnified along with every touch. Oversensitized, I whimpered, still needing to come, but feeling too *much* to get there. I needed help, something to push me over.

Diesel gripped my erection between our bodies. His huge hand dwarfed my dick, and he gripped tight, knowing the exact amount of focused pain I needed to rip from the edge and fall into bliss. "Now, baby boy." He didn't bring me an orgasm as much as he yanked one from me. "Paint my hand with your cum."

The world went shimmery and then... "Oh my...fuck! Diesel, I'm coming!"

My body became a rippling beast, contracting and tightening as I rode my orgasm like a wave that refused to crest. Diesel's hard dick fucked me through my climax, pushing it farther than I would've thought pleasurable and continuing even as my dick went limp and my groans softened into mewls.

"One more time, my omega," he demanded hoarsely with his face pressed against my neck. "Let me see those lips open in ecstasy one more time."

With Diesel, nothing was done by halves. Concentrated and undiluted, he was everything in every moment and never apologized for it. And now, he was the man bringing on my second orgasm, somehow stronger than the first, perhaps because now I knew how his body vibrated when I came all over his dick.

His arms tightened around my back, clasping together at my spine as he pulled me tighter and thrust deeper. So relaxed from my orgasms, I felt the extra inches push in, but it didn't hurt. My body sucked him in deeper, wanting all of him even if getting all of him split me apart.

I dropped my gaze between our bodies to where Diesel disappeared inside me. His unyielding length glistened with his cum and saliva—not even half in.

My world narrowed. Anything that wasn't my alpha's dick disappeared. Though brutal in their intensity, Diesel's thrusts remained even and controlled through my climax, until the waves of pleasure ebbed, and he threw his head back in a loud roar. His thick neck muscles corded as the sound lengthened into a continuous growl. His teeth pressed against my skin, sinking his incisors into the crook of my shoulder before letting loose a burst of molten hot liquid that warmed me from the inside.

My alpha. His cock and cum. He was claiming me in the way only a shifter could. With his teeth and scent, he marked me. My head drooped on his shoulder, rolling with his thrusts as my eyes fluttered with ecstasy.

I knew what was happening but was damned to add anything meaningful to the moment. Finally, Diesel had done what I'd fantasized about him doing since I was younger than was entirely appropriate.

My alpha had broken me. I was ruined. No other man would ever compare, and as terrifying as that thought should have been, I didn't give a damn.

10

DIESEL

QUINLAN FIT PERFECTLY beneath my arm. That had always been a Quinlan-sized space; I simply hadn't had Quinlan to fill it.

I did now. Just as I finally knew exactly how sweet my omega was. I'd never forget the way he tasted on my tongue, all lust and honey. He walked with a slight limp, a fact that made me preen like an asshole. My omega felt me with every step, and he'd better get used to the feeling.

"You might not talk out your thoughts like I do, but I know what you're thinking, big boy."

I arched an eyebrow at him. "Big boy?"

"I'm trying it out. You have such *good* names for me." He didn't try to stop the shudder that trembled through him.

My wolf preened. My omega loved being my baby boy.

"How about you call him 'fucking late to an important meeting?'" Knox called out from the operations room.

My chest rumbled with my growl, and I used the arm wrapped around Quinlan to lift him closer to my side, bringing his toes high enough to graze the ground as I walked. "Don't snap at my omega," I snarled back, coming into the operations room in the same moment.

Fuck.

Judging from the scents coming down the corridor, the pack, minus Siobhan, Jamie, and the children were in the room. I'd known that, having detected their scents the moment we stepped into the corridor. I hadn't known they'd be sitting, facing the door, and smiling like maniacs. Even the Walker representatives beamed, though the two of them couldn't have any idea what this moment meant.

"Your omega?" Knox said without judgment or doubt. His eyes remained on Quinlan.

My mate nibbled on his bottom lip, before nodding shyly.

"Well, good," Knox said with twice as much pride in his face than was in his tone. He cleared his throat and squeezed his mate's hand when Jazz grabbed his fingers. "Now that that's finally dealt with, we can move on to the important matters of being attacked by fucking water."

"*Fucking* water?" Kansas said, his face twisted with confusion as he looked to be trying to imagine that.

Wyatt patted the back of Kansas's hand, kissing him softly with a grin that bordered on proud. "Why don't you repeat what you said before, for those who weren't present?" he suggested gently.

"Right!" Kansas shook his head like he was trying to dislodge the mental journey he'd just gone on. "That thing you were fighting when we got here. It wasn't really alive, but it had living energy."

"How would that happen?" I asked, and Knox made a sharp noise. I assumed he'd asked that question the first time they'd all talked about this, and he hated going over the same things.

Kansas acted like he hadn't heard Knox's irritation. "I've never come across anything like that. I mean, except for me. I can consume energy. Well, I kind of *have* to every once in a while, or else I go a little...loopy."

"You're an energy vampire?" Storri whispered, tucked deeply beneath Faust's arm.

"Yeah, I guess. But *I don't kill people.*" Kansas craned to face his mate as he emphasized.

"Totally not creepy that you feel the need to mention that," Jazz quipped.

Kansas laughed like Jazz had told his favorite joke. "Hollister told me you were funny!"

"Anyway..." Knox all but snarled.

If I had the slightest artistic ability, I would've drawn his face at that moment and hung it on the wall beside his room.

My boy could draw and paint. I needed to make sure he had the supplies to do that. I twisted to turn to the door before Quinlan tugged me back, reminding me what was going on at the moment.

I couldn't help it. Caring for my mate rose above everything else. But keeping him safe was caring for him, and his safety was the most important thing.

"So, yeah, I used to only be able to draw out what I consumed. I've been practicing...and *stable* for a while and I can control more. Which is good because that living energy was some of the foulest I've come across. It didn't feel human—at least, not *mostly* human. I don't know what used its energy to create that water thing, but it's strong, and I'm gonna go ahead and say he's evil too." Kansas's face sharpened into an expression far removed from his bubbly personality to this point. "You don't attack babies if you aren't evil."

That was a reasonable benchmark that I could get behind.

"As helpful as that information is," Faust leaned forward over the table, bringing Storri forward with him, "we still don't know who attacked us. I'm comfortable in guessing the why."

"It's Portal, right?" Isaiah asked. "Can't we assume that as well?"

"Yes, but at this point, it isn't enough to just say Portal." Knox turned to a monitor beeping on the table behind him. "Badger's here. I'll bring them in. They should hear this."

"Oh cool, it will be nice to see them again," Kansas chirped after Knox had left.

Wyatt drew his mate in, pressing their foreheads together. "Kitten, we can't stay long."

"But what about the message from the council?" Huntley asked.

"And why did they send you instead of a council representative?" Jagger added his question to his mate's.

Wyatt's expression of love turned sour as he looked from his mate to us. "Technically, I'm a council representative."

Sitka frowned. "You don't look happy about that."

"Nana made him," Kansas whispered.

"She didn't make—" Wyatt took a deep breath. "She asked me—"

"—and he wouldn't ever do anything to jeopardize his spot as favorite."

"My sweet omega," Wyatt said through clenched teeth. "Why did I bring—"

Kansas squeaked, and Wyatt turned to face two bright blue eyes a blink away from tearing up.

The fight left Wyatt as quickly as it probably had when Nana had asked him to be a council representative.

As they made up, Quinlan whispered, "I like him."

A kiss and nose rubbing later and both faced us again. "The council is officially expressing their vow to assist in this Portal business however needed. If you all accept it, I'm to be your liaison, not because you can't speak directly to the council, but because I'll be able to get what you need faster. Soldiers, weapons, equipment. I've been advised to spare no expense. If demons open a gate to hell, that's gonna be bad for everyone."

The council hadn't been a friend to my life, but not because they were an enemy. In my experience, they assisted when they weren't needed and disappeared when they were. And thanks to Jazz's inheritance, the pack could probably equip a large army with the latest weaponry, but soldiers were a thing we could not buy. At least, not the type of men you wanted fighting by your side. I'd know; I was one.

Knox returned, smelling of the biker pack as well as one more man—old and *unclean*. "Wyatt, if it isn't pressing, I want you to stay. The men brought back a Portal agent who wants to negotiate."

I blinked, and my gaze went red, seeing through my rage—like before, when Quinlan had been dead. "The fuck? We don't negotiate with Portal."

Knox growled, and I growled back. Neither of us would back down, so Knox didn't wait. "Which is what I fucking told him," Knox bit out. "He seems to think he knows something that will change our minds. I told him it wouldn't," he added before anyone could object. "But he's insisting, and I won't say no to information."

It was standing-room only in the interrogation and *gentle persuasion* room. The biker pack stood clumped in the corner behind the human Portal agent. Wyatt and Kansas remained and stood in the middle of the rest of us. Only Hallie and the doctor elected not to come down.

The Portal agent sat tied to a chair in the middle of the room. He was gagged but not blindfolded. His eyes weren't opened wide with fright, but moving, sliding from face to face like he was memorizing what we looked like. Dressed in torn silk pajamas, he had a full head of gray hair and a face that looked decades younger than his hands. I wanted to punch my fist through his skull, but Knox seemed to think he'd tell us something useful and not purposefully misleading.

Knox strode forward, yanking the gag from the man's mouth. "Again. No matter what you say, we will still very likely kill you because you literally sold your soul to a demon. And that makes you not okay in my book."

"He also supplies drugs to the majority of the school-aged children on the east coast. Targets children specifically. He doesn't even need the money. His Portal contract made him a billionaire several times over. Don't worry. We found our own list to work through at this piece of shit's house." Badger ran his fingernails through his cropped black hair.

"What do you have to tell us?" Knox asked.

Jazz leaned back, putting a few more inches between him and Knox, but getting closer to where the other nephilim, and Kansas, huddled together. It didn't look like any of them even noticed they'd migrated.

"You won't kill me." The Portal agent stretched his jaw as he spoke. He had dimples; there was no way those were fucking real. "Portal isn't trying to open a gate to hell." He sounded amused, like he was gossiping at a party.

"If you're just going to lie..." Knox reached for the knife in his belt.

"No, no, wait," he pleaded, clearly not aware we could detect his lies. Riling him up had been Knox's only goal. "They aren't trying to open the gate because they already did. Days ago."

"Bullshit," Faust sneered. "They needed blood, large quantities of nephilim blood."

"And they got it. A monastery down in Mexico. A whole congregation of them. They'll need more, but the initial sacrifice has been made. You can't save them, but I can tell you who's tasked with doing the next pickup. He's using my vehicles. I know his name."

"What do you mean they'll need more?" Jagger snarled.

The asshole waited an extra second before responding, just because he could. "The cracks between this world and hell have already begun to form. Already, the demon kings are breaking through, and when the gate fully opens, every beast of hell will be able to travel through."

His zeal grated in my wolf's ears. Blind devotion only ever meant empty-minded followers, a useless trait to have in a pack member. "Why do you sound so excited? You die same as us when that happens. Or do you think your masters will save you a spot at their feet?"

Finally, his dimples flattened. I'd struck a nerve, and his face contorted with malice. "They wouldn't ignore their faithful servant."

"Which is why you're here, needing to beg for your life by spilling all your secrets. They've *already* ignored you."

"Perhaps. Or maybe they're waiting for you to lead them right to what they want. If I help them kill the halfling? I'll get my own *palace* in new hell." I already hated that Quinlan was in here. I hated any of the nephilim were, but Quinlan especially. He'd seen enough evil. He didn't need more. But when the agent's hungry eyes landed on my boy, I saw red.

"What the fuck does that mean? Why him?" We knew Portal was after the nephilim, but he made it sound like Quinlan was specifically being targeted.

"The halfling cannot be permitted to live," the man parroted like it was a sentence he'd said and heard spoken often. Quinlan was half angel and half human like the others.

"He said that a couple times on the road here. Figured he meant the nephilim," Badger said. "We weren't followed here. I made damn sure of that. He's grasping."

"It won't matter if you let me go. My masters are here. They'll forgive what I've told you. If they can forgive the traitor Pierce, they'll forgive me." He swallowed and set his dark gaze back on my mate. "He's the one insane for the halfling. The halfling will wish he died after Pierce gets—"

My lip curled. "What about Pierce?"

"He failed, lied, tricked the hand that fed him. But he proved his worth with the nephilim from the monastery, and now he's back in their good graces."

My wolf howled at this new information. We'd already known Pierce was under contract with Portal, but we'd assumed killing the pack had been his task. Now it sounded like Quinlan had been the target. But he'd left Quinlan alive. Wondering about Pierce's reasons for doing what he did got us nowhere, so I didn't try, except now it sounded like Quinlan was both the target and the prize.

Protect. He's threatening your mate. Protect him. Protect your omega. I clenched my fingers into a large fist, prepared to punch a hole through the agent's skull, when Knox stopped me.

"Take the others. I'll handle this. He's told us all he's good for."

The agent's smirk hardly faltered. At some point in the interrogation, his faith in those he'd sold his soul to had eclipsed his sense of self-preservation. No one would come for him, especially not now that he'd given us a name. We witnessed, firsthand, what Portal did to its employees. Jazz's father had been killed for much, much less. All this man's devotion told me was that the humans who worked for Portal were just as dangerous as the demons.

———

Knox and the rest of the team left that evening with the bikers to stake out the location of the man tasked with obtaining the next shipment of nephilim. Wyatt had left, promising to fill the council in on what we'd learned, while preparing their soldiers so they were ready when needed.

No one wanted to dwell on those nephilim who had already been lost or that Pierce might have discovered the nephilim pack's existence while here at the hotel. He'd sat quietly in each strategy meeting, all the while memorizing what he could to bring back to his angry owners.

Though Quinlan and the others had never met the slain nephilim, they took the news of their deaths hard. Knox didn't want to be away from Jazz in that state; neither did the other alphas. Since they'd already been taken out into the field, and this was reconnaissance only, the nephilim left as well, leaving a skeleton crew at the hotel.

Until we knew why Quinlan was specifically being targeted, there was no way I'd let him leave the hotel. Nor would I leave his side. The others didn't need my help to watch a person, and they had extra eyes anyway.

"You could've left with them. We would've been able to handle it here." Quinlan narrowed his eyes on where I stood in the corner of the sitting room. He held Onyx over his shoulder to burp him. The doc had taken Angus while Isaiah, his daughter, and Jamie took the girls. Hallie had already made plans with Alejandro, but swore she'd come back if we needed her to.

Quinlan had to look over his shoulder to see me from where I stood. He likely didn't know I'd chosen this spot so I'd be free to readjust. This wasn't the first time I'd witnessed Quinlan holding a baby, but it was the first time I was seeing it after making him mine, and it made me and my wolf *very* happy.

I couldn't help but to imagine what Quinlan would look like, swollen with my child. Of all the lives I'd imagined having with him, mated and pregnant hadn't been among the possibilities. At that time, it hadn't been one. Now that I knew what he really was, and what would happen when we came together, I couldn't hold back the mental images. When—not *if* —he got pregnant, we'd know in the same way all the others had found out, with a sparkling pile of vomit.

I grunted, pushing off the wall to retrieve the empty bottle. "I won't risk leaving you."

"You'll have to eventually. You're Alpha to this pack too."

"I know that, and I will, when I know you're safe."

"Can any of us ever truly be sure that we are safe?"

"Quinlan."

My omega shivered, closing his eyes briefly before lifting his gaze to mine. He blinked away the desire burning there, or tried to. He couldn't make his cheeks stop burning. "What?"

"Finish burping the baby so we can put him down."

Quinlan's spine stiffened. "Why should I be the one to finish the baby tasks? You're just as capable."

He knew I had no problem caring for the babies. I'd assisted often in the nursery in our old pack, which meant he was saying this to get a rise out of me. It had taken some getting used to, but I preferred this version of Quinlan, who didn't only possess a sharp wit and bratty rebellious streak, but showed it. As long as he slept in my arms at the end of the day, I'd accept every new, burgeoning facet of his personality with ease.

"Hand him here, then. He likes me more anyway."

Quinlan glowered, the expression only deepening when Onyx let loose a happy coo when he was passed over. "He just doesn't know me as well yet. That's all."

I was only interested in teasing my mate when his feelings weren't actually being hurt. With Onyx over my shoulder, I patted his back while also dropping to my haunches in front of Quinlan. His lip stuck out, and his arms crossed tightly over his chest.

"You're right, Quin. Soon, he'll wonder why he ever liked me in the first place."

It looked like he was trying to keep his pout but was experiencing difficulty. "No, it's okay, I want him to—" Quinlan stopped speaking the moment the baby made a wet burping sound.

The smell came next, and I knew it wasn't magical bubblegum pregnancy puke I felt soaking into my shirt.

"I'm sorry. I should've given you the towel," Quinlan said between laughs. He got to his feet to walk behind me and started to laugh harder. "He likes you, all right. A whole lot."

Quinlan's voice changed, turning higher as he cooed at the baby. "Do you have any milk left in there, little mister?" He grabbed Onyx from my shoulder. "Let's see if you aren't ready for a nap."

"You set me up!" I yelled after him as Quinlan ascended the stairs with the baby. He didn't reply, but I heard his sneaky giggle bouncing all the way to the second floor.

11

QUINLAN

My WARRIOR's muscles glistened as his arms bent, bringing his body almost to the ground before pushing back up. I could sketch his body for hours and had asked to repeatedly as a teenager. He'd always refused me, but maybe now he'd reconsider. I'd have a lot of chances to sketch him since he was stubborn as a redheaded mule and refused to leave my sight, despite it being days since the others had returned from their fact-finding mission.

Figuring out which nephilim were being targeted next was going to have to wait until the man was released from jail. While our men had been watching, a half dozen police cars, blaring their alarms, had swarmed around the place. Thankfully, Knox and the others were far enough back they hadn't been discovered, but the man they needed to question had been escorted from the location minutes later in handcuffs and was currently still sitting in jail.

At least that had given the pack extra time to absorb all that we'd found out.

Nephilim were already dead, the blood drained from

their bodies and used to open a gate that—if the agent could be believed—was *already* opening.

The night of my rescue, after I'd fainted, Diesel had said there'd been an earthquake that they hadn't been able to explain at the time.

They had thought the earthquake had been related to me, but we knew the true culprit now.

Which meant we could also be terrifyingly sure of who was responsible for sending the water beast.

Shake all of that together, stir, and you got an alpha who refused to even go downstairs to the gym to work out without his mate near.

"You're making me hot and bothered. I'm going to go find Jazz."

Diesel pushed himself up and continued into a standing position. "Where can you sense him?"

I should've known that the second I'd mentioned leaving the room, his workout would be over. That hadn't been my intention.

It had taken me a shameful amount of time to notice, not only how believing he'd lost me had changed Diesel, but the hurt and worry he carried from those years.

I cupped his face, fighting back my own tears at how much misery he must've been in. "I promise not to leave the hotel, I won't even go outside. I'll be okay down the hallway, Diesel."

"I know you will, baby boy. I'll be with you." His words allowed for no argument and I wouldn't push him anymore on this. Not when his eyes were bright with an edge of panic at the thought of me leaving the room without him.

My butt sank into the mattress we'd shared every night since Diesel had moved me in. I reached to my nightstand

and grabbed my whetstone and my whip. "Finish your workout. We'll find Jazz when you're done."

He shook his stubborn head, which only made pulling his hair back all that much more difficult. "Wasn't Jazz going to teach you something?"

My nephilim brother had talked about doing illusion training. He believed if I felt better able to spot an illusion when it was used on me, I'd feel more in control of my surroundings. I wasn't sure how well that would work. Thinking of my life with Pierce, of the nightmares and solitude, felt like thinking about something that had happened to someone else. That life belonged to some other unfortunate soul. I only wanted to think about the time I had now. My second chance. But forgetting the past meant you were doomed to repeat it, so I'd agreed to train.

My wraiths slunk in through the door, having spent another night and most of the day in my old room. They swore they weren't mad at me, but more and more, they elected to not be around me.

"Oh look, it's my once best friends who have since abandoned me."

Diesel snorted in that happy way he always got when I directed my ire at someone who wasn't him.

Quiiiiinlan, they cooed, swirling up my body.

"At least you're happy to see me," I grumped. There was no reason to put on an act. The wraiths could literally read my mind and knew how glad I was for them, but I did it anyway. They curled over my shoulders, massaging me as they pulsed. I turned my head like I refused to accept their hugs. "Do I have to get kidnapped by a psycho for you two to care?"

That got a growl out of Diesel that clearly said, *too soon.*

Jaaaaaazz waitssss.

"He does? Where?" When they didn't immediately answer, I closed my eyes and focused on my brothers. "Gym. Come on, sweet cheeks."

Diesel accepted my hand, but dug his feet in the ground. "That's a no from me on sweet cheeks."

For as much as he complained about the attempted new nickname, his eyes crinkled with happy smiles.

The moment my foot touched the hallway carpet, I heard a sharp gasp, too tense and frightened to be a noise of pleasure or ecstasy. I trusted Diesel to let me know if the sound really was an overheard intimate moment but kept pace with me, holding tightly to my hand as we went the opposite direction of the gym.

Our feet stopped just outside Hallie's door, shut but for a sliver where we heard more sniffling and quiet crying

"Hallie? Are you okay?" Hallie and Diesel clearly had a special relationship. He was gentler with her than he would be to his other alphas, and he was more open with her than he was with the rest of the pack.

When I'd discovered how she'd helped Diesel pull through long enough for him to find me, I knew I didn't just like her—I owed her my life.

"I'm...yeah, I'm f-fine."

That certainly sounded believable and not at all an act —if we were celebrating opposite day. "Hallie, are you very sure you're fine?"

"Yes," she replied weakly. "I'm f—" A coming sob choked out the lie on her tongue. She might not want to talk to us about what was going on, and we would respect that, but Hallie clearly wasn't fine.

"Can we come in?" I asked, my voice urgent. Something was wrong, and if she was willing, she needed her pack around her.

My mind spun with possibilities. Her boyfriend, Alejandro was a gentle soul, but her ex-husband was trouble. If he'd hurt her, the man would pay.

We still couldn't barge into her room uninvited.

"Ye-e-e-es," she said between sobs.

Diesel burst inside, lifting me off my feet in his haste. "What happened? Did he hurt you? Tell me if he did, Hallie." Diesel's growls erupted between his words, making all that he said nearly unintelligible.

Hallie shook her head. She sat at the edge of her bed wrapped in a purple satin robe tied with a gold ribbon and her hair twisted on top of her head in a towel.

I could be sure I wasn't the only one of us looking our pack mate over, searching for injuries. She looked in perfect health, all except her hands that trembled, clenched around a thin piece of plastic.

"Are you pregnant?" I whispered my question.

Hallie inhaled deeply, centering herself before nodding. It didn't take long for the nod to go a bit wild as the truth of the moment seemed to hit her again.

"Who was it?" Diesel snarled in a voice that didn't at all belong around the joy slowly filling the room.

Those hadn't been sad sobs, but happy ones. My big oaf was just too blinded by his concern.

Hallie's eyes turned into daggers directed at Diesel's face. "What the hell do you mean who was it? The man I'm dating!"

"Does he know?" Diesel shot back nearly before she'd finished speaking.

As much as Diesel liked seeing me turn my inner brat on someone else, I wholeheartedly enjoyed watching my pack mates rake him over the coals.

"How could he know? I just found out before you barged in!"

"If he doesn't jump for fucking joy..." Diesel warned.

Hallie's face twisted, preparing to spit forth what I was sure would be a well-placed, and highly entertaining, string of curse words, as well as suggestions for what Diesel could do with his attitude, but it was time to turn this car around.

"Hold on, hold on, hold on." I stepped forward, sliding my body between theirs. My voice went high with evil glee. "Are you telling me that me and Diesel are the first people you've told?" It was a rhetorical question. Obviously, we were. We heard the gasp; she was holding the pee stick. But they weren't quarreling with each other anymore, which was all I'd wanted. "Jazz is going to be so ma—"

"What is it? What's happened? I felt it!" Jazz's yell grew louder as he ran toward us down the hallway. He burst in through the open doorway in the next second, red-faced and panting. "What's happened? I know it's good. I brought everyone."

On cue, most of the pack joined him. Only Storri and Sitka's cheeks matched Jazz's. The others clearly hadn't run here.

During this, Hallie's eyes closed, and she'd stopped crying. Angling her face toward the ceiling, she moved her lips in a murmured prayer. "Please, God, grant me the patience to deal with this group of nosy people who I swear I love."

Jazz snorted, unaffected. His eyes dropped to Hallie's lap before widening. "Are you?"

"I think yeah, I am." She bit her lip as her eyes filled with tears. Only now it was clear they were joyful. "I've been here before but—I don't know. This feels good."

"We need the doctor," Diesel growled, turning and

lunging toward the door—my hand still in his—where he caught himself from barreling into the person in question.

"I'm here. And I know this isn't the popular answer but, the best thing for Hallie right now is rest." She stepped forward to address the small crowd and clasped her hands in front of her. "I'm sure she'll want to talk about this at length with each of you, but let's try to do it in small doses, okay? At least while we figure everything out."

Hallie looked relieved that someone else had saved her from asking, but Jazz's expression turned murderous. He opened his mouth, a clear rebuttal on his lips, when Knox shook his head, smirking as he hooked the arm that wasn't holding Angus around Jazz's middle and carried him out like a duffel bag.

When we reached the hallway, Diesel pulled my hand, directing me away from the others and toward the other end of the corridor. "Jazz won't be able to do anything but talk about Hallie."

"Yeah, I know. I want to talk about Hallie!" I cried out but he kept urging me the opposite direction down the hallway.

I wasn't sure where he was taking me. There wasn't anything on this side of the corridor but more empty rooms and then the wall.

Diesel stopped at what I thought had been a random spot until he pressed the pistil of a flower carved into the decorative molding. It depressed under his finger with a click, followed by a sharp swooshing sound. The bottom panel smoothly slid open, revealing a dark, squat passage.

"You have to duck for a bit," Diesel murmured, his face close enough behind me he nibbled at my earlobe while I shuffled.

"Duck?" I twisted my neck around to look at him

wondering if he'd forgotten the obvious difference in our heights. "What do you have to do? Crawl?"

His head tilted to the side, pinning me with a disparaging look. "I do not crawl, boy," he grunted.

The brat living in my head replied with a silent, *challenge* accepted, I turned my head so he didn't have to see my amused snort.

He still heard it though, and his replying growl sounded deeper than normal. Animalistic.

I whipped my head around when I recognized why the growl sounded different and stared into the loving eyes of my alpha wolf. Diesel's *wolf*.

He was a gorgeous man, but a damn majestic beast. While on two legs he operated as an alpha with a job and only felt as good as he did about the work he'd put in. He wore his confidence differently as a wolf. He could be proud of himself, and—as sad as it was that my mate couldn't truly see himself—his pride was a sight I craved.

Diesel let me look my fill, just as humble as he was when he stood on two legs. When he'd decided I'd looked enough, he pushed me forward with his nose at my back.

The passage would've been creepy if I wasn't with my knight in a fur coat. I didn't end up needing to crouch all that much, but Diesel did. His wolf was still taller than I was. As the ceiling got closer, he had to drop into a crouched shuffle that I wouldn't call a crawl, but only out of respect to him and a burning desire to later see and taste the heat he packed.

After thirty seconds or so of crouch-walking, the tunnel opened into an elegant hallway. The décor matched the rest of the hotel but it was more pristine here in this dark, dry space. *This* must've been what the Hotel Royal Paynes had looked like in its day—stuffed floor to ceiling with elegance and class.

"Where does the hallway go?" My voice echoed off the arched beams in the rapidly rising ceiling. We'd gone from a dark tunnel, feeling the building brush the tops of our heads, to a corridor that made me feel like I was walking through a palace.

Diesel's human hands lifted and spun me around so we faced each other. It was only instinct to wind my limbs around him as he whispered, "I'll show you."

"But then later we can go outside maybe and do some more stuff in your wolf form, right? I've been thinking over this fantasy of a boy lost in a forest, and he's found by a huge wolf who happens to be a lonely alpha, willing to *take* what he—"

"Quinlan," Diesel said with a strained edge. "We're definitely fucking doing that at some point," he said before pushing open a large door that groaned as it swung. "First, I'm showing you this."

He carried me to the center of an enormous open room, longer than it was wide, with gold painted arches. At the top of the long outside wall, plate glass windows let in the only natural light the room would see. This deep in the hotel, we had to be partially underground. Those windows had to be at ground level or just above. "What is this place?" I slid slowly out of his arms, unwilling to look away. My skin prickled, but not just from the chill. The room was empty, but it felt *full* of shared memories and past emotions. There'd been joy in this room, happiness, love.

"It's the ballroom. We never made it this far in our repairs, but as you can see, it's the best kept place in the hotel. The regular entrance is over there, up the double stairs, but I thought you'd appreciate the secret passage."

He'd thought correctly. A few minutes ago, I would've wagered the tunnel was the coolest thing I'd see that day. But that was before I saw this space.

"It's my favorite room," Diesel said softly.

I frowned. That didn't track. Not because of any rude reason toward Diesel, but because I knew he preferred functional things. To him, a room was a space you did something in. Though this place had surely once been a proud addition to the hotel, the room was empty save for the chairs stacked along the walls. "What do you like the most about it?"

His chin dropped, and his hair swung forward to cover part of his face. "That it would've been your favorite. I've spent entire days in here, imagining the way you'd bring the walls to life with your paintings. I dreamed of you painting a mural right there." He gestured to a portion of wall, peeling with old wallpaper visible from every angle.

My chest tightened picturing Diesel as he'd been, lonely and heartbroken. "I'll do it. I'll paint a mural."

I hadn't picked up anything more than a pencil in years. Pierce had supplied me with paints and drawing paper, but I'd refused to use anything that man gave me that wasn't for my survival. I lifted my arms, prompting Diesel to stoop over enough for me to wrap them around his neck. He brought me off my feet without ever grabbing hold. I didn't need him to especially once I locked my ankles together at the top of his butt. "I won't promise it will be good, but I'll paint you something." I slumped down, making Diesel cup my ass to keep me from falling. "Except I don't have any paints."

With Diesel's face pressed against my neck, his breaths made my skin tingle and I felt his smile before I saw it. "I thought of that."

His fingers slipped between my cheeks as he carried me over the dusty floor. My ass clenched, suddenly concerned with how very empty I was and how close his fingers were to remedying that. Diesel knew exactly what he was doing to me. His fingers hadn't slipped by accident. I kept hold of my desire as tightly as possible, paying attention to the room instead.

Cobwebs decorated the high corners, particularly along the windows on the long wall, trailing down as dust and gravity collected on the silken strands. This room had still gone through decades of neglect, but it was drier here than in the other parts of the hotel, so while things had begun to crack and crumble, there wasn't the mold or mildew common in the other neglected spaces.

He set me down in front of a lumpy, folded drop sheet making sure my body slid over every inch of his along the way. "When your paints and the scaffold ladder come, I'll bring you down here every day, if you want."

That gave me some time to restart my creativity. When I'd been held captive, every ounce of my focus had been diverted into thinking of ways to keep myself safe and to keep Pierce away. Now, I could dream of beautiful land-scapes and rolling hills dotted with trees, their branches heavy with leaves that burned the bright colors of autumn.

Like the tub, Diesel had planned this for me. While I'd been shaving a stretch of chain into a deadly weapon, he'd been staring at these walls, grieving.

"Thank you, Diesel. For...all of this. This room is gorgeous. Perfect. My favorite."

That was only a tiny lie, since wherever Diesel was, was my favorite.

He made a low chuffing sound and nuzzled my neck, clearly pleased that I was so happy with this gift. There wasn't any music, but that didn't matter when Diesel began to sway, holding me closely to his chest.

My Diesel wasn't a gentle giant, but he was a giant who could be gentle. And light on his feet. As we rocked back and forth, Diesel's delicate steps and featherlight touch had me leaning into him. We already touched in all the spots we could—with our clothes on—but it wasn't enough. He kissed my neck as he moved, humming first softly and then louder until we spun around the floor to the music he provided.

With my hand in his, he spun me away from his body, acting as my anchor as I twirled out and then back like a boomerang. He caught me with my back to his and held me against his sculpted body. One hand dropped to my hips, tightening in a way that made my knees week. I didn't have to worry about something as silly as standing on my own two feet, not with my alpha around. Whether he was holding or spinning me, Diesel did it with such care, I couldn't help but feel loved.

While his cock was exactly where I wanted it, prodding my ass through my jeans, it wasn't *enough*.

The non-existent music took me over. We didn't need a drum or a piano, not when we danced to the beat of Diesel's heart and my hips rolled to the melody of his adoration.

But, even that wasn't enough for long. My pants felt both too tight and too thick. Any boundary between our skin was too much. Unwelcomed.

"Diesel," I moaned, wrenching my top half around at the waist where I found his mouth.

He kept the kiss light, much too gentle for the touch I craved. "What's wrong, baby?"

I bucked, enjoying his hiss while hoping that got my point across. Diesel just growled softly, the only indication that I was testing his will was the way he'd squeezed my hipbone.

"What is it?" His tone was way too tender for me to believe he truly didn't know what I wanted.

Besides, I probably smelled like an animal in heat.

"I need you," I whimpered.

Suddenly, the fact that I hadn't yet taken his full dick was unacceptable. I didn't want there to be any part of Diesel that I hadn't claimed with my body and though I'd surely run my tongue and hands along that gloriously veiny skin, I hadn't taken him inside me.

How could I be Diesel's full mate with only a partial dicking?

Diesel snarled in response to the thought I hadn't meant to voice. "Is that what's wrong, baby boy? You're hungry for my cock?"

Fucking hell, now I was. I'd been before, but now I was man-stranded-on-a-desert-island-for-a-thousand-years level of hungry. Words left me. I could only bite my lip and nod like a pitiful street urchin only asking for a bit of change—and also to get railed.

My mountain of a man spun me without difficulty, catching my ass squarely. The new position was heaven and hell. I had friction against my own aching erection, which was an improvement. But now, I didn't even have the warmth of Diesel's body at my backside.

I didn't know if I should whimper or whine and ended up doing both. For several long seconds, all Diesel did was watch me work myself into a frenzy, bouncing and hanging off him like a jungle gym. But I could only get so much friction and soon became frustrated. "Diesel, please. Please..."

I didn't care that I was finally begging like he'd asked days ago. I was too overcome with my lust to care. In fact, if begging got me what I wanted, then just call me Fido because I was willing to cry until I got that bone. "I'm so empty, alpha. I need your heat. I need you in me. I want to take you, all of you."

Diesel grabbed the waist of my pants and pulled, tearing at the seams. I bounced back, releasing them from where they'd snagged between our bodies. He made short work of my shirt, leaving me in his arms, completely naked while he was still fully clothed.

His lips claimed mine in a searing kiss that left me panting. "Shh, baby boy." His lips still touched mine as he spoke. "I have what you need."

His warm palm hugged my cheek and I pressed into the touch. My alpha would take care of me. He had what I needed. I just had to trust him and—

Why was I still empty?

I let out my own growl—not nearly as impressive or boner-inducing as Diesel's—and reached between our bodies. I'd let him take his time, teasing and drawing it out, *after* I got my fingers around my throbbing dick.

But, of course, Diesel wouldn't allow that. He pulled my hands back. "Around my neck, omega."

At any other time, I would've taken him to task for the gruff command, but my skin felt too tight with arousal to do anything but obey. I wrapped my arms around his thick neck, holding my hands together in a hope that extra compliance would get me what I wanted faster.

It at least got Diesel to undo the button of his pants. His fingers disappeared under the fabric returning with his cock. A sparkling bead of pre-cum glistened at the tip, gathering and growing in size before it became too much and had to slide down the shaft—or drip on the floor.

I shuddered at the idea that my alpha was literally dripping with desire for me. I licked my lips and hunched over, trying to dive between our bodies to get my mouth around him. He stopped me—a classic Diesel move. We'd do this his way. I could suggest, beg, plead and scream, but Diesel still made the choice.

Thankfully, I had a caring alpha who wanted me as much as I did him.

He carried me over to where the drop sheet sat folded on the ground and reached beneath it, removing the lump I'd noticed earlier.

I cocked my head to the side. "Coconut oil?"

"Trick I picked up from the twins."

I laughed loudly. I was pretty sure he didn't mean he'd learned while using the coconut oil with the twins, but if that was the truth, I couldn't say I hated it. Could I handle seeing a Diesel, Huntley and Jagger sandwich? Probably not. But I could ask Sitka if he'd ever imagined the same thing.

"Whatever you're thinking, you're wrong," Diesel grumbled before pumping oil into his palm. With one hand, he rubbed the oil around to coat his fingers.

"Too bad, I was thinking how good those fingers are going to feel inside me." That wasn't a lie, since I did wonder about that. Just not at the moment Diesel was asking about.

"I guess if you can't feel good, I'll settle for you feeling *owned*." He slid the first digit in my tight ring, letting my body adjust before he wiggled it around, gently stretching my rim.

"Mm, yes, yours, Diesel. All yours."

One finger turned into two. It wasn't just my brain that was eager to take a trip to Poundtown, my ass was eager as well, evident by how quickly my hole opened to accept him.

"You're going to try to take all of me?" Diesel stopped his thrusts and spread his fingers out inside of me, making a W that he used to stretch me further.

My chin hit my sternum in my zeal to respond. He slid all four inside and I gasped but bore down on his hand, rotating my hips as wildly as he'd allow. "I need to. I need all of you. So you're really mine."

"I'm already yours, baby boy, but I'm glad you want me. It's okay if you can't. If you never can—"

The playful arrogance in his words said he was *mostly* joking—though I was sure if I ended up not being able to handle it, he wouldn't be disappointed.

In my mind, that wasn't a possibility. "Diesel." My keening wail finally drove him to slide his dick to the place on my body begging for his attention. He didn't push to far, only letting the head of his cock prod against my greedy opening.

"Fuck, baby boy, your ass is drawing me in. Clinging tight. Don't worry, I'm done teasing you."

I wouldn't have believed him all the way if it weren't for his next hip thrust.

With my arms around his neck, Diesel's hands were free to grab my ass where he stretched the cheeks apart and slid in that much more.

I bit his shoulder, clenching my teeth into the fabric of his shirt. This was fine, I'd done this much before, but with as much as I had to convince myself I could take it, it might as well have been my first time.

"Are you okay? We can stop whenever. I'll be just as happy getting my tongue in here as my dick.

Forgetting for a moment that no one in the history of the world would be "'just as happy" to not get fucked, I didn't want that.

"I'm okay. Keep going. I want you."

He kept going.

And going.

And going...

When our bodies finally met, flush together, my teeth clenched together I was stuffed so full. I couldn't see how we would move, how I'd be able to do anything but live the rest of my life like this, stuck on my alpha's monster dick.

But, as was his way, Diesel showed me what my body could do. He lifted my hips, sliding out slowly before letting me fall gently back down. My feet hooked over one another at the small of his back but he didn't need my help keeping me upright.

He highlighted this fact as he spun around, resuming our dancing sway while he pumped into my body at an excruciatingly slow pace.

"No," I whimpered. "Not gentle. I don't want gentle, Diesel."

His throat rumbled. "Quinlan, we have time to go slow."

We might've had the time, but I didn't have the desire. I couldn't stand the idea of him keeping any part of himself from me, whether that was his sarcastic quips, or his primal stamina, I loved *all* of him and wanted *all* of him.

I didn't recognize the sharp, plaintive mewls coming from my mouth, but Diesel did.

His fingers flexed tightly—he'd be upset about the bruises he was leaving later, but I loved how it felt too much to stop him.

Growing up, Diesel had assumed many roles in my life. But no matter who he was to me, I craved him with an intensity that bordered on obsessive.

Okay, it *was* obsessive.

But at least it was an obsession we shared, and one that

hadn't changed with time so even though his cock stretched me wider than I thought physically possible and his hands held me tighter than a lottery winner held their winning ticket, I wouldn't change a single thing.

Diesel worked us into a rhythm, swaying and swinging his hips as he fucked me in circles over the dance floor.

That familiar fizzle in my balls brought an orgasm that raced to the finish line. It was impossible to hold back or even slow. Not when I was concentrating everything I had just to take him.

"Why do I ever doubt my omega?" Diesel crooned. "What a pretty sight you make, trembling, stuffed full. Fuck, Quinlan, the nights I spent imagining the ways I would wreck you. They didn't do the reality justice. That's a good thing. I'd have walked around permanently hard for you. Really, it would've gotten embarrassing."

I managed an amused snicker before he pulled his hips back in preparation to pound the air out of my body. It was while gasping for air that my orgasm gathered, building at the base of my spine and lingering, almost as if my body was waiting for permission.

"Diesel, I'm so close. Diesel!"

He roared and wrapped his huge hands not only around my waist, but ass as well. I had no control in this position. Only Diesel had the power to use me as he liked, thrusting into me with beautiful, brutal strokes.

"Come, sweet omega. Come on your alpha's dick."

That was all I needed to hear. My back arched immediately, climaxing with the force of a runaway stallion. Diesel kept moving, pounding over and over, drawing every drop of my climax out of my body.

Spent and boneless, I couldn't even wrap my legs around him anymore. My thighs shook along with my arms but I didn't need to do anything as my alpha took command, meeting my needs before his own.

But not that much before.

His fingers spasmed and though I knew to expect his climax, I hadn't expected it to feel so much or so *hot*. I imagined my alpha scalding me from the inside, cleaning away everything that wasn't him and me.

When I could breathe evenly again, I mumbled into his neck. "You've never taken me dancing before." I let my chin rest against his shoulder, baring my neck to my alpha as he hummed and rocked from one foot to another.

"I still haven't," he grunted. "This doesn't count. As dancing."

His hair tickled my nose, and I rubbed my face to try and scratch the itch. "This counts. I'm not taking a single thing with you for granted."

"I want you to." He pulled me back, putting more space between our faces than I liked, especially with the way our sweat cooled on my skin. His thick arms had no problem lifting and holding me as he pleased. "I want you to take it for granted—to expect that I will satisfy your every need. That's what I want from you, Quinlan."

My throat closed with too much emotion. My gaze turned watery, but I nodded. "Okay."

Satisfied, Diesel took his shirt off and draped it over my shoulders before returning to our lazy dance. He looked so happy dancing that I didn't care his still-hard dick hadn't moved or that my cum was drying on my skin.

I had Diesel's hums, broken only so he could whisper in my ear, describing all of the paint supplies he'd bring me. From dirty sex talk to dirty art talk.

As he requested, I didn't thank him, but I did kiss him

and hold him tight. I rubbed up and down his chest, covering him with our combined scent.

There'd been a time when my alpha had roamed this room alone, propelled only by his grief, but that time was over. I was here now, and if we were going to roam, we'd do it together.

———

"STORRI, *do you want butter on your popcorn?" Jazz hollered from the doorway.*

Movie night was only ever as good as the snacks.

"Extra butter, please," Storri replied, tucking each of his girls around him on the nest he'd made of blankets.

That looked comfortable. Maybe Diesel could grab us some blankets from our room. "Darling..." Darling? *That was a new one from me. I shook off the weird feeling that thought gave me and turned to find Diesel standing by the door. Jazz was just outside, walking in, carrying two steaming bowls of popcorn.*

"Diesel, could you—"

Diesel smiled, the expression so full of malice my stomach leaped into my throat. Something bad was going to happen. Something—

Jazz grunted and dropped the bowls. Popcorn flew everywhere, but all eyes were on Jazz's chest, blooming red.

Diesel pulled the knife free of Jazz's chest. As Knox charged inside the room, Diesel caught him, bracing his palm against Knox's forehead as he brought the knife—still covered with Jazz's blood—across his throat.

Knox dropped the same moment Storri cried out for his mate, but Faust was still upstairs. Knox's and Jazz's bodies lay in crumpled heaps, spilling twin pools of red that Diesel carelessly stomped, like a child through puddles, to get to Storri.

I ran like a coward out the door.

If this was real, I never would've been able to leave my brothers. Storri had been screaming in terror, but I kept running until his screams grew faint.

No. This wasn't Diesel. This wasn't him. He'd never... I was dreaming, but these weren't my thoughts.

If this wasn't my dream, and I was sleeping, that meant one thing. I needed to wake up. I'd never learned that skill before—waking up after realizing you were sleeping. I'd always had my wraiths to—

My wraiths!

They weren't here, in dreamland, but they knew what was in my head. Maybe, if I screamed for them, they could hear me. "Wraiths! Please wake me up! Wraiths! Wraiths! Can you hear me?"

I screamed so loud my throat burned, but I didn't stop. This wasn't real pain; this wasn't real.

"Quinlan!" Diesel roared, stomping through the grass, holding a knife covered in blood that dripped down the handle. "I'll give you something to scream about!"

Pierce needed to get some new material. If I hadn't already caught on, I—

My eyes popped open, and I was immediately aware of something covering my face. I scratched at it, kicking wildly until I realized it was one of my wraiths wrapped around my nose and mouth, preventing me from taking a breath. Though my lungs screamed for air, I settled, trusting my wraiths not to kill me. The other returned, swollen like a ball that covered my head—replacing the wraith already there.

Air baaad.

Beside me, Diesel grunted, his eyes closed. I pushed his shoulder, as able to rouse him as I was to turn him over.

"Wake him up!" The air felt too thick inside my wraith air bubble. My throat constricted, fooling my mind into believing there wasn't enough air, that something was wrong with it—I needed to calm down. The air wasn't thick —that was my anxiety—but it was limited.

Nooo. The wraiths flashed from black to silver like police lights in an old movie.

"Why can't he wake up?"

Stuuck.

He was stuck dreaming? Maybe whatever Pierce used to plant nightmares kept him asleep as well? Where was Pierce? This was his doing, no question about it.

Outsiiide.

I told myself it wasn't cowardice but practicality that had me asking my next question. "Can you just go knock him out or something?"

They flashed again, the intensity rising from police light to strobe.

Pierce only had a few tricks, and he reused the same material, but I couldn't discount his effectiveness. I could sense the other nephilim were in their rooms, but knew somehow that they were all unconscious, the same as Diesel. If I hadn't had years of recognizing my nightmares, I'd probably be in the same state. "What about the babies?" I asked, bending down to pick up my whip.

Neeeed to huuuurry.

That wasn't the answer I'd hoped for.

I ran over my options. If I couldn't wake Diesel up—and I could only assume the wraiths knew it would scramble his brain or something—then I had to handle the threat on my own. And with Pierce on pack lands somewhere, I couldn't wait for the gas to clear and hope Pierce wouldn't have moved on to the next stage in his attack by then. I squeezed the familiar handle, holding the length in a coil that would keep it from dragging. "Where outside?"

The wraiths flashed a muted silver, indicating they weren't fans of the plan, but they escorted me down the unusually dark hallway anyway.

I knew Knox had installed motion-activated nightlights in his unending mother-henning, but there wasn't a single light on the entire way to the stairs.

Pierce must've cut the power, which likely meant he'd planned on coming into the hotel and wanted to keep everyone as disoriented as possible.

My foot missed the first step down to the main floor, forcing my wraiths to catch and hold me steady. How could I stay steady when my knees knocked so loudly it should've been enough to wake the whole pack? What the hell did I think I was doing, stalking through a pitch-black hotel toward a homicidal killer? I wasn't trying to die or get kidnapped—again—but there were lives at stake, for more than one reason.

I'd had a chance to kill Pierce once and swore when I failed I wouldn't again. It was time to see if I could keep that promise. At the bottom of the stairs, the wraiths switched, giving me a new supply of clean air. We kept to the shadows, creeping along the back wall toward the side door of the sitting room.

The wraith not providing me with clean air pushed the door open, releasing a light yellow fog into the outdoors.

Other siiiiide. Treeeee line.

I exhaled and cursed how shaky the breath was. *Is he alone?* I didn't dare speak now that we were outside, Pierce was an alpha shifter, after all.

Yeeeesss.

Here for me?

They didn't reply, but that was my answer. Even if I was terrified to face my personal bogeyman again, the choice was simple. The pack was in danger. I needed to protect my pack.

Diesel would never want me to charge into a fight alone, but he'd also never forgive himself if something happened to one of the children.

I crouched, slinking around the side of the house. The ocean roared in the distance, matching the droning in my head. At the last corner, I ducked behind a row of bushes, spotting Pierce sitting in the grass a few feet from the wall closest to the main bedrooms.

Before I could finish wondering why he was sitting down, I was distracted by the thing on his head. Not quite a hat, not quite a mask, it was white like ivory.

Or bone.

The brow of the thing was more pronounced than on a human skull, and the eye sockets were both too long and too narrow. There was no bottom jaw, but the top held a row of fangs, the incisors larger and pointier than the rest. Two gnarled horns shot out of the bone headpiece, spiraling out from opposite sides.

A demon's skull?

Was that what I was seeing? What he was wearing? I'd never seen the thing on his head in his possession before, but if Pierce only wore it when I was sleeping, that made sense.

If that thing had something to do with Pierce controlling nightmares, then I knew what to do. Slowly and soundlessly, I stretched my arm out preparing to flick my wrist the moment my body cleared the bushes.

The wraiths didn't stop me from counting off in my head, but I felt their apprehension. Swallowing it all down, I jumped from my position, sending the links of my whip sailing forward, where the tip wrapped around one of the mangled horns. I yanked back with the dexterity of a fly fisherman and reeled in my catch.

Pierce roared, twisting his head my direction. His eyes met mine, flicking quickly away to where the skull piece had landed on the dirt. My wraiths slithered down my body and I assumed they were going to pick it for me, but they veered away at the last second, hissing as if in pain.

If I'd been in a position to allow terror to fill me, that would've done the trick. Nothing had ever hurt my wraiths. If they couldn't touch the thing, could I?

I wouldn't take the chance. I had more than a hunch that the skull piece was the very thing that had made my life hell, and it wasn't just because Pierce looked like he wanted it back very much that I would enjoy destroying it.

I grabbed a rock, not a word passing between us before I smirked at the rage in his face turning into terror.

He stumbled over the grass between us and my wraiths shot forward punching him back, and holding him down as I lifted the rock in the air and slammed it against the tangled bone.

There was a dull pulse of power—a shockwave that made the contents of my stomach rumble. I managed to keep everything down, looking up in time to see Pierce slide two fingers into his pocket.

"Come!" I screamed the second after Pierce flicked his fingers, releasing a dust that made the wraiths *squeal* with pain.

At the same time, it felt like a red-hot iron had been plunged into my heart. The wraiths fell from him, writhing and wiggling as though they were trying to wipe off the pain.

Hot pressure built behind my eyes, but if there was ever a time I shouldn't cry, it was now. I understood why I'd want to. The situation didn't look good for me from my point of view. Sure, I'd smashed his toy, but now he had a powder that put both me and my wraiths out of commission. He hobbled toward me, clutching his bandaged left arm to his front. The gauze at the end was dirty and loose, like it hadn't been changed in a long time.

He moved more slowly too, weakened either by the fight or from using that thing. Shifter or not, Pierce had never had the ability to regrow his hand, but if he'd been healing as he should've, the injury would've scarred over by now. Dark shadows hung beneath his eyes, and there was a long cut across his forehead that was still wet and open.

It could be helpful that he was no longer healing as he should, but his injuries wouldn't matter as long as I couldn't move.

I hated the whimper that escaped me seeing his approach and closed my eyes, picturing Diesel asleep in our bed.

The gas smothering the babies as I lay rolling in pain.

"Quinlan."

My spine turned to ice at my name coming from those lips. I'd forgotten the way he said it, like a prayer. It had always fucked with my mind. How could he claim to love me and want to care for me, but keep me locked away from the people I truly loved?

"I'm so sorry, little bird. I blame myself for leaving you for so long. You should've stayed where you were safe. Where I could keep you from his gaze. I can't protect you if you don't come with me now. That's what I'm here to do, *save* you. He knows you're here. He's already attacked once. He wants you dead, baby. I'll find us a new home, where we can live together. Come with me, let me save you." Despite the utter crazy in what he said, his tone and affect remained authentic, earnest. His eyes shone with dark worry. He wasn't screaming, but *pleading*.

Too late, I noticed he'd gotten close enough to step on the end of my whip. I flicked it back, but his shoe was thick and the razor just lodged into the sole. With my wraiths and whip out of commission, I had no illusions to how long I'd last in a scuffle. Pierce might've been weak at the moment, but I was pretty sure a weak alpha was still stronger than a human.

The air around us grew violent, whipping the branches of the trees back and forth. Thick mist rolled in from the ocean, blanketing the space in fog that, despite how fiercely the wind blew, lingered densely on the grass around us.

A loud crashing sound punctuated by shattering glass and splintering wood, pulled my attention back to the hotel. Every window and door was wide open, hanging from their hinges as they flapped in the harsh wind.

Pierce stumbled away, off my whip, with his mouth dropped open.

I knew I wasn't that scary—moments before he'd been trying to save me—and I also wasn't the one controlling the wind, which had to mean there was something I didn't want to see behind me.

"You want to see me, demonling," a rich voice cooed.

I didn't trust the voice, but I also wasn't afraid of it. There was something eerily familiar about the way his words danced through the air. I turned my head back and found myself staring at a demon. A real one, not the skull or animated beast of one. But an actual man-sized demon with deep red skin and a body like that of a god that Greek gods prayed to.

I wasn't attracted to the demon—the very idea made my nose wrinkle—but I recognized his strength.

"Alright, rein it in. I'm actually very attractive."

I gasped. It was reading my—

"It? My name is Claus."

A booming roar sounded from inside the hotel and I immediately recognized Diesel's brand of anger. It seemed like Pierce did too because the sound knocked him out of his stunned stillness.

Claus waited for him to take his first step toward us before leveling his red glowing stare Pierce's direction. "You want to leave now."

Whatever Pierce had planned for us, it didn't involve facing a demon. He turned with a grunt, shifting before he ran in the opposite direction, abandoning the bag he'd brought with him.

His scraggily wolf disappeared in the trees and I started after him, but Claus grabbed the back of my shirt.

"What?" I hit at the demon's hand like he was a pestering fly. "No! He needs to die now."

"Demonling, if I let you go after him, he'll just use that devil's powder to subdue and, if you're lucky, *just* kill you. You can't be his favorite person now that you've destroyed the Skull of Arach—we'll talk about how we could've handled that differently later—which'll have him hurting for a while. Besides, I just found you, I don't want you to get hurt, and I can't technically kill anything. Yet."

That was, of course, the first thing Diesel heard as he ran through the grass, his eyes glowing with rage.

12

DIESEL

I KNEW before I opened my eyes that Quinlan wasn't beside me. The bed felt cold, like it had before, and *empty*. The window above the bed hung open, and I *hadn't* left it that way.

Panic swelled in my chest, sinking heavily to claw at my gut. Quinlan was gone, of his own will or taken? My lips opened in a howling roar, both calling out for my mate and alerting my packmates to danger.

I hit the wall of the corridor, unable to get my legs to move as I wanted. There was a taste in the air, one I hadn't fully noticed when all I could concentrate on was Quinlan's absence. It was sweet, but sickly so. Wrong.

"No! He needs to die now!"

Quinlan's voice drifted softly in the air. He wasn't in the hotel, but he was near. I heard the others stirring and trusted them to account for the rest of the pack while I surged outside.

I sprinted toward the tree line but stopped, my claws tearing into the ground, when Quinlan's scent drifted from the other way. In a flash, I was back to five years ago, tearing through what was left of our smoldering home, searching with dumb fucking hope that would only be stomped on, pissed over, and lit on fire.

When I spotted him in the grass beside the hotel, I felt so light, I could've flown the rest of the way. Until I noticed he wasn't alone. It was a testament to how scared for him I was that my first thought was that the figure was just a man.

My nostrils flared. Not a man.

His hand gripped Quinlan's shirt, his words muffled in the wind. "I can't technically kill anything. Yet."

It couldn't have taken more than two seconds for me to shove between their bodies and push the demon away from my omega, but it was two minutes too long.

Quinlan clung to my arms, holding me back while the demon stumbled. He gained his footing and wiped the front of his body as though he was more annoyed I'd gotten his clothes dirty than that I'd put my hands on him.

I surged forward, held back by Quinlan's hands around my wrist. "No, Diesel, wait! He helped me. Saved me from Pierce."

My wolf wouldn't let me calm down enough to listen until I shoved Quinlan's body behind mine. Him resisting was the last thing my wolf wanted to see, which meant I had to hold two things back, my instincts and mate. "Pierce was here?"

Quinlan's shoulders dropped. "Yeah, um, there's good news. I broke the thing that let him make me dream."

The demon wailed mournfully.

"But he got away and would've gotten away with me too if Claus hadn't have come."

"If he saved you, it's so he can kill you when he wants.

Get back to the hotel." The others would be coming any minute and I was certain Quin would run into them before getting too far away, alone.

He didn't run. His fingers rose to my forearm, and held on tight while the wraiths flew chaotically in the air above our heads, likely sensing Quinlan's emotions—or warning us to get the fuck out of there.

Quinlan was scared, and the bitter scent of pain lingered, but he wasn't lying. He believed this demon had saved him from Pierce, a man whose grave I would soon be dancing on.

The alpha team, including Dog, circled around our position. Quinlan's wraiths darted for the canine, circling around his neck like a hug. Dog huffed, but made no effort to shake them off.

Knox would've ordered the rest of the pack into the panic room at the first sign of danger, which explained why the other nephilim weren't clamoring to get to Quin.

That still left five angry bodies, sizing up the very demon who'd decided that moment was the best time to flick dirt from beneath his nails.

"Listen to the demonling. I saved you. All of you."

"Don't call him that," I snarled, bringing Quinlan under the protection of my arm since he clearly was refusing to return to the hotel.

"Whether I call him one or not, he still is, Alpha."

We knew Portal likely had profiles on each of us by now, but it wasn't outstanding having it confirmed. "If you truly saved Quinlan, then, your job is done. He's mine to protect. Leave now." My omega must've sensed how I was barely holding on to my control. The scent of Quinlan's pain, the scent of Pierce, Quinn's fear, the demon's presence, all added up to an agitated wolf who would bite first and ask questions never.

Knox growled and I met his stare. He was crouched behind the demon, ready with claws and teeth, to take it down.

"I can't make any promises for your safety if you stay." I nodded to my pack mate.

Claus smirked. "You can't kill me."

I dropped my arm from around Quin's shoulders to his waist. He let me hold him but for some fucking reason, I felt interest and curiosity, all directed at the red devil at my twelve. Why would my mate care so much about a demon? He'd saved him from Pierce...

Cold dread rolled down my spine, catching on every notch. "Quinlan, were you about to *run after* Pierce?"

"See, yes! He was!" Claus shouted as though relieved. "And I kept him from doing that too. So really, demonling, I saved you twice. So you shouldn't even try to kill me. Besides, when you fail, I would pay back the favor like *that*." He made a slicing motion over his neck.

"You can't kill us either. Yet."

The demon rolled his human-shaped eyes, but his lips were a wide, tight line.

That bothered him, that he couldn't kill.

"Okay, no, I can't kill any of you. Right now," he added, turning his head as he spoke to address the wolves closing in on him. "I can hurt a few of you, though, and if this fight lasts, say, a few days or so, then I'll be full strength. *Then* like *that*." He made the same slicing motion.

A cold breeze blew, chasing away the thick, gray blanket of fog and revealing a beautiful dawn morning. The sky brightened so suddenly it seemed as if I'd taken off a pair of sunglasses. "You would kill us?" Hopefully if Quinlan heard the demon admit to wanting to *kill us*, then he'd stop leaning just a tiny bit forward—but enough to make me want to throw him over my shoulder and run.

Claus narrowed his eyes, like he knew exactly what I was trying to do. "No. Then I *could* kill you. I would have the capability to." He swung around suddenly, pointing a clawed finger into the air. "You know, if we're being real pedantic here, then I should say I could kill you now. I'd just have to be creative. I could...blow that tree down and knock you off the cliff."

"That was yesterday's activity," Quinlan quipped.

The demon smiled at him. Luckily for the demon, there wasn't any attraction in that smile, only a fondness.

But I still hated him smiling at my boy.

"We've gotten off track." Claus waved his arms in broad gestures as he spoke. "Abridged version, the scoundrel Pierce returned tonight to nephi-nap Quinlan and the other angs."

"Angs?" Quinlan asked.

"Half-angel." The demon flicked his hands like he was beating a drum. "I'll be here all night, folks."

"No, you won't be," Knox growled. "Where is Pierce?" Knox looked over the demon's head, making it clear he was addressing the question at me.

"Ran. Gone."

The news that our old leader had made an appearance agitated all of us. Neither twins had spoken since rushing outside. They circled around the demon like caged panthers and from the look in their eyes, the demon had no idea how close we were to testing out that "can't kill him" theory.

"Hey, private bubble," Claus shouted, flapping his hand

at the twins, who'd crept up even closer behind him. "*Anyway*, Pierce was here with the Skull of Arach, a fact he likely regrets now since this capable demonling here destroyed it."

The demon sighed, making it clear we hadn't given him the reaction he wanted. "That's kind of a big deal, guys. To lose the item you sold your soul to obtain?"

At once, the alphas crouched low and growled in tandem. I steadied my hold on Quin, preparing to get him out of here no matter how much he fought. My baby boy was already in hot water and I was in too dark a mood. "How do *you* know he sold his soul for it?"

"Because I'm very good at putting clues together, and there's literally no other way for someone in this world to obtain the Skull of Arach, without it being part of a soul deal. It is a *powerful* weapon." He shook his head sadly. "Seeing that shifter with it was like watching a toddler stumble around with a flamethrower. Nearly *useless* in his hands."

Before anyone could call him out for likening shifters to toddlers, a mouse ran toward us through the grass, squeaking loudly, with a slip of paper curled in its tail.

The demon stared at the small animal, one eyebrow raised as Faust dropped to his haunches and held out his hands for the mouse. It delivered the paper before scurrying off.

"Well? What does the mousemail say?" Claus swept an expectant hand out in front of him.

Faust looked to Knox, waiting for his nod before reading out loud. "If there's no danger, you better come get us now."

Quinlan laughed, trying poorly to hide the sound between my ribs. "That sounds like Jazz."

"It's his handwriting," Faust agreed. "And Storri's mouse."

The demon clapped his hands and continued clapping in time with each word he spoke. "Can we get back on track?" He turned in a circle like an angry teacher scolding his boisterous students. "Quinlan destroyed a weapon of horror and anguish. The Skull of Arach has brought kingdoms to the ground, turning entire cities insane, leaving the people ripping out their hair and clawing at their eyes."

"Then how come all Pierce did was make me dream?" Quinlan's body hung loosely under my arm, his body relaxed despite the demon's continued presence.

Whatever strange relationship they'd formed before I arrived, it was one they both felt.

"Because, demonling, he is a stupid human shifter—" The demon cleared his throat. "I will not say sorry," he gasped, affronted by a suggestion I hadn't heard voiced. The demon continued to look to Quinlan, his lips twisting with distaste. "Fine! He is an *overly ambitious* human shifter who didn't realize he wasn't equipped to properly wield the weapon he coveted."

"He was greedy," Huntley said, having straightened from his I'm-going-to-kill-you crouch.

Jagger's body mimicked his, though he stayed near to his twin and slightly in front. The sky was bright, no longer dawn, a fact that sent Knox's gaze repeatedly to the hotel.

We couldn't stand out here all day, the nephilim wouldn't stay put, for one. But I had many more questions, and the demon looked as longwinded as he did pleased with himself.

"I can only assume you're correct, Alpha Number Two. I don't really know the guy. Figures he'd be Thalasso's. That demon king of drowning has taken one too many trips to the Cave of Eternal Silence, if you know what I mean."

"How would we know what you mean?" Quin shot back with a tone that was far too familiar.

"Is it my fault I expect a certain level of culture and sophisti—"

"Quiet." Knox made the time-out gesture with his hands.

The demon closed his mouth and waited patiently, with a smirk on his face.

"Tell me why I should trust you in my home. You are a demon, correct? The things that want the nephilim dead?" From Knox's tone, it was clear there wasn't a whole lot Claus could say to get him access to the hotel.

"You are half correct. I am a demon, but I don't care either way if the nephilim die."

Quinlan's lips parted in an affronted scoff.

I lifted my mate, puffing my chest when he easily wrapped his arms around my neck before readopting my glare. "How can we trust anything he says?"

The demon tilted its head to the side like it had suddenly become too heavy to hold. "*Because* Quinlan seems to like you all, and since he's my half-brother who I'm finally meeting, I'm not keen on upsetting him."

My wolf snarled hard enough the sound rumbled at the back of my throat. "Everyone get inside," I barked, snagging the demon's wrist as he sauntered by. "And if you make one wrong move, just know, even at full power, you couldn't kill us all before we ripped you apart."

———

I PULLED Quinlan's chair closer to mine, watching the other pack members file in, look up, freeze, and then stumble forward. The doctor, Siobhan, and Jamie remained with the babies in the panic room, listening through the monitoring system. The others took their seats, filling the chairs around the table in the meeting room from the back up.

Claus sat at the head of the table. A position he'd immediately taken and that seemed to please him greatly. He folded his red, clawed hands on the table and beamed at each entering body, flashing sharp, silver teeth, including large canines that resembled fangs.

When all had entered, Claus gave a sweeping, summer camp wave. "Hi, new faces. I'm Claus."

"Hi, Cl..." Storri started to respond loudly, but when he noticed no one else talking, he sat back, finishing with a whisper. "...Claus."

Claus gave Storri a grin so cocky, Faust growled and dropped his arm over his mate's shoulders.

Claus rotated his index fingers around each other as he spoke. "So, should I just start from the beginning? Or does someone else want to do the recap?"

Quinlan leaned forward, speaking like a racehorse hearing a starting pistol. "Claus is my half-brother, so he says, but I feel like it's true. Pierce somehow filled this place with the same gas he used to pump into my room. We went to sleep. He made us see dreams, though I don't know why he would've done that instead of just knocking us out and coming in."

"The effects wore off quickly after the gas was cleared," Faust said. "He would've had to have been fast to apprehend you all."

Claus lifted his fist to his face like he was a gameshow

host speaking into a mic. "Ding. Ding. Ding. However, you didn't make the bonus round. Pierceypoo has been using something that is tearing him apart from the inside. His body can't handle it, and it's starting to show. The poor guy looked all banged up. He couldn't have carried you in that state—why else would he have devil's powder? That shit is not cheap, and getting it couldn't have been easy. You could sell your soul and the soul of everyone you knew and still not afford a pinch of it."

Quinlan rubbed his chest. "Why? What's it made of?"

"Shavings collected from the devil's horns." Claus looked to Hallie, sitting closest to him on the right side. "He likes to keep 'em pointy."

"The devil? The actual devil?" Quinlan didn't sound scared as much as he did shocked.

"The one and only. The powder can hurt demons. A king such as I wouldn't be so affected, but you can see why it's such a rare item. Demons hoard it, and the devil isn't in a habit of arming his followers with weapons that could destroy each other."

"You all sound pleasant," Quinlan quipped, making Jazz gasp and reach for Quinlan like he thought Claus would attack him. "But why did it hurt me? And my wraiths?"

Hearing themselves being mentioned, the wraiths glided up from Dog's side and hung over Quin's shoulders.

Claus looked to the ceiling like he was praying. "Oh dear lord, give me the patience to educated my wayward brother. Put the blocks together, bro. The powder hurts demons. The powder hurt you. You are..."

"No *fucking* way," Quinlan seethed and shoved back from the table. His wraiths expanded, looking more like black wings that cast a shadow over the room before hugging around him like a pod.

"Did he say, brother?" Sitka whispered.

"Why *else* would I call you demonling?" Claus asked, still sitting.

Quinlan's wraiths burst apart revealing a gaze that was only eerie because now both eyes were black. "This isn't funny."

Despite there being no window open on this floor, a strong draft circled the room, continuing back around instead of going out the door. The wind circled again, around and around, picking up the lightest items in the room, flower petals, bits of paper, and what looked like a chunk of lasagna from dinner a few nights ago.

The spinner rapidly grew into a full-blown tornado that nearly lifted the pack from their seats.

Though I wanted to hug and console him, I stayed near, but didn't attempt to touch him. Enough guilt streamed from me, the shifters in the room frowned. I'd pushed that moment when we'd returned to our old pack lands out of mind. There wasn't anything wrong with my baby boy and worrying about the dead tomato plant leaves would achieve nothing. Still, I should've told my mate instead of keeping it from him in an attempt to save him hurt.

A hurt he ended up experiencing anyway.

"You feel that power, brother?" Claus whispered, his lips curling like he was enjoying this. "That's your demon side. My presence must help you open the door to your demon, and that power you feel right now, making all your no-no places warm? It's only possible because of that."

The shadow covering the room disappeared the same moment the tornado died. Quinlan sank into my arms and the wraiths shrank, hanging once again over his shoulders. "I don't want that kind of power," he spat.

"I thought so," Claus quipped, turning back to the others

like Quinlan had simply asked a question out of turn instead of nearly reenacting a scene from *Twister*. "I don't know what the fuss is about. You aren't even full demon. You're *half* demon and half nephilim."

"But that's two halves," Jazz said. "That isn't all he is. He's more human than demon," Jazz said as if his determination could make it so.

Claus rounded on him. "Yeah, except the demon and the angel cancel each other out and make a human... Sometimes."

"That isn't possible." Jazz didn't sound like he cared that Claus was a demon, not when the topic was Quinlan. "Your math is shit."

"Fine! I accept that! Moving on!" Claus sliced his hand through the air repeatedly. "Pierce wanted to sleepwalk the nephilim out, and I'm spitballing from what I overheard here, but I think he planned on taking Quinlan and—if it were me—kidnapping the others to appease my master. A servant as banged up as that can't be in his master's good graces. And because of that banged-up-ed-ness he could likely only succeed in taking you all if everyone was deep under the control of the Skull of Arach. In Pierce's hands, sleepwalking you out of here is the extent he could do with the skull. In a demon's hands? A demon king? Horror *and* anguish? I'd have been unstoppable." He stuck out his bottom lip, crossing his arms to pout.

"Not sorry," Quinlan murmured.

"All this tells me is that he's still trying to serve his demon king. Thalasso is as forgiving as a rusty needle, so whatever Pierce did to get on his bad side he must be scrambling to remedy. This..." He gestured to himself. "It isn't supposed to happen. We aren't supposed to get passes out of hell. We kings do go out, but only on the devil's business.

For Thalasso to use his soul contracts to make this happen means he must have an endgame. Otherwise, he's ash when he goes back."

The wraiths skimmed the ceiling as they zoomed back and forth over our heads.

I grabbed Quinlan's hand. "What are they saying?"

"Nothing. They're just...scared? They're scared."

Dog whined and jumped on the table, barking up at the wraiths, who paid him no mind.

Claus pushed back from the table, reaching up like he was trying to catch the wraiths.

"Stop! Don't hurt them!" Quinlan cried out, sounding so much like a little brother pleading to his older sibling that I couldn't refuse the fact that these two beings were related.

"I'll get them for you," Jazz said, shifting as he jumped forward. He flapped his wings and lifted feet into the air, and I wasn't sure if Jazz's ulterior motive wasn't to show off how much he'd been working on his flying. The space was too small for a jumping dog, leaping demon, and flying wolf, with the wraiths weaving around it all like bullets that couldn't make up their minds.

The chaotic sounds drowned out everything else, which meant none of us knew someone was here until the front door opened, and Alejandro stepped inside with a teenage girl.

"Hola, I let myself in. I tried calling Hallie's cell and then knocking—for a while—but..." Alejandro turned like he was moving through wet cement, slow and dramatic. His eyes landed first on Claus, unapologetically demon, stretching his clawed hand toward the ceiling. He gave Dog a brief glance, but seemed to decide that wasn't behavior too out of the ordinary. But then he spotted the wraiths and

Jazz—who'd crashed to the table, tangling up in his wings, the moment he realized we had guests.

Hallie pushed back from the table and stood, both hands cupping her tummy. "Al! I forgot—"

Alejandro grabbed the teenage girl's hand and walked out the door.

13

QUINLAN

"ALEJANDRO!" Hallie took off after her boyfriend.

The rest of us weren't far behind. Diesel didn't wait for me to get to my feet. He lifted me like a mother monkey and chased after Hallie with Jazz hot on our heels.

"Wait, I can ex—Fuck!" Hallie stumbled over the first step and caught herself against the pillar. She doubled over, clenching her teeth in pain.

"Hallie!" Alejandro had made it to his car, but doubled back when he saw Hallie trip. He dropped to his knees beside her.

The pack gathered in a half circle on the opposite side of Alejandro.

"I'm fine. I'm fine." She waved us off but still clutched the pillar. "Just lightheaded. There's a lot going on right now."

Alejandro peered up at the crowd, all still in their pajamas, except for Claus, who was topless with brown leather short pants, like what a pirate would wear.

Claus let out an outraged scoff.

It hadn't seemed like he could read anyone else's mind,

so I assumed it was just a demon brother thing—*man, that is weird.*

Claus nodded.

If he could read my thoughts, did that mean I could read his?

Claus shrugged. Diesel noticed the gesture and glared at the air between me and Claus before stepping to the side with a huff and blocking my view entirely. I wound my arms around his waist, weirdly giddy after nearly having a hell-inspired meltdown.

Doctor Tiff pushed through the throng of concerned bodies, coming to Hallie's side and grabbing her wrist. "All right, let's get you inside, lying down, and *staying calm.*" The doctor spread her commanding gaze to each person, stuttering as her eyes fell on Claus. She shook her head like a mother whose children would *not stop* bringing home stray animals. Her eyes landed on Alejandro last. "Since it looks like the cat is surely out of the bag..." Doctor Tiff stooped over, picking Hallie up with ease. "Alejandro, you and your niece follow me. The rest of you..." She shook her head. "I don't know...go eat breakfast?"

———

"AN ARCHANGEL AND A DEMON KING? Star-crossed lovers born on opposite sides of a war. How did they meet?" Storri swooned, opening his mouth absentmindedly so Faust could feed him more pancake. He'd been too entranced with Claus's story to touch his breakfast.

"On the battlefield," Claus whispered dramatically, like he knew how much it would please Storri.

"Oh yes," Storri sighed. "That's the perfect place. Then what happened?"

I couldn't be upset with Storri for finding my parents' tragic love story entertaining, not when Claus told it so dramatically. Like before, everyone sat clumped on the other side of the table eating their breakfasts, but that was only because Claus had already knocked his own plate on the floor *twice* with his wild gestures.

"It was love at first sight. My demon sire had the angel pinned, readying the final blow..."

Claus spoke faster, rushing over what should've been the most dramatic part. I'd only known the demon for a few hours and already knew he had a flare for the dramatic. I stared, unblinking, at Claus's temple. There was more to the story, and maybe if I concentrated really hard, I could see Claus's thoughts like he could mine.

I gasped at the flash of change. His words echoed like I'd turned on a radio in my brain. "That wasn't it!"

That jerkhole.

"My archangel mother had our demon king father pinned."

Diesel's chest rumbled unhappily. "I share your head with the wraiths already. Now this guy?" His tone flirted between jest and jealousy.

Claus waved his hand as though he was erasing what we'd said. "History is written by the victors. *Anyway*, neither could do it. They couldn't kill the other, but the enemies around them had no such reservations. So they ran, both deserting their posts, becoming wanted fugitives on both sides."

"And then they had you?" Storri asked.

Claus laughed warmly, his black eyes narrowed with something that looked most like affection. At this point, I thought he just liked seeing Faust bristle. "No, sweet angel, I am Quin's half-brother. We share a sire, but, Quinlan was born. Demons are not *born* in hell. Some, like my sire, were once humans who, through repeated evil deeds, were taken to hell, where their evil festered and reproduced like maggots in rotten flesh. If a demon doesn't die before coming to full power, they become demon kings.

Then there are demons like me, created of my sire's flesh. He ripped a rib from his chest, fed it with unwilling blood from a living vein, until *utter perfection* was created." He put his hands out like a magician's assistant at the end of a trick. "This all happened centuries ago. By the time my sire became a general in the thousand-year war, I was a demon, ready to become a king."

"What are you king of?" Storri's eyes were wide, utterly enraptured by all that he'd heard.

"Demon king of missed opportunities."

Storri's pink lips pouted. "Well that isn't as dramatic as I'd hoped."

Faust smiled wide and pulled his mate into his lap.

"Isn't it? And what would've happened if I'd climbed from hell and headed to the nearest brothel instead of following a familiar scent? I never would've found my half-brother, and you would likely be bound in the back of a van right now. An opportunity not grasped is a very terrible thing, little neph."

Storri's mate was more than happy to play knight when Storri squeaked and hid his face in Faust's chest.

"Going back to the story..." Claus looked only slightly offended. "Once little Quinlan came into the world, the two went on the run, pretending they ever had a chance of a happy family. They reached the end of their rope, plain as that. I was told from the demons on the front line. They fought to the end, running until there was no more road. No direction to disappear into."

I hadn't been expecting a parental reunion like the ones the others had gotten. Until now, I didn't have a reason, other than it didn't *feel* possible. If our archangel parents were only allowed to speak to us in a time of great need, then, I should've spoken to mine years ago. "So, my parents, they're both...dead?"

Claus nodded, his face empty of his usual sarcastic charm.

Diesel's warm arm squeezed my shoulders. "How do you know all of this if you were in hell?" he asked

"As I told you I am stunningly adept at filling in the gaps. I knew when my sire had died because I heard the story from those who had killed him. I knew I had a brother because I felt his creation, here, in my abyss." He tapped the middle of his chest. "I knew where the demonling was because I could smell him, just as I'd smelled Thalasso on the former Skull of Arach owner."

"And you never told *anyone* you have a half-demon brother? Not even your... boss?" I stumbled over what word to use. Boss wasn't correct, but it felt rude to assume.

"You mean the devil? No, we aren't pals. For the most part, in hell, everyone does what they're supposed to do. You only hear from the devil if you've done something to get his attention. No one wants the devil's attention, not unless you've got some bargaining chips."

Jazz's nose wrinkled and his knee bounced. "What does that mean with Portal? We thought the devil was, like, CEO and founder."

"Portal?"

"The company behind all of this? The guys who hired my dad to kill me?" Jazz rolled his hands over each other with no small amount of exasperation.

"Ohhh, the *figurehead*. It hasn't always been *Portal*.

Travel from hell to here isn't common, but has been necessary to get the job done. We also need an organization on earth to keep up with soul servants. Souls are the highest form of currency in hell, and humans are always willing to give theirs up for the most ridiculous thing, so it's a program that works. Runs itself most times, but when it doesn't we need a stronghold and since time moves in circles in hell, any stronghold built here will likely be dust the next time it is really needed. So we borrow ones that already exist. We've used companies, organizations—cults are easy because the followers hardly notice a change. Any demon is allowed to utilize the stronghold, but the majority are on a strict telecommuting level, trading souls for servitude. I assume Portal could've briefly once been a true business, but from now until it becomes unsuitable, it's every demon's headquarters on Earth."

"What was the figurehead before?"

"I believe it was once an organization called the Freemasons and then, more recently, the Illuminati."

"Those things still exist!" Jazz cried out.

Claus winked. "Or do they?"

Diesel brought his lips to my temple, and my cheeks warmed. He touched me so freely now. That hadn't been the case before, and my stomach still flipflopped when he reached over to squeeze my thigh or kiss me.

My wraiths came back into the room with Dog walking beneath them.

"It's strange seeing them on the outside." Claus jerked his prominent chin at my wraiths.

My forehead wrinkled with confusion, but before I could ask, Claus began to explain.

"Demons don't have as much soul as a human. I am the

only demon produced from my sire's ribs. Why mess with perfection?

"That means I have about half the amount of soul as my sire has, since souls diminish with each generation. There are some demon lines that stretch so long, they don't have any soul in them at all, but a soul isn't just a bargaining chip. It has a purpose. It's a driving force, what turns a hunk of gorgeous muscle..." He flexed. "...into a sentient being. So demons have wraiths. Technically, they are a part of you, though, it seems, on the outside, they have their own identity. They weren't always on the outside?"

I shook my head, using too much strength for how light it felt. My wraiths were demon soul replacements?

"Technically, you don't *need* them. You've got a bright soul shining in there." He stuck his tongue out like he found that fact distasteful. "And I'm not sure why they would suddenly burst out of you. I suppose if you'd lived a life of utter and complete happiness, with your every whim met, then maybe your demon side laid dormant?" He said all that like he doubted that was actually the case. The following silence made his eyes stretch wide open.

That had been my life with Diesel on our old pack lands. I hadn't constantly been smiling and laughing, but I'd always felt safe knowing I was just where I was meant to be. Diesel had made sure my life was perfect, saving me from ever having to face my demon side.

"Your nephilim power likely had something to do with that."

A record scratched in my head, halting all thoughts.

I whipped my head back to my demon brother. "I don't have a nephilim power."

Claus looked me up and down—ridiculous, since I sat at the table, and he could only see half of me. "Oh yes you do, demonling, and may I commend you. It's fiendish really. More insidious than anything I could've thought up. Leave it to the angels..."

"What the fuck are you saying?" Diesel barked, speaking the words in my mind.

With his nose lifted as though he'd been personally insulted Claus replied, "Quinlan attracts. He's a human lure. People get within ten feet of him and feel all warm and fuzzy." His black eyes found mine, staring me down. "You didn't get teased a lot growing up, did you? No one's ever rude to you at a grocery store."

That was a no to both, but what did that prove? Diesel made sure I didn't get teased, and if I'd ever traveled to a grocery store off pack lands, Diesel would've been there too, to make sure no one was rude to me.

"Demon." Sitka addressed Claus from the farthest corner of the room. He'd stayed pretty silent throughout everything, but I could feel his unease and knew it was because of his time in the Portal lab. That he addressed Claus at all was already shocking. "Are you saying Quinlan's power is that people like him?"

"Short version, yeah." He rolled his eyes. "An angel's charm."

I made people like me?

Sitka could disappear, Storri could persuade a herd of bears to dance the Macarena, and I got to never know if someone really liked me or if they were just responding to my *charm*.

I pushed my plate away, my stomach turning with vomitous intent.

Had I forced every single person in this room to care about me?

I'd *cursed* them without their knowledge or consent. My

throat shook, my breath trembling as I searched for anything to make this not true. "But what about Pierce? He'd kept me locked away. That isn't something you do to someone you like."

Claus shook his head slowly, obliterating my hopes that I'd found the crack in his explanation. "For some humans, love becomes obsession."

All this time I'd wondered why? Why me? Why was Pierce so infatuated with me? I'd felt so sad for myself, believing the universe picked on me specifically.

I knew it now. The fault wasn't with Pierce, but with me.

Everything—the bomb that killed my mother, my being kidnapped, Diesel's years of grief over an omega he'd loved more than *anything*—it was all *my* fault.

14

DIESEL

I FELT my mate slump the moment his distress flooded my senses. There were so many possible causes, but I knew which was the culprit. He'd discovered so much about himself in the last few *hours* but not even learning of his half-demon status had made him feel as anxious as discovering his nephilim power.

It wasn't surprising to me. I'd always known my Quinlan was a charmer and had spent plenty of afternoons growling from behind the curtains as I spotted my boy being flirted with by yet *another* interested shifter. He never noticed the lingering touches or coy smiles, and had been too trusting to believe a person would come to talk to him for any reason other than what they'd claimed.

Even regular, non-angel people had god-given talents; this wasn't any different from that. It couldn't be reason enough to prompt his distress. "Quin—"

"No, Hallie," Alejandro's authoritative voice shot in from the stairwell, lifting my hackles. He stood at the bottom of the stairs, in view of the meeting room.

Who the hell did he think he was talking to Hallie like that?

"I have no problem with people who turn into animals or flying specters, but I won't have my child raised in that. You said so yourself that dangerous things have happened here, *as recently as last night.*" He exhaled harshly, looking through the front windows where his niece sat in the car with her face pressed against the window, staring at the hotel. "I cannot knowingly bring Maria into danger. Come *with* me, Hal. Come live with me in town. You can visit all the time and—"

Everyone huddled at the table who'd been pretending not to listen got up at the same time, rushing into a bottle-neck at the archway to the foyer. Alejandro stood at the bottom of the stairs, reaching up, to Hallie standing at the top, hugging her stomach with one arm while holding a balled up tissue.

That fucker made her cry.

My forward lurch was stopped by Quinlan's tight grip around my arm—and the wraiths gluing my feet to the floor. "This isn't your fight," Quinlan whispered sadly.

Looking around the group, I wasn't the only person who wanted to jump in the middle. We all fought back the instinct to protect our packmate—even when the danger wasn't physical.

Her eyes were full of tears, but her voice was strong. "You asking that only proves you must not really know me, Al." She nodded toward the door. "You should just go. I'll let you know when the next appointment is, and then after, we'll...work something out."

I couldn't be proud of the way Hallie kicked Alejandro and his shitty ideas out the door when she sounded dead inside. Empty.

Alejandro had noticed her tone too. He watched her face, his eyes searching. "I can't...Hallie, don't..." Alejandro took a deep breath and looked over at the young girl by his side. "You said there was danger here, Hallie. I don't care about any of the other...stuff, and I won't tell anyone." He scratched the back of his head. "I *really* won't tell anyone. But I have to think of Maria and my future child. Answer me one question, Hallie. How many times has your life been in danger while living here?"

Fuck. The answer to that question was incriminating, but it was also a really shitty question. He must not have known Hallie if he believed that would prove anything to her. She'd put herself in danger more times than I enjoyed thinking about. I never should've let her, but I also knew I didn't control a single thing Hallie did. If there was something she could do to help protect her packmates, she would do it.

Hallie shook her head softly. She wiped the tears from her eyes, and none rushed to replace them. "I'll text you the time of the next appointment. All of my appointments will be here, so you're going to have to decide what you will do about that." Hallie turned and disappeared down the corridor before Alejandro could come up with a reply.

Camel—a shifter much too pretty to be responsible for the heap of bloody remains visible on the screen in the back corner of the room—wiped his hands clean of the gore that covered them. "He got taken off the neph job because of his little stint in jail. Weirdest thing though..." His tone would've made more sense if we were co-workers gossiping at the water cooler. "He told me who got his spot. It's a name we all know."

"Pierce," Knox snarled.

"That's the one. Didn't you guys say he's half-speed—not healing? What the fuck is he doing on a mission as important to the demons as that?"

That was a good question that I'd ask Pierce when we caught up with him.

I'd decide when I got there if it would happen before or after I ripped off his dick and stuffed it down his throat.

"Where is he going? Who are the nephilim?" Knox was already on his feet, reaching for his knife holster.

"Intel says it's a single family living in a picturesque cabin by a lake in northern Idaho. You'll need to leave now to get there. I already contacted Badger, and we don't have a rider within six hundred miles."

"Understood. Thanks, Camel." Knox lifted his finger like he wasn't quite finished. "Did that guy give you trouble during the interrogation?" Knox had also observed the state of the clearly dead *heap* in the background, the former Portal servant tasked with snatching the next group of nephilim.

"None at all, sang like a canary," Camel replied. He blinked, and then, "Why do you ask?"

Knox jerked his head in farewell, cutting the call without answering. "None of you will ever be alone with that guy," he announced to the pack.

Jazz smiled from his seat in the rolling chair next to his mate's, but his amusement was short-lived. "So this means..."

"That you stay home, love," Knox replied, not unkindly. "I won't bring my nephilim omega to a mission where the targets are on a mission killing nephilim. There's no strategic reason."

I didn't want to leave Quinlan, but I couldn't sit back on another mission. We knew where the danger was, for the most part, and Faust would stay with Dog. If we were gone for more than a night, the pack would sleep together in the panic room.

Quinlan grabbed hold of my index finger and pulled my hand into his lap, looking down at where we held on to each other. "I know you have to go. And I know why I can't go even though my help would be totally beneficial—"

"Mine as well," Sitka shouted, unhappy about staying home. He crossed his arms over his baby, using his son like a shield to separate him from his alphas.

The twins gave each other a look and then came in from opposite angles, trapping Sitka with their lips on either side of his face. "Don't be mad, hotness," Huntley said between kisses. "I know deep down you understand."

"Hmph." Sitka still frowned but had made no move away from either of his mates.

"Claus, you'll go, right?" Quinlan turned to face his half-brother, working his bottom lip overtime. As he'd warned us, Claus grew stronger as more time passed. He could manipulate his appearance and, for some reason I couldn't understand, wanted to look like a hipster Paul Bunyan. "You'll go, though. Right, Claus? *Brother?*"

"You point that charm somewhere else, demonling," Claus grouched, waiting a beat before sighing loudly. "Yes, fine, I'll go and protect your poor, widdle alf—"

I growled sharply. "Watch it."

———

IT WAS the type of day too pretty for anything bad to happen. Puffy, white clouds lazily glided through a bright blue sky. Between a mountain and a lake, the position made me twitch, but nothing could keep that mirror-glazed lake from being gorgeous.

Fucking awesome. I got my mate back, and now I was spewing poetry.

Pretty day or not, five miles ahead, a cabin of nephilim unknowingly waited in Portal's crosshairs.

Each of us—minus Claus, humming as he stuffed the candy he'd stolen from a gas station into his mouth as quickly as he could unwrap it—checked over our equipment, making sure if anything went wrong, it wasn't something that could've been easily avoided.

The Walkers and the council knew of our mission and were on standby, ready to provide more assistance if it was needed, but ultimately, we were the ones best trained for the job.

Knox slowed to turn right off the highway onto a road that wound around the lake.

I could see a family of nephilim living in a place like this. There hadn't been information on whether the nephilim were a found family or blood-related, but I was relying on the mates to get that information at some point.

Knox curved the vehicle around the last turn, and a sprawling log cabin appeared in front of us. The windows—of which there were many—reflected the day's sun, lighting the cabin with an ethereal glow. The home stood behind a ten-foot, wrought-iron security fence on three sides, with a long dock and lake making up the fourth. There were cameras at the mechanical gate and an intercom with a single button. The buzzing in the distance told me something, somewhere was electrically charged. My bet was the gate.

Knox pulled the car up to the intercom and pressed the

button. If they didn't let us in, we'd just let ourselves in, but it would make everything flow more smoothly if they came willingly.

The black asphalt driveway wound through a pristinely manicured lawn. Three cars, all black Kia SUVs, were parked on the blacktop closest to the front door. There was a four-car garage to the right, the doors closed, with a stand-alone basketball hoop placed between the middle garage doors.

"This place looks like a postcard," Huntley said with a tone that wasn't appreciative.

"It's too perfect," Jagger added.

I stared at the windows, attempting to see through the glare and inside. "Why aren't the cars parked in the garage?"

"Hello?" a soft woman's voice replied through the speaker.

"My name is Knox. I'm the man who called and left a message? I know you likely think I am insane, but I swear to you, your lives are in danger, and we are here to help."

The woman didn't immediately scream for him to leave or threaten to call the cops, so there was a chance we wouldn't have to do this the hard way.

"I...um...I actually b-believe you. I sometimes...see things and...just come in." Her voice shook. Breathy and distressed.

The gate swung open, and the electric hum stopped.

There was picture perfect, and then there was too fucking easy... This smelled too fucking easy. "You think they don't trust us?"

Knox didn't reply with words; all he offered was a scowl. "We have to go find out. Whether they want our help or not, there's no way they can handle what's coming for them." He cut the engine and opened his door slowly.

Leaving the vehicle outside the gate ensured our fastest mode of transportation wasn't locked behind an electric fence.

The security cameras followed our progress, tracking our movements through the gate and up the driveway. With a swift but cautious pace, we stalked closer to the picturesque home.

Claus surged between me and Knox, skipping ahead toward the house like we were arriving to a barbecue. He'd changed out of a ridiculous flannel but had replaced it with a colorful button-up Hawaiian shirt. The unbuttoned shirt flaps billowed as he stretched his arms over his head before scratching his hairy human gut. "You're all so gloomy all the time. Maybe something is just going right for once? Think of that?"

Knox grunted, slowing the closer we grew to the door. "Too much isn't adding up."

He froze, and loud footsteps sounded from inside the house. With seven members in their family, the footsteps wouldn't be alarming if it weren't for the fact they all sounded like heavy-duty boots. Their breaths and heart-beats were close enough to hear through the cabin walls. Some breathed more rapidly than others, but it was a single heartbeat that stuck out above all the others.

Slow, steady, calm...the heart of an alpha shifter.

Knox turned back to the vehicle the moment the gates swung closed and sparked, igniting with an electric whir. Annoyed and furious, Knox muttered, "Fuckin' trap," as he faced the cabin, his hand reaching for a blade.

"Your streak is over." I refused to give up the chance to ridicule Knox. His plans always worked; the opportunity was rare. We dropped into formation, backs together in a circle so we were ready for an attack from any direction.

"Fuck you, Diesel." Knox grabbed Claus's bicep and jerked him from his position of most-likely-to-get-shot-first to a place in formation between Knox and Jagger. Claus was getting stronger, but I wasn't stupid enough to believe playing human dress-up was the only strength that'd been restored. "You try next time, dick. I'll gladly give the responsibility—"

The front door opened, swinging slowly with a low, anticlimactic groan. "Do you ever tire of being a step behind, Knox?" Pierce slunk out the front door. We'd all been expecting him the moment we'd heard his heart. Ten men, all dressed in black tactical gear, marched out the door, dividing to either side of Pierce, standing with their weapons aimed and ready. Inside, I counted no less than thirty additional men. Pierce *would* bring an army, too weak to face us unless the odds were stacked.

"Where are they?" Knox wouldn't indulge Pierce in his evil banter.

But Pierce didn't need indulging. He already had a small tape recorder in his hand. "*I...um...I actually b-believe you. I sometimes...see things and...just come in.*" His smile widened. "That's what she told me a few days ago when I called to *save* them. They're dead. They've been dead for days, actually.

"None of you are good for much, but like good doggies, you can follow a trail. I knew you'd make it here—*too late for it to fucking matter*. And I could kill two birds with one stone. Get the blood to Thalasso, take care of a thorn in his side, all while the gate grows wider and—"

Before the words could leave Pierce's mouth, Huntley's snarl sliced them in two. "Are you honestly monologuing? Hurry the fuck up and get to the part where you *try* to kill us."

Pierce traded the recorder for his pistol, immediately cocking and training it at Huntley's head.

Jagger's growl couldn't be heard, but felt. He moved to cover Huntley.

Pierce watched it happen with a smug smirk. "Fucking idiots. All of you. You fight with your hearts instead of your heads. None of you had any business being Alpha, then or now."

Was his plan to hurt us with his *mean words*? If the nephilim family was already dead, he could've intercepted us at any point between the hotel and here. Lying in wait somewhere along the way wasn't Pierce's style. He wanted us to *know* we had failed. He'd always gone for the overkill in the field, and it was our stupid mistake believing that brutality ended once the missions were over.

"...the whole thing was my fucking idea..."

I'd stopped listening somewhere around the time he started whining and had no clue what he complained about now. Knox was as restless as I was, and Claus had started hopping from foot to foot like he was trying to keep warm in the cold.

"...pack would be nothing without me—who the fuck is this guy?" Pierce gestured with the barrel of his gun toward Claus. He didn't realize he'd met Claus already. Claus didn't just look human, but smelled human too. "Is this my replacement? I'm offended. I'd rather that bitch Hallie than this—"

I surged forward, but Claus stood squarely in my way. "This is why I'm here." He winked and spun to face Pierce.

"I'm defecting!" he called out, lifting his hands for a scant second before prowling forward like a tomcat. The sight of him in his Hawaiian shirt, sandals, and cargo shorts was made doubly ridiculous when he faced off against Pierce's heavily armed men.

Pierce holstered his weapon. "Who the fuck are you?"

"Well, you actually already know my name," Claus chirped. Pierce looked like he couldn't decide if he was entertained or annoyed. His senses were telling him Claus was a regular human—one just bold enough to make Pierce curious, if only for the moment. "I am hurt that you don't remember me, but am glad to see you. Joining these packs should come with a return policy or something. I'm so totally done with those losers." He threw a frustrated hand our direction. "Maybe if I told you my whole name, you'll remember, and then we can start talking benefits. I'm going to need a fair amount of vacation time because, you see, I'm really—"

Pierce cleared his throat and leaned toward Claus like he wanted to tell him a secret. He gestured with his chin for Claus to do the same. The moment Claus leaned forward, Pierce stabbed him in the gut. "I don't fucking care."

Claus grunted and groaned, making it clear he wouldn't be winning an Oscar anytime soon. "Ohhhh, ouch, ooooh. You cut me off. Rude."

It was Pierce's turn to look shocked. He let go of the knife handle, but Claus snagged his hand, squeezing it back in place as he stepped forward, reforming into his demon king body as the rest of the blade and then the handle—along with Pierce's hand—sank into Claus's gut. "My *whole* name," Claus purred while his horns sprouted out from his head, curving toward the sky, "is Claus, Demon King of Missed Opportunities." He looked down at where he had Pierce's arm trapped *inside* his body. "But I won't miss this one."

Claus lifted a clawed hand. At the same time, Pierce

turned his chin to his shoulder, snagging part of his vest between his teeth and into his mouth. He exhaled hard, sending a plume of dust into Claus's face.

Claus stumbled back, releasing Pierce before sneezing so violently, a stream of fire shot from his mouth like a flamethrower. The men fell back, firing and forcing us to find shelter behind the parked cars. Claus sneezed again, one after another. Each as loud and violent as the first. When his face started smoking, I wondered if demons could go into anaphylactic shock.

Pierce screamed for a retreat, and as the bullets receded, we surged forward, getting to Claus as his sneezes began to ebb.

"I'm—"

Huntley yanked Jagger back, saving him from another fireball.

"—sorry about that." Claus rubbed his nose with a flat hand. "I really screwed the pooch on that one. So much for my awesome kill-you line. That would've been so cool. Could've ended this whole subplot. Don't know why I didn't expect the bugger to have *more* devil's powder. Next time we meet up with him, remind me to ask about his supplier."

"We aren't chasing after?" Jagger stood at the corner of the cabin, peering through the trees in the direction Pierce and his men were fleeing.

"No. He has too many men to hide behind. He'd just leave them to die and buy himself more time. We need to get back. Huntley, call Faust. Let him know what's happened and to go to threat level severe. Claus, you're... good?" Knox gestured vaguely at his stomach.

"It hurts a lot, and I want a nap..."

Satisfied, Knox went back to the plan. "We'll do a search

of the house, in case there's any information on who these people were—*fuck.*"

We'd all heard the telltale click and dove away from the building at the exact same moment, getting as much distance as we could in the fraction of a second before the house blew up.

15

QUINLAN

When Diesel limped through the door, still in pain after the drive back, I knew I could add this pain to the mountain I was already responsible for.

They'd almost died, all of them except probably Claus—and he didn't sound like he had a great time either. He told his story with dramatic flourish that had Storri on the edge of his seat and Faust rolling his eyes.

The men reclined in the sitting room, refusing the infirmary like the alph-idiots they were. The blast from the explosion had forced them all to go flying. Bones had to have broken and likely still were broken, but all Diesel would let me do was put a cool rag to his forehead. "Your forehead is warm. I'm going to get some ice." I stood from Diesel's side, making it a few steps before Diesel pulled me so I lay sprawled on top of his body.

"Your presence is all I need to heal me."

More than one person groaned in the background. They probably hadn't seen how Diesel had grabbed tight handfuls of my ass as he spoke.

I wanted to laugh with him, to tease and flirt while he

pretended he didn't hurt all over. But I couldn't ignore that much of his attraction to me was due to my nephilim power. I'd unknowingly influenced his emotions, and the worst part was that I didn't know how to turn it off. If I could, I'd switch it off forever, and if, when my effect wore off and the pack—as well as Diesel—realized they'd have less trouble without a member who was half-demon, I'd leave without a fight.

I'd pondered leaving while the alphas had been away. I thought about it for so long, Sitka, Jazz, and Storri showed up at my door. We'd watched the children play, which I was happy to do anyway, but I knew they'd sensed my thoughts. If I left without learning to turn off my power, then they would just chase after me. They wouldn't be able to help it. Maybe in the beginning, but Claus had told me after that the effects magnified with time.

"Mate?" Diesel squeezed my butt cheeks, shaking slightly to get my attention.

I met his gaze but shook my head. Diesel often knew what I was feeling before I did, and there was no doubt he'd sensed my trepidation. I felt paralyzed, not wanting to move too much or make too much noise.

For a second, I was sure he'd challenge my reply. His eyes narrowed, and I dropped my lips to his, kissing him softly. He took over the kiss, nibbling my lips for a bit before pulling back to whisper, "Later."

"And you're sure the nephilim family is gone?" Jazz curled deeper against Knox's chest. His pink lips turned down. He carried a sorrow we all shared. I hadn't felt the moment of death or anything like that, but with the men's return came a heaviness that felt ironically like a missed opportunity.

"Yes." Knox nodded, never one to mince words. "Pierce

was never stupid. This would all be easier if he was. He's greedier than I ever suspected. I spent the most time with him early on. I should've recognized who he was instead of making excuses for a pack brother."

"We aren't playing the blame game again." Hallie lay on one of the couches, a cool cloth over her head. "You're right. Pierce is smart. He's also right in saying he's been one step ahead. So, what do we do? How do we close that gap?"

"Forget the gap." Knox stood abruptly, taking mate and son with him. "How do we close the gate? Claus?"

"I've never opened one. I'm not stupid enough to ask for that wrath, nor am I brainless enough to learn how without reason. We know nephilim blood is a key component."

"But you escaped hell, same as Thalasso," Diesel pointed out. "That doesn't matter?"

"I wasn't responsible for opening the gate, just being near enough to sense it. I'm a demon. I can't be blamed for being a little naughty whenever given the chance. As for closing it, we'll have to figure out the ritual he used to open it. Find that, and the other information should fall in place."

"So we...research?" Huntley didn't sound pleased that the next steps weren't immediately jumping into the action. "Where do you even start looking for a thing like that?"

"No idea. I'd check the devil's grimoire if you have the stones for it. There are a few copies on earth, pages pressed from the wood of trees used to hang the innocent, bound in virgin leather. I can probably sniff out a copy on Earth."

"Virgin leather?" Storri asked.

"Don't tell him," Sitka cried out.

Jazz patted a bewildered Storri's arm. "Okay, you get this creepy book. We figure out how Thalasso opened the gate, close it, and then..."

"Dance?" Claus's grin was evil.

Was that redundant? Like saying the yellow school bus was yellow?

"All we need to do is search the *creepy book* that is, last I checked—since the grimoire is ever-growing—seven billion words long and written entirely in Enochian."

Jazz winced, possibly imagining having to turn the pages and hold a book like the one Claus described. "Could we get the ebook version and Google translate?"

"WE SHOULD STAY and help the others." I planted my feet on the floor in front of the steps, bringing Diesel to a stop. Claus had left immediately after the plan had been set, in search of a copy of the devil's grimoire. Without knowing how far he'd have to travel to find the book, we didn't know how long we would be left on watch and waiting.

Claus believed more nephilim wouldn't be killed until right before the next sacrifice. In the meantime, Knox had the Walker County pack and the shifter council working on tracking down more groups of nephilim. With the information Badger and his men were collecting, there were several leads, and once the nephilim were found, they could go into protection. It wouldn't be easy convincing so many that they could be trusted, but at least they'd be warned. The nephilim family in Idaho clearly had known danger existed. Their security system was too advanced for them to be unaware, and they'd still been overcome.

Before he'd left, dressed in tan linen pants and a red Baja hoodie, he'd explained that lesser demons wouldn't be able to pass through the gate until it was fully open, which was a thing he'd said was best avoided. "But as the gate grows, more demon kings will notice it, and they aren't as warm and cuddly as I am."

"Why are you helping us?" Hallie had asked, her arms crossed over one another.

Claus didn't look at all offended. "I'm not just here out of the goodness of my void. The devil will fry the demon who opened the gate but likely reward the demon who had a hand in closing it."

Knowing he had something to gain seemed to have been enough to soothe Hallie's distrust for the time being. Since Alejandro had left, ending their relationship in the process, Hallie had acted like she didn't hurt, but we all knew she did. We felt it through our pack bond, and the alphas could sense it every time they scented her. But if Hallie wanted to push her problems away for a bit and concentrate on something else, then the possible end of the world was a great option.

But then he'd left and everyone else had split up, to make calls or tend to young ones, leaving me with an excuse that clearly wasn't true.

Diesel made a show of looking around us. "What others?"

I shrugged. "Something could come up."

Diesel bent over, wordlessly hauling me to his shoulder as he ascended the stairs. This wasn't the first time he'd carried me through the halls, but it was the first time it made me want to cry instead of smile.

"Baby boy, the moment we're alone, you are going to tell me what is making you feel like that."

For not the first time, I cursed shifters and their stupid senses. I hadn't been bothered all that often being the only human in the pack, but when I had been, it'd been because of something I was trying to hide and had no possibility of succeeding.

He carried me into our room and shut the door. The click of the lock sliding into place always made me shiver just a little.

"You shouldn't have carried me," I whined the moment he set me down on the bed. Climbing up the mattress, I sat at the head, clutching the comforter to my chest. "You're hurt. You could've died. That was what Pierce was there to do. Kill you."

Diesel sat on his side of the bed in the same position. "But he didn't, so I don't know why you're worried about it still."

"I just—" It hadn't been until I'd gotten a bit older that people started commenting about my relationship with Diesel. Never very loudly, and only ever from the mouths of unmated shifters who were clearly just jealous—hence the reason why I never told Diesel about it—but I'd still heard what they'd said. That Diesel was whipped. They'd implied I'd performed some amazing sexual feat that had earned me a spot by Diesel's side. Little did they know I'd wished for Diesel to let me touch his body, but he'd rebuffed my every attempt. But he never stopped taking care of me. I'd taken it for granted that his feelings were real and his adoration was pure. "Just don't die for me. Not ever. Don't do it."

Diesel growled low but immediately swallowed it like he'd opened the door to a lion's cage and slammed it shut as the beast roared in your face. "Why is this something you're worried about, Quinlan?"

This new Diesel was sneaky. He'd been easier to read before. He'd worn his feelings on his sleeve, which was how I'd seen them so clearly. Now, he zigged when he would've zagged, and I was left uncertain of his motives.

I couldn't share my fears and expect Diesel to understand. He was stuck under my spell, after all. He looked at me like I was the moon, sun, and stars, and I never once worried it wasn't real, that he didn't actually love me. When I thought back to his reluctance, the way I'd pushed our relationship forward every step of the way, it made me want to drop to the ground and cry.

But I couldn't have a tantrum, and I couldn't let my nephilim curse draw Diesel any deeper under my spell.

I got up and walked to the desk, taking a seat in the chair. I spun around and crossed my legs at the knees. "I think after learning what we have, if you want to reflect on certain choices you've made..." *And maybe decide the half demon you were forced to adore isn't actually what you want.*

Diesel looked at the carpet between the bed and the desk. "Omega, why are you putting space between us?"

My face burned, both in shame and arousal. This would all be easier if I didn't want Diesel so badly. "I don't know— maybe I just needed space! People need space sometimes." Could I annoy him out of caring for me? Or would that just make being forced to love me that much more unbearable?

"Is that what you need, mate? Is you needing space the reason why your scent went so sour downstairs?"

"No." He'd know if I tried to lie, so I didn't attempt it, adding as much disrespect as I thought I could get away with instead.

"Tell me the truth, Quinlan," Diesel cooed, sliding to sit at the end of the bed.

He braced his forearms—each wider than an average man's biceps—against his knees as his eyes roved my body, pausing on where my legs were crossed and my arms folded over my chest. His eyes softened, tilting slightly down in his amusement.

There was nothing funny about this. "Why aren't you mad?" I hadn't intended to scream, but that's what ended up happening.

"About you not telling the truth from the moment we stepped in here? I can get mad about that if you want, or I can wait for you to be a good boy and tell me what's going on."

Damn him. He knew that hearing the words *good boy* from his lips made my dick cheer like it was ringing in the new year. Being praised by Diesel was like a warm hug that quickly liquefied into a deep yearning. My spine straightened, imagining the words dancing from vertebrae to vertebrae, electrifying the nerves and shooting warm tingles to the rest of my body.

I loved this mountain of a man, plain and simple, but while my heart yearned for his nearness at all times, only one of us could trust our emotions. His desire, his *need* for me, wasn't real. I'd been tricked again, but this time, I'd been the deceiver as well.

"It's not real."

"What isn't?" Diesel leaned back, his question was as crisp as an apple in autumn.

I hadn't said anything and already felt like I wanted to disappear. Everything going on around us, it all pointed back to me and at more than one time. I was the common denominator here, and my absence would—

"Speak," Diesel ordered, managing to say the one thing to pull me from my misery and replace it with fury.

I pushed to my feet, clenching my hands into fists that hung at my sides. "I am not a dog."

"I didn't call you one. Now answer the question."

I'd burned too brightly and lost steam just as quickly. Realizing that even now, I was influencing the moment and dictating Diesel's needs was enough to push me back into the chair, my chin low.

Diesel's footsteps were measured. I couldn't see his boots until he stood in the square of floor I could see with my head down.

I just wouldn't explain. No one could make me, and if I said I was leaving with enough conviction, then maybe they'd believe me.

Strong fingers wrapped around the hair at the back of my head and pulled, forcing my face up to his. "Tell me what has you so worried. What isn't real?"

"You heard Claus. You know what my nephilim power is. What you feel isn't real. I'm making it happen, Diesel, and I'm so sorry for that. I've ruined your life...I've stolen it! You could have done anything, lived a long happy life with a mate who—"

He kissed me because, well, *Diesel*. Though his lips felt like home, I had to make myself remember they were more like those staged houses where the lemons were plastic and the TV was made of cardboard.

"Quinlan, I love you so much. I think you are smart— brilliantly creative—and sharp as a whip, but that was the stupidest fucking thing I've ever heard. Your nephilim power isn't making me love you. Maybe it got you a few extra scoops of ice cream a few times. It could even explain how many times you got me to let you stay up late on school nights, but it doesn't *make* me love you. I do that on my own, and to suggest otherwise is suggesting I don't know myself. Is that what you think?"

"No...but you have no choice!"

Diesel's arms rippled as he lifted me from the chair. "I have a choice, Quin. I choose you, always, baby boy. How can you not know that?"

I dropped my face a second time, but this time in shame. Hearing Diesel explain it, I felt silly for my worries, but Diesel did have a way of talking away my worries just so I wouldn't hurt. "It isn't that I don't know it. I don't know how to trust it."

He growled and smashed his mouth to mine, losing the tight control he had on his reactions. "You trust me," Diesel whispered hotly, speaking with his lips pressed against mine. "Trust me."

I wanted to, and not just because my hole clenched for this man, but because he was my alpha. Trusting my alpha was my natural response. If he told me that my nephilim power wasn't the thing making him love me, how could I tell him he was wrong? If our roles were reversed, I'd threaten to cut off a body part if he refused to believe me when the topic was me. "Okay, alpha." I tilted my head, bearing more of my neck as I nibbled at my bottom lip. "I love you so much, Diesel, I can't stand the idea that any part of us might be coerced—fake. But I do trust you. I do."

His thumb grazed over my lips and cheek while he caressed my nape with his index finger.

I shivered, fluttering my eyes closed at the sensation before finding his gaze again.

"*Good boy.*"

His kiss was shorter than I expected before he set me down and turned me in the other direction.

"Hold on to the post," Diesel ordered with his lips tickling my earlobe.

I reached for the wood post obediently, giving a questioning hum only after I'd done as he asked.

"Somehow, at some time, you got it in your head that your gift is what made our relationship. You must need me to remind you." Said from a different pair of lips, that might not have sounded so threatening, but his casual tone hid unwavering intent.

I licked my lips, careful to keep my hands where they were. "How will you remind me?"

Diesel grinned. He looked like he'd enjoyed the tremble in my words that I hadn't been able to hide. He was my protector, but Diesel would always first be a predator. He stood behind me, nuzzling the side of his face against my neck to deposit his scent while taking mine in. "First, I'm going to undress you."

He pulled my pants down in one fluid motion that took my underwear with it.

I squeaked, feeling the strangest urge to cover myself. Not only had Diesel already seen everything I packed—I wanted him to see me. But the move had been so sudden, like a table suddenly without its cloth. Ta-da.

My shirt met a worse fate, splitting apart under Diesel's claws.

He kissed my now naked shoulder, spreading the kisses down my arm to a spot on my wrist that he rubbed against his cheek.

I closed my eyes, getting lost in Diesel's gentle lips and soft caresses.

"Quinlan..."

"Hm?"

"Who is your alpha?"

He wasn't asking me who was Alpha of the pack, but who my alpha was. If I hadn't already been flying so high, I might've protested the possessive name game, but the only thing I wanted to do at that moment was please him. "You. It's you, Diesel. You know that."

Diesel nodded his head like we were in the middle of an interview and he was jotting down my answer. He suddenly dropped to his knees behind me, and I craned back to see him, but couldn't twist very far while keeping my short arms attached to the post.

My question was answered in the next minute anyway when Diesel spread my cheeks open and buried his face between them. For several glorious seconds, the sounds he made were messy and loud, sounding vaguely like a velociraptor receiving its daily cow.

I howled and attempted to drive my ass back.

Diesel already had hold of my greedy hips, keeping me where he wanted. "And what is an alpha to you?" He lifted his tongue from my butt crack long enough to ask his question before returning to his task—going from educator to master and commander of my ass.

After several swipes that made my toes curl, I realized he expected me to be able to answer while he worked me open with his tongue and index finger. "I...um..." I exhaled and pressed my forehead against my hands. "My alpha takes care of me."

I felt his smile press between my cheeks.

"He...protects me and cares for me—"

Diesel's teeth chomped down on my butt cheek. "You already said care."

This test would end in sex despite my answers—at least I hoped so—but I was still disappointed in myself, as if I'd studied but couldn't remember a thing. "I—well—How am I supposed to concentrate with you doing that?"

The warm wet heat disappeared. "No!" I arched my back, pushing my ass toward him and into the air. I didn't care what it made me look like, how shamelessly I presented myself to him. I needed that feeling back. "I'm sorry. Just let me think a little. Um...the alpha also...fucks me?" I cocked my head to the side, stretching my lips in a hopeful grimace.

Diesel laughed, but I could only hear the sound. I couldn't feel it. He still wasn't touching me.

He didn't say anything for so long I gave up trying to entice him and dropped my butt to peer under my arm. I would've felt slightly rejected if it weren't for the sight that greeted me.

Diesel had his shirt on, a tight black tank top that outlined his chest muscles like a comic book hero. He didn't wear pants or briefs, which would've been the most exciting thing, if it weren't for the grip he had on his monster cock. He stroked with a firm hand, but slowly, bringing his palm over the head before sliding back down, leaving his length glistening with lube.

It wasn't just pornographic, but straight-up obscene. A single man shouldn't possess something so powerful.

He stood there even after he knew I was watching, staring unabashedly at my nude body while he stroked himself.

Would he come like that? Not even touching me but using me to get him off? Another important question: why did that sound so hot? I groaned, my eyes fluttering back as I pictured him rubbing himself to completion as I waited, ass up for the hot stripes to splash against me. Would he rub it in?

"You are so fucking filthy," he groaned, his expression dazed.

"Takes one to *ohh*." I clamped down on the finger in my ass, feeling full but manageable.

He worked his pinkie into me, utter concentration on his task as he switched from pinkie to the next finger over. Slightly larger, it still wasn't hard to take, especially after the slight stretch. Diesel continued down—there was something especially naughty about being stretched by only his middle finger—spending more time on his index finger before sliding his thumb into place. Though shorter, the digit was thick enough to make me gasp.

"Let's recap, shall we?" Diesel started again with his pinkie, moving much more rapidly from finger to finger like a lewd version of the knife game.

I bobbed my head, but I didn't think he was waiting for an answer.

Once he was able to fit in all four, Diesel paused and rubbed my ass gently. "You know that your alpha *fucks* you. He takes care of you and protects you. That you should *trust* him."

It wasn't a question, but I answered anyway, nodding no less than a thousand times. "Yes! I do trust him. I do."

"Why?"

I blinked. It felt like a trick question, and the answer wasn't going to come quicker once he started moving his hand, in and out, stretching my rim.

Why?

Because likely wasn't an acceptable answer, but I was pretty sure if I didn't answer with something, that dick might get lifted off the table, and that simply could not happen. "Testosterone?"

He pulled his hand free, whistling softly at what he saw. I was ready to moan my displeasure at being left empty, but Diesel's cock replaced his fingers, sitting heavily against the rim.

My heart beat like a jackhammer. My hole fluttered as if trying to grab hold of what was knocking and suck it in deeper.

He flexed his hips and slowly...*slowly* sank into my heat. "Because your alpha loves you," Diesel whispered as he settled into place, having bottomed out, bringing our bodies together like corresponding puzzle pieces. "Say it." He snarled and palmed my neck, pressing just enough that I could breathe but knew it was because he allowed it.

"Because my alpha loves me."

Diesel pulled back only to slam immediately back in. "Say it again."

"Because my alpha loves me!" I wailed, losing control of the sound when Diesel repeated the move, pulling nearly all the way out before driving forward and forcing my body to make room for him. "Because my alpha loves me." My vision went white the moment Diesel switched angles, slamming into that special spot that made me roar. "Diesel!"

He growled continuously, the noise rumbling just enough for me to realize he was speaking. "Say it again."

No sooner had I deciphered his words did he slam back inside, setting an unforgiving pace.

"My alpha loves me! My alpha loves me!" I chanted like a man possessed.

His snarls filled the room. If there was more to this lesson, it would have to wait because Diesel had clearly stepped aside, allowing the beast to take over. He panted with his forehead pressed between my shoulder blades. The grip he had on my hips would surely bruise and likely was already. There'd been a time when Diesel had been gentle—for him. He'd wanted to wait, to give me time to get used to his size and strength. The training wheels were off now, and I could see the difference.

I felt and heard it too, but the most important sense at the moment was the lightning fizzling in my balls like carbonated water. I didn't stop my cries, screaming, "My alpha loves me," throughout my orgasm until I was on the other side, gasping with the words still on my lips.

Diesel lifted his left hand from my waist, pressing his

splayed fingers against the middle of my chest instead. His right hand held more tightly to my hip, keeping me in place as he thrust forward, sinking to the hilt. His roar ceased when his teeth found the crook of my neck, but he still growled, thrusting through his climax.

There was no way the entire hotel, enhanced senses or not, hadn't heard that. I'd be more embarrassed later, but while safe in Diesel's arms, I couldn't summon the energy to care.

16

DIESEL

I nodded to the wraiths, offering my thanks for them keeping an eye on Quin while I made him a breakfast tray. They rippled out the door back down the hallway to Quinlan's old bedroom that they'd claimed as theirs. The wraiths had bits of Quin in them, if Claus could be believed, and that changed my view of them dramatically.

Quinlan's off-key singing warbled in from the bathroom. Grinning, I set the tray down and leaned inside the doorway, enjoying my mate's soothingly discordant wailing.

"So, tell me what you want what you really, really want!" Quinlan's pitch changed along with the key. "I'll tell you what I want, what I really, really want!"

For a while, Quinlan had wanted to be a pop star. He'd put on concerts, most times to an audience of myself and his mother. I'd volunteered to watch each one, not to support Quinlan—though that was an appreciated side benefit—but to save some poor hapless soul. Thankfully, he'd picked up a paintbrush soon after and realized he loved painting more than glitter shoes and microphones.

But he still gave it his all in the shower.

"Like a bridge over troubled waters," Quinlan howled, making an artistic choice to spontaneously create his own melody. "I will lay me down!"

I studied his blurred form through the shower door. "I'm gonna lay that ass down."

"I heard that!" Quinlan yelled.

My nostrils flared, getting a whiff of concentrated mate. His sweet scent was especially succulent today and called to me like a siren's song, luring me to the shower door. I reached for the door, but if I saw my mate all glistening and wet, covered in soap that slid down his skin, by the time we got to the breakfast tray, all the food would be cold. "When you're finished in here, I have breakfast ready." I'd made him his favorite, strawberry pancakes with whipped cream and sausage links.

"Why don't you join me first?" he purred, setting my dick off like a needle on a compass. Quin was my magnetic north.

"Because you need to build your energy back up. Can't have you tapping out an hour into riding on my dick."

"Diesel!"

He couldn't see my grin, but I let it stretch wide. His smell thickened with his arousal, as I'd hoped, adding to the existing bouquet. "Hurry up, my sweet, helpless omega mate."

"Helpless—? You come back here and say that to my face!" Quinlan squealed from the shower.

I shut the door.

Less than a minute later, Quinlan emerged, dressed, but his clothes were already wet in spots where he'd been in too much of a hurry, and his hair dripped. "I'll show you help—pancakes!" Quinlan dropped to the mattress, bringing his legs to fold under him as he eyed the plate. The righteous anger that had propelled him out here disappeared in the face of sugary goodness.

Some of the whipped cream had melted, mixing with the juice from the strawberries, but the sausage was still warm.

"Let's get you comfortable." I lifted him to the head of the bed and tucked his bottom half under the blankets. With my face already close to his neck, I didn't miss the chance to scent him, drawing in a lungful of *Quinlan*. "Did you use a different kind of soap?" Instead of turning to grab the tray, I buried my face against his neck and wet hair.

"Okay, I smell good. I get it. Pancakes!"

When my boy's tummy rumbled, I pulled away—with difficulty.

Quinlan clapped as I returned with the tray. I loved the way he got excited about food, like it wasn't just something he had to eat so he didn't die. His joy at seeing his meal arrive at the table never failed to make my wolf preen, proud that we'd provided him something that made him so happy. Now, his meal sat on his lap. He ignored the fork and swiped his finger through the whipped cream topping.

Suddenly I wasn't worried about breakfast or anything that wasn't getting Quinlan to do that same thing on my dick. There was whipped cream left. I could make it real good for my boy.

"Diesel..." Quinlan laughed, drawing my attention to the fork in my hand, stretched toward Quin's mouth with nothing on it.

I stabbed a chunk of pancake and returned the fork to its position. "Your lips are damn distracting."

"They are?" he asked, all wide eyes and innocence. He licked his lips slowly, revealing all that doe-eyed naivety as the act it was.

I capture his lips with mine, thrusting my tongue inside his mouth to get more of his sweet taste. It wasn't the strawberries I savored, but something that was all Quin, natural, but new, with a weird hint of bubblegum—

Adrenaline shot through me in response to the smell. My wolf howled, inconsolable as long as Quinlan wasn't in our arms. He needed protecting, now more than ever. "You're pregnant."

"No, I'm Quinlan," he joked. When he looked up and noticed my stillness, he dropped his sarcastic smile. "How can you even tell? Hey—wait!"

Quinlan reached over my shoulder for his breakfast, but if what I thought was coming came, he'd want to be in the bathroom.

"Actually..." His voice quieted, and he sank off my shoulder and into my arms. "I think I'm going to—"

I had him at the toilet, seat up and his hair pulled back as the first jet of rainbow surprise splashed into the bowl.

"It's okay. You're okay, baby boy." I rubbed his head, stopping only to comb my fingers through his hair. Quinlan wouldn't like strands sticking to his forehead.

Luckily, the rainbow explosion was always dramatic, but also brief, and Quinlan soon straightened to wipe his mouth with the rag I handed him. "Is it weird that I just want to sit here and stare at it?" He didn't have his head in the bowl anymore, but his face turned down to the sparkling, swirling mixture.

I wouldn't have minded sitting and staring, but not at a toilet of puke—at Quin's dazed wonder. Now that I knew what the extra scent was, it came at me tenfold. My mate was pregnant. Quinlan was going to give magical birth to a child, and if we were lucky, the pup would inherit the majority of Quin's genes.

In two weeks' time, we would bring our baby into the world...

Into this *world?*

The same world with a gate that was slowly opening and connecting our world with hell.

Put that way, it didn't sound unwise to be procreating, but irresponsible.

If my wolf had the ability to bite me, he would've at that moment. I wanted this child and couldn't wait to watch Quinlan hold and rock our baby. But while my human side knew to face the realities of the moment head on, my wolf operated on instincts alone, which were telling us to protect Quinlan and keep him wrapped in something warm and safe. Nothing would hurt him because I wouldn't let anything near him.

While half our pack lay in the crosshairs of a demon organization, that was the only way I could see to be certain. I needed to find someplace to hide him, where our enemies didn't know to look and where he could ride out our battle with hell safely and out of danger. I'd have to be certain the place was truly safe, or I'd never be able to leave him. He shouldn't be alone, but Quinlan wouldn't go anywhere without his nephilim brothers, and they didn't belong in danger either. None of the pack did.

I should have put my foot down in the beginning with Jazz. If I had, the omegas wouldn't have gotten it in their minds that they were somehow also responsible for protecting the pack. Knox had been wrapped around Jazz's finger from first sight. Faust and the twins weren't much better. The other alphas might not be able to say no to their omegas, but I...

Couldn't either.

But when it was Quin's life and the life of our unborn at

stake, I would.

I'd been waiting for the other nephilim to burst inside, alerted by either their pack or angelic bond. It hadn't taken this long when it was Hallie, but Quinlan had sounded so excited then, so happy.

"Quinlan, do you want to be pregnant?"

"Of course I do."

His reply came too quickly for me to believe it. "What is it? Are you worried about staying safe in the hotel? That's a valid concern, and I want—"

"No, I'm not worried about safety." He snapped at me like he'd been able to sense I'd been about to suggest something that would make him angry. "I'm just...I'm a guy? That isn't a question. I am. Being pregnant wasn't something I grew up wanting. It hadn't been a possibility, but even if it had, I don't think I'd have wanted to get pregnant back then."

"Back then?" My insides turned into ice, reimagining all of those warm, happy moments, Quinlan swollen with his hand on his belly, but this time, he was *frowning*.

"Back then." He nodded. "I think because I didn't have you. You weren't officially mine. And I'd always been so worried that something would take your attention from me. I know that's selfish now. You were right. I wasn't ready back then." He lifted his face to meet mine. I was glad for it since I'd been seconds from doing it for him. I needed his eyes, even if the sadness in them would hurt.

His dichromatic stare wasn't sad. He was radiant.

"I'm ready now because I *have* you. I have a pack. I'll miss our old pack forever, but if I had to start from scratch, I'd want to with the people in this hotel." He blew out a heavy sigh. "So, yeah, I don't know how I've got a bun, or where exactly my oven is..." He peered at his midsection.

"But I do want to be pregnant. I'm happy," he added resolutely.

The soft knock on the door acted as an immediate fact checker. "Quinlan?" Sitka called through the wood. "Can I come in? I felt something—"

"I'm coming, Quinlan!" Jazz's scream sounded like it came from quite a ways down the hallway.

Not ten minutes later, the entire pack loitered inside our room, getting their stinky smells all over everything. I preferred only my mate's scent in my space. Sensing others in a space where my baby boy was often vulnerable made my jaw clench. But even a man as stubborn as I could make allowances for special occasions.

Hallie sat squeezed between Siobhan and Sitka on the bed with Quinlan. I'd felt her eyes on me and tried to catch her attention, but she was lost in her thoughts. "You're so lucky you don't have to worry about a natural human birth," she said. "A Diesel-baby is going to be huge."

"The baby could take after Quinlan. His petite frame and Diesel's shaggy hair," Storri suggested.

"Like Cousin It, short and hairy." Huntley laughed.

"Hey!" Quinlan whined when more than one person's laughter joined Huntley's. "Don't make fun of my baby! Whatever the size or hair level, my baby will be perfect!"

I'd have swooped in to comfort my pouting mate, but a puppy pile of Sitka, Siobhan, Storri, and Jazz beat me to it.

When Jamie jumped in, I barely contained my growl. It wasn't the kid's fault he was a reasonably okay-looking shifter male who was closer to Quin's age than I was.

Moments like this made our pack stronger anyway, and I wouldn't do something to stop that, even if Jamie was getting mighty close to snuggling my mate.

I wouldn't do something to stop it *right away*. "That's

enough. Give him room. He's breathing for two."

Quinlan rolled his eyes, but they'd been filled with so much joy.

"Congrats, man." Knox clapped his hand on my shoulder. "Has the panic set in yet?"

"Fuck yes." I checked to make sure the others were occupied before continuing. "Claus said we were only safe from lesser demons while the gate is opening. We can't guess how many more demon kings crawl out or what they'll want." Quinlan's laughter brought my attention back to the bed. They'd started coming up with names. I had nothing against Sitka, but we were *not* naming the child *Howler*. "Thalasso won't be weak forever. Claus can already play-build a body at whim, and when Thalasso's strength also returns, he'll come for the nephilim."

"What's your point here, Diesel?"

Our huddled conversation had drawn the attention of the twins and Faust.

"We need to take them someplace safe. Where we aren't sitting ducks."

"I agree," Huntley grunted. "But Sitka would only leave kicking and screaming."

"What are you guys talking about?" Jazz skipped with Angus from the bed to our huddle.

Knox fit his arm over mate and son, kissing Jazz on the temple. "Diesel wants to ship you all off to an impenetrable fortress. Regular first-time dad jitters."

"Diesel—*what?*" Quinlan shouted at a pitch normally reserved for dolphins.

The others scattered from the bed. At least now I'd get everyone out of my room. But they left me with a mate staring at me with unbridled fury.

Fuck.

17

QUINLAN

"You will have to talk to me at some point, Quin."

If I had Diesel's hearing, I would've sensed him walking down the stairs into the ballroom. I'd been so engrossed in my task, his voice startled me and sent my pencil careening off the paper. I growled and accepted the eraser my wraiths handed me. "You made me mess up."

"Looks like an easy fix," he replied unapologetically.

Why would I expect him to be apologetic? He was unflinchingly bold. He might not have been the type to take control of a room, but he was the type to do the work himself while everyone else wasted time bickering.

And he loved me. Fiercely. I knew that, but none of that excused him wanting to separate us the very day he found out I was pregnant. At a time when we'd need each other the most, he would have us separated?

I longed to go back to the day before, when the pack had sat with me on the bed and we'd joked about naming the baby Organic. The alphas hadn't been the only ones disappointed Diesel hadn't gotten a face full of puke. The others in the pack hadn't been able to hide their disappointment either when they heard. I'd promised them if I ever got pregnant again, I'd be sure to throw up on his face. Now I didn't want to get close enough to the man for that to be a possibility.

"Yeah, easy fix," I snapped. "Just erase it, push it out of the way like it doesn't exist. *Ship it off.* That's how you solve problems, right?"

"Omega," Diesel growled out in warning.

I brought my attention back to my sketchbook and continued my sketch. "What?"

My wraiths slithered between us. They'd been helping me sketch, acting as reference points on the wall. Yesterday, I'd wanted to do a large portrait of the pack and had begun sketching many of them out, tweaking their images as I spent time with them throughout the day. Then we found out I was pregnant, and I realized a portrait of the pack would never reflect the pack because we would always be growing. And I might've also wanted to paint *individual* portraits at some point. I'd woken early this morning from a fitful sleep and padded down here with a lemon tea to keep my hands from freezing. After a few starts and stops, I had something that would light up the room, while hopefully seeming like it could've been painted there when the hotel had first been built. I'd put pencil to paper and came back with an ocean at sunset. Wild waves sent spray into the air as seagulls skimmed the water. Along the sand, beachgoers lounged on canvas chairs, while a toddler chased after a brown Labrador puppy. Though the ocean was stormy and turbulent, everything on land was blue skies and puffy clouds. I liked how, depending on the viewer, it could seem like a storm approaching an unsuspecting family or the aftermath of a storm rolling out to sea.

Diesel moved around the wraiths, approaching from

behind me, but my wraiths slid with him, mirroring his movements. He snarled and quick-stepped to the side. The wraiths were there before he got a step closer. "Do not separate us, omega."

I snapped my pencil in half, letting my sketchbook fall gracelessly to the floor as I leaped to my feet. "Oh, that's *rich,* coming from you."

"Quinlan..."

"No! Right now, you don't get to *Quinlan* me. You found out I was pregnant, and your next thought was to *ditch* me. I knew guys like that existed in the world, but I—"

Diesel's growl shot through me, setting off warning bells.

A small part of me was glad he'd derailed me from saying something that I'd only wanted to say because I hurt. Diesel wanted me, and he wanted this baby, but just not at the same place as him.

"If you're angry I wanted to put you someplace safe, then too bad. That's what I do, Quin."

He was my primal warrior. Stubborn, brash, and rough, but at that moment, I hated it.

I wouldn't cry and blinked rapidly to keep the pressure back. I wasn't pushing the emotion down because I didn't feel comfortable showing my tears, but because I didn't want it to seem like I was trying to manipulate him in any way.

He'd gone through enough of that already, but that didn't mean he wasn't wrong now. "Diesel, all I know is the last time I was separated from you, I didn't have a really great time for a long while after. There's danger here. That's not the argument. When you're fighting hell, the danger is *everywhere.*" I bent to retrieve my sketchbook and broken pencil pieces, holding the book tightly against my chest.

"I've been scared too, thinking about everything coming after us, and I've comforted myself by remembering that when whatever is coming comes, and I am afraid, *you will be there*. Right beside me. But I guess that's not what you want."

Maybe it was unfair to flounce immediately after, not giving Diesel a chance to respond, but there wasn't anything he could say. We'd both claimed that we wanted to be near the other always, and only one of us meant it.

———

DIESEL ENTERED THE MEETING ROOM, head swiveling as he searched the packed room for me. His brows lifted when he saw me in our usual chairs around the table. Jamie and Isaiah set out all the toppings and shells needed for people to make their own burritos. The twins and Sitka already had theirs made. They'd had difficulty stuffing so much inside, and all three had needed more than one shell.

Diesel sat in the chair next to mine like he was expecting the legs to give out under him. The prospect of my sabotaging his chair out of anger wasn't so off-base, but I couldn't argue we should be near each other always and then refuse to be near him.

That was just hypocritical.

Besides, he hadn't chased after me in the ballroom this morning, and by now, he must really miss me.

When the chair held, Diesel sighed with relief, checked my plate to make sure I'd put food on it, and then got started on his own.

A true professional, he recognized the folly of one huge burrito and made three large ones instead. The pack as a whole could eat, and none of them was all that shy about it.

I'd helped Siobhan care for the children one day and, during a single conversation, watched her polish off a sleeve of macarons, *after* I'd witnessed her catch—and eat—an entire duck— as a wolf, of course.

It didn't take long for the bowls to empty, and with such an elaborate setup, there were stacks of dishes to wash. I'd already finished, and Diesel had a surprising two burritos left still, so I got to my feet and gathered the dishes that were already empty.

The kitchen was a disaster. Every vegetable must've gotten its own cutting board. The stovetop was piled high with dirty pots. One was still on, frying a crisp layer of refried beans to the inside. Amid it all, shredded lettuce was scattered atop the counters like Christmas tinsel. I dropped my haul on the counter next to the sink and returned to the meeting room for another round.

Jamie met me at the door with his own stack.

"Don't worry," I said. "I can do these. You already washed dishes after breakfast." I'd feel better getting lost in a mindless task anyway—instead of spending that time dwelling on Diesel.

"Should you be doing strenuous chores for the next two weeks?" Storri asked, sitting closest, his face wrinkled with worry.

"You all realize pregnant people can do almost every-thing not-pregnant people can do?" Hallie called out from the other end of the table.

Dr. Tiff snorted into her tea. "She's right. There's no reason Quinlan can't do dishes if he wants." She didn't sound like she knew why I'd want something like that. The doc wasn't big on housework, but she was an amazing doctor, so it all worked out.

With verbal permission from the woman who would

know best, I continued stacking dishes, feeling Diesel's eyes on me the entire time. He didn't say anything as he ate and tracked me.

I was elbow-deep in soapy water when I felt him approach from behind. He was still feet from me, but close enough to feel that heat. My anger for him had died out before lunch—before I left the ballroom, if I was being honest. But now, I was just hurt, and that felt so much worse. I'd rather mask it in anger.

"Do you need help?" he asked softly, setting his dish down on the counter.

"I'm fine, thank you." I pulled my eyes away from him with a silent eye *pop*. He was a gorgeous man; it would be hard for anyone to look away. I could still hold my ground and appreciate his form. I was an artist, after all. It was my job to see inspiration in life.

The corners of Diesel's eyes crinkled as he grinned. "What are you talking about?"

Gah! Every time I thought I'd broken the habit...

"Nothing. Have you heard from Badger recently? They must be getting near the end." Those guys were a little too efficient at making people disappear, but at least these were evil people.

Diesel said nothing, his silence only interrupted by Sitka, who'd come with the rest of the plates. Once he'd gone and it sounded like the rest of the pack had cleared out, Diesel's face tightened, and he reached for the sponge from my hand. "Let me do it," he offered like a plea.

I shoved my hands under the water, stubbing my finger against the bottom of the sink in the process.

My finger throbbed while Diesel murmured, "So stubborn."

I pretended not to hear or hurt and grabbed the next stack, letting them plop messily into the soapy water.

"Did you check for knives?" He sounded just like he used to, fatherly but also terrified I'd somehow manage to cut my throat before I finished rinsing the last cup.

I didn't want to keep fighting but couldn't think of anything to say that wouldn't sound like a challenge, so I kept my mouth shut, bravely washing dish after dish despite the danger of *possible knives*.

Diesel did nothing but watch me work for a few minutes. I reached for the next stack, and he pushed off the wall, bringing his heat directly behind me. He leaned in, speaking quietly since his lips were already so close to my ear. "You've done half. Let me do the other."

There was no way I'd done half, and all the worst pots and pans were still left. "Oh, we're equal now?"

So much for not fighting.

Except Diesel didn't fire back. He sighed and slid his arms under mine. His hands dipped under the water, and he found the sponge in my hand. I didn't fight him when he tugged the sponge from my hand, leaving me in place as he wordlessly took over washing like I was wearing a mechanical Diesel suit.

His breath was soft and warm against my ear, and it was all I had not to push my ass back and really get acquainted with that hard body. I hadn't touched it in nearly twenty-four hours. I kept my hips in check and thanked the stars Diesel couldn't see how I'd gone hard instantly.

I knew when he smelled my arousal because he growled, soft and low in his chest. He continued with the dishes, letting my desire froth and foam at nothing but his proximity.

"I lost it yesterday, and I'm sorry." Diesel nuzzled the back of my neck and took long draws through his nose pressed against my skin. "You were right. I found out we were going to have a baby, and I went into lockdown mode. Having you—*not* by my side, because there's no way you're fighting while pregnant, and that's the end of that discussion—but having you near me, on pack lands, makes me stronger. Makes the pack stronger."

He kissed my cheek, and my body turned into a wet noodle. Diesel anticipated my drop and slid one of his legs between mine, propping me with his thigh against my groin. I didn't even try not to ride him, but I had no power or momentum, and I gave up with a pitiful whine. "Does that mean I'm forgiven?"

The scoundrel knew exactly what he was doing. "Why would you think that?" I rolled my body like one of the fitness models in Jazz's stripper aerobics DVD.

I got immediate gratification in the form of Diesel's rumble, reverberating in my chest. "Forgiven or not, baby boy, I'm still your alpha. You're only pregnant for two weeks. It isn't too much to let me help you with your chores."

"And after?" I smirked.

He sounded personally offended. "You'll be too busy with the baby and recuperating to do chores then."

My alpha could be rough around the edges, but if the largest problems I had with him were about him being over-the-top protective or wanting to do all my laundry, then I was very lucky.

"Okay." I played it up, like agreeing to be doted on was a hardship. I knew what was coming next, and I couldn't wait.

He brought his lips to my ear so I'd feel him say it too. "Good boy."

I sagged against him. Thousands of sex-butterflies fluttered inside my body, making me feel like I was made of nothing but tiny wings.

I could only hope Diesel was keeping an ear out for intruders when he lifted me onto the counter because I would do nothing to stop him pulling my pants down and taking my throbbing length into his mouth. His head looked almost obscenely large against my narrow hips. I grabbed hold of his hair, gathering the locks like reins that I mostly used to try to push him harder.

Really, he moved his head as he liked. I could no sooner force a motion from Diesel than I could stop the orgasm that hurtled right over embarrassingly quick and leaped into premature.

Diesel laughed knowingly. With the way his tongue pressed against my still-spasming dick, I felt every chuckle.

———

CLAUS CALLED LATE the night before to say he was getting close. He was pretty sure he'd found a copy of the grimoire —since they weren't the types of books people really advertised owning. He needed to do a little more digging to confirm and be sure there wasn't anything stowed with the grimoire that could possibly hurt him, like devil's powder. There weren't many items, and many of them were rumored to be destroyed, but apparently there were items on earth that could kill and hurt a demon king.

Immediately after Claus had first left, the pack seemed to have been able to push the blanket of doom lowering slowly over our heads out of mind. As the days passed, worries grew, and waiting became the hardest thing any of us were doing.

The mood in the hotel may have explained the reason

why the pack woke up to an indoor putt-putt golf course that Knox and the other alphas had built. I walked beside a long ramp that sloped up and then down at the stairs. There was a cup built into a wooden holder at the bottom landing, where I assumed a safe golfer could roll the ball down the stairs, or a risky golfer could go for the hole-in-one from the second floor.

Breakfast became something everyone raced through, and thanks to the way Knox encouraged, and at times delivered, shit-talking, the pack was eager to show each other up.

They used to do the same things in our old pack: arranging outdoor movie nights or clear nights where they made a bunch of fires, laid out blankets, and invited everyone to stargaze. My favorite activities had been the ones that required Diesel to take off his shirt.

Unfortunately, putt-putt wasn't that strenuous of an activity, and even though we were on hole ten, Diesel didn't look at all close to flashing some abs. He did insist on carrying me the several feet from hole to hole, so at least I got to feel some of what he was packing.

"Am I just meat to you?" Diesel grumbled softly on our way to hole eleven. This shot had another ramp that extended out the sitting room window and then back inside the next window over.

I pressed into him. Would he still be able to hold me tightly when my stomach got rounder? It was already sticking out a little with a golden ring around my belly button that made it look like a target. "Yes, mouthwatering and juicy."

His lips turned down in the corners, and though I knew we were joking, I rushed to console him. Damn pregnancy hormones made me all soft and paternal. "I like your brain too! And your mouth."

"What brain?" Faust walked toward us with Storri and the girls. Too much longer, and they wouldn't be able to carry the bundles of energy everywhere anymore. Florence wiggled constantly to be set down already. Faust set her down to scoot along the carpet. The moment she was out of his arms and out of range of friendly fire, Diesel pegged Faust with a golf ball.

Faust didn't do anything but laugh, though Storri kissed the spot Diesel had hit repeatedly and glared at him like a mountain lion protecting her cubs.

I separated myself from Diesel, expecting this to turn into something more like a battle, but both alphas tensed at the same time and turned to look at the door. When both growled, I rushed to pick up Florence. If we needed to run to the panic room, I wanted to be ready.

Diesel hooked his arm around my waist and scented my neck, a gesture that calmed us both. "It's Alejandro," he explained. "He just pulled up in the driveway. The guy already broke Hallie's heart and still lives. If he ruins putt-putt day, Knox won't be so forgiving."

My relief that hordes of demons weren't tearing through the forest toward the hotel was short-lived. Hallie hid her emotions, especially ones like hurt. She'd just started actually smiling again. As a pack, we'd helped her decide where to put the nursery and how to decorate it. The doc seemed especially excited for a long-term birth and went all out getting Hallie several body pillows, heating pads, and acupressure bands for her morning sickness. Though she wasn't so lucky as to be done and over with the pregnancy in two weeks, so far, her morning sickness wasn't that bad and truly stuck to its name.

"Are you going to send him away?" I asked.

"And face Hallie's wrath when she finds out?" Faust replied. "It's your funeral."

He made a good point.

The others were already at the landing, along with Hallie. I slipped out from Diesel's arm and joined the others circled around her like a protective wall.

When Alejandro knocked, Diesel answered the door.

I almost felt bad for the man. It couldn't be fun walking by so many angry men who he now knew were capable of literally ripping his head off. He faced the gauntlet with dignity. Now, he just had to get through us.

"I figured everyone would be...well, you're all just together...*all the time.*"

The doc snorted, but it was Hallie's reaction that mattered, and her face had remained stony.

"I think I understand that more now," he rushed to say. "And I'm ready to do this in front of your family if I have to." He sucked in a deep breath. The man really didn't look like he'd had a great couple of days. The bags under his eyes broadcast just how much sleep he hadn't gotten.

He looked worse off than Hallie, and I was petty enough to be happy for that fact.

Learning your girlfriend was pregnant was big enough news to swallow, but he'd also had to come to terms with the fact that his girlfriend's *roommates* weren't at all what they appeared.

Alejandro scratched the back of his neck nervously. "I love everything about you, Hallie, and have since high school. I told myself you were better off with *him*, that you were happy and cared for. But you weren't. I should've fought for you then, and I'll sure as heck fight for you now. I love your bravery and resilience but also your loyalty. I shouldn't have asked you to leave this place, and you were right to be angry. But I won't stop loving you or our child. I got something not many else get, a second chance, and even though I blew it and don't deserve a third, I'm hoping you'll let me try. I love you, Hal. I want to be where you are, whether that means living here or outside in the woods. I don't care. I'll make it work."

Hallie's expression hadn't changed, but her voice shook with emotion. "What about your niece? I know you have a duty to keep her safe, and I really can't promise there will always be safety here."

The leftover bullet holes in the foyer were proof enough of that.

"I'll make it work, Hallie. Besides, I'd already thought long and hard about that, and the way I figure it, these guys..." He gestured to the alphas. "...are the most intense, protective people I've met. If they're here, living comfortably with their children and...husbands?" He cocked his head to the side.

"Mates," Hallie supplied.

"Mates. If they live here with their mates and children, they must be relatively certain of their ability to keep them safe."

That was quite literally the point of alphas. Shifters could be volatile and distrustful. Alphas existed not only to care for a pack, but to give shifters that anchor, a net of safety. The world was dangerous, but in a pack, you didn't have to face those dangers alone.

Hallie pushed through the throng of people separating her from Alejandro. He held out his hands, and Hallie grabbed hold. Their foreheads pressed together.

"I love you so much, Al—"

"Who is walking up our driveway?" Isaiah peered out the narrow window next to the door.

Faust brought the surveillance feed up on his phone and we all—including Alejandro—peered over to see his screen.

"That guy was on the side of the highway when I drove here. I figured he was a lost tourist. The surfers who come to this part of the coast are always a special kind of crazy."

I could see how Alejandro had come to that conclusion. With sandy blond hair long enough to fall into his eyes and a tan, fit physique, he certainly looked like a surfer. The man looked up like he sensed the camera's lens on him and smiled.

"Panic room," Knox grunted.

Before any of us could comply, an earth-shaking explosion rocked the back of the hotel, coming from the direction Knox wanted us to head.

Dust sprinkled overhead as the twins shifted and herded the pack into a group—Alejandro included—that the alphas circled around. We remained that way long enough for the guys to pull up the other video feeds.

Faust grunted. "We need to evacuate. The back of the hotel is on fire."

On cue, smoke drifted up the hallway.

"Who is it?" Jazz had to raise his voice to be heard over the screaming babies. He bounced on the balls of his feet, patting Angus's bottom.

If Knox knew, he would've answered his mate, but the man outside was completely unfamiliar. The fire out back was a pretty big clue that he wasn't here to surf, though.

"Assume demon," he growled.

"Not Claus?" Storri asked hopefully.

"Not Claus," Faust rumbled in reply.

With a fire in the back and a demon out front, we had

nowhere to go. Running upstairs would just trap us further if the fire spread.

"Come on out," the man outside yelled. "I just want to talk."

"I don't believe him," Alejandro whispered to Hallie, tucked behind him.

I was pretty sure we all shared his feeling, but that didn't end up mattering as the man-shaped demon outside lost patience. He erupted out of his laid-back surfer suit, splitting the skin as he burst out like a sausage left too long on the grill. The remaining demon was surely a king, as big as Claus with large horns that stretched back instead of up, curving down at the ends into twin points. His skin was a dark, muddy red that reminded me of an infected wound. Though his horns were smooth save for the segmented ridges, his body had the wrinkle of a hand left too long in water. Black eyes stared into the camera, unblinking. We all suspected who the demon was, but our suspicions were confirmed the moment we spotted Pierce hobble to his master's side.

"He looks like shit." Knox sounded pleased by the fact.

He wasn't just being mean, either. Pierce's cut on his forehead looked infected. The shifter probably wasn't used to worrying about things like infection.

"That's what happens when you're a backstabbing prick," Diesel snarled.

Thalasso stepped out of his human suit, and everything that was left dissolved into ash. "You lot have caused me enough trouble. It's high time we truly meet." He paused as though waiting for us to rush outside and curtsy. "No? You didn't tell me your friends were so shy, Pierce."

The old pack Alpha winced when Thalasso said his name. His breaths were short and jerky, like he was trying to breathe around a few broken ribs. I could only imagine Thalasso hadn't been happy the last time Pierce had a chance to kill the alphas and chose to showboat instead.

"Don't worry. I'll start the introductions." The demon bowed to the camera. "My name is Thalasso, Demon King of drowning, and I'm tired of talking to a machine." He lifted his arms, and a funnel of water shot all the way from the ocean at the bottom of the cliff to our front door.

We had a half second to prepare before the door burst in. Jazz, Storri, and Sitka shifted and flapped their wide wings, bringing their children to their backs and safely above the water. A second spout, wider than the first, burst in from the sitting room, sending a flood of furniture surging into the foyer.

My wraiths wrapped around my body the moment before the water covered our heads and flushed the pack out the front door.

"There we go." Thalasso's voice echoed above the roar of rushing water. "These dogs are who have been causing such a ruckus?"

My knees hit solid ground. Around me, the others were coughing. I'd lost track of half the pack, seeing only Jazz flapping with wet wings. He had the most trouble flying, and it showed with the effort it took him to stay off the ground. I wanted to call his name and get closer, but didn't want to attract attention.

The alphas were on their feet, everyone in their wolf forms but Hallie, Alejandro—the man likely regretting everything he'd said not ten minutes ago—and me.

...and Pierce. But with the terror clear on his face, I wasn't sure he *could* shift anymore.

I scrambled to my feet, bumping into Storri, the girls safely tucked between his wings. As they grew, they slept less while in puppy form. All four had their ears down and their soulful brown eyes peering over the bend of Storri's wing at where the rest of the pack snarled, heads low to the ground as he they circled around the demon.

Thalasso didn't look at all concerned, but Pierce did. He dropped as he shifted—shocking me with the ability. The wolf he became wasn't the wolf he once was. He'd been powerful once, stately. Now he was a withered shell of the beast of his past, hair dingy and falling out, revealing loose, sallow skin.

He was so small, he had no trouble darting between Jamie and Siobhan—neither of which had any business attempting to take down a demon king. I considered chasing after, but disregarded the idea in favor of running with Storri and Jazz. Sitka barreled up behind us, dropping his head between my legs so that I landed behind Onyx on Sitka's back.

Thalasso wanted nephilim blood, so the smartest thing for us to do was stay far away. But what good would running do if we left our pack to be slaughtered? Sitka must have been thinking the same thing because he paused at the forest line and turned back to the standoff.

To the surprise of no one, Diesel was the first wolf to lose his patience. He lunged forward, getting a chunk of the demon's calf between his teeth. He jumped back, tearing the demon's flesh from his body, but not before Thalasso got in a kick with his other leg that sent Diesel soaring. I tracked his flight, wincing when he hit the ground hard.

He jumped to his paws and shook it off before searching the space. When he found me astride Sitka, he barked loudly, and though I was no wolf whisperer, I knew exactly what he was telling us to do—run. Sitka shot forward after Jazz and Storri. Both winged wolves had only made it a few yards before the woods began to move. The forest floor rippled. It looked like shadows leaking from the ground, but when one stood, we saw they weren't just shadows, but water demons, each a quarter of the size of the water demon we'd faced before. I counted ten marching for us before Sitka turned in the other direction to the back of the house.

Every yelp of pain that came from the fight felt like another fiery poker stabbed into my heart. I didn't know who had been hurt or where Hallie and Alejandro ended up. I could only hope they'd managed to run and hide.

The water demons had no trouble keeping up and then some. When I looked up, several of them were already ahead, waiting for us. Like while we'd been running, they'd been directing us where they wanted.

One of the demons shot out of the ground, pouring ice cold water on the three of us. Onyx didn't cry. In fact, none of the puppies were crying. Maybe Storri was able to console them while they were all in their animal bodies. The water demon reached down, his dripping fingers heading for Onyx. I hunched over the baby at the same time a loud growl erupted beside us. Dog bounded toward us, wraiths on his tail. He jumped between us and the water demon, thrashing the demon with his teeth, but getting nowhere.

The demon reformed faster than Dog could tear it apart. It dropped a heavy fist down, hitting Dog's flanks and shoving him into the ground with bone-cracking force.

The wraiths made a shrieking noise I'd never heard them make before, each turning the color of a glowing coal. They shoved their bodies forward, *inside* the water demon. For a terrifying moment, I thought they'd made a mistake, that the water demon had them trapped.

Then it began to steam and bubble. Sitka jumped back,

putting space between us and the boiling hot water monster. Giving the water demons more ways to hurt us couldn't be the wraiths' plan. They glowed brighter, and my chest warmed, like my heart glowed right along with them. All of sudden, the water demon erupted with a loud hiss, turning into steam and dissipating in the air.

Back at the main fight, Thalasso roared in pain. Either someone got a good shot in, or hurting the water demons hurt him. The wraiths fluttered to the ground, dark again, and rubbed against the side of Dog's face. He let out a soft woof as a second demon slid in to replace the first.

The wraiths repeated their actions from before, but already, it was clear they weren't burning as brightly. My chest didn't grow nearly as warm, and when they shoved their misty bodies into the demon's core, it took twice the time to turn him into steam. At least Thalasso screamed again.

"Storri! Hurting the demons hurts Thalasso. You need to tell the others!"

He nodded and took to the sky, soaring above the danger. Storri did not have trouble flying, but none of them could sustain flight for very long.

A few minutes later, the demon screamed again, and the water demon closest to us dropped, becoming a large puddle.

While we'd been figuring out how to fight back, the fire at the back of the hotel had spread, jumping the lawn, to the closest branches of the forest.

We waited for Storri to return before heading toward the fire as a group, dodging water monsters while we ran into a burning forest. None of us got very far before the water demons gathered together, forming a wave too powerful for any of us to hope to swim through.

There was no direction left to go but back, which was probably exactly what Thalasso had planned in the first place. To think we'd worked so hard only to wind up in the same place made me want to burn hot like my wraiths, but they were clearly exhausted from the effort and refused to leave Dog as long as he was down.

Back at the front of the hotel, the pack still had Thalasso surrounded. Several of the smaller wolves limped or were actively bleeding. But the demon king bled as well. He looked like an old chew toy. His right knee was nothing but a wet chunk of flesh. The demon's blood ran dark, and I wouldn't think about what it probably tasted like. He was missing most of the fingers on one hand, and his legs were completely covered with bite marks and missing bits of flesh.

I couldn't spot Diesel in the middle of the action and panicked, searching the ground for his body.

The pack worked together, keeping the attacks constant but brief. If the demon got his hands on any one of them, he could've torn them apart, but facing four alpha wolves and the rest of the pack to boot seemed jarring enough to knock him off his bearings.

This wouldn't last for long. Soon the wolves would tire, or Thalasso would regroup, and then everything would be over.

Despite the futility of it all, the pack kept pushing Thalasso off the lawn and to the cliff.

Without a warning I could see, Storri howled, and the wolves jumped back at once, leaving a wide berth around Thalasso. He pulled back, eyes flitting from wolf to wolf, but not to the school bus tearing through the grass toward him. The shifters cleared the way at the last possible moment, leaving Thalasso just enough time to inhale before the bus made impact and sent the demon flying over the cliff.

The front of the bus teetered over the edge, and for one heart-stopping moment, the back tires lifted from the ground. Knox, the twins, and Faust were there at the bumper, keeping the bus stationary long enough for Diesel to jump out. When the others let go, the bus teetered once more before resting at the edge.

"Diesel, check the—"

Thalasso rose above the cliff. He hung suspended above our heads, a smirk on his face that said he knew he'd won. We'd thrown everything we had at him, and he was still coming. Worse, it looked like his time over the cliff had given his body a chance to heal. His knee was back, along with most of his fingers.

I jumped from Sitka's back and raced over the lawn toward Diesel. If we were all going to die now, I'd do it by my mate's side.

"Are you finished?" Thalasso mocked. "I could go a few more rounds..." He let his gaze land on the torn-up lawn and our pack members, beaten and bloody, to the hotel, where large clouds of black smoke billowed from the back side. "It doesn't look like you can. Look, you don't all have to die. I'll even let you keep your nephilim, I have more. Just give me the half-breed."

I wrapped my arms around Diesel's waist and held tight.

There was a loud crash, like Thalasso had landed on the roof of the school bus.

"Demonling, I leave for a few days..."

My head popped up while still keeping my arms around my alpha.

Claus stood on top of the school bus, his horns shining beneath the sun.

"Claus," Thalasso snarled. "You're standing on the wrong side."

"When has that stopped me?" He gestured his head at the mayhem surrounding us. "Devil know what you're doing?"

Thalasso's feet hovered hundreds of feet above the surface. "He will be pleased, when he finds out. The devil doesn't want anything to do with this world, only the souls that come from it. Imagine what he'll do when hell fills with souls. He'll let us rule earth together. Remade, a place where we will rule. Me, and every demon who has seen my vision. I'll give you only one chance—join me."

I wasn't worried for a second that Claus would switch sides, but he sure made it look like he was considering it. He shrugged and faced the floating demon. "Nah, I already joined a club. But how about this—to say I'm sorry, I'll give you a blowjob."

Thalasso's frown was likely shared by many on the lawn, but I didn't look from my half-brother to check.

He inhaled, his chest barreling outward, before he pursed his lips, and blew.

Thalasso shot back like a feather in front of an industrial fan. In seconds, he was no larger than a red dot, hovering over the horizon of the ocean before he disappeared completely.

"That just bought us time." Claus jumped from the school bus and looked around. "But it looks like time was what you needed. I'll put out the fire. Grab what you need, and then we should probably skedaddle."

18

DIESEL

In HINDSIGHT, the school bus would've been the best vehicle for the pack to flee in, but we made it to the private airport outside of Portland in one piece.

Thank fuck for Jazz's shitty dad and the money he left behind. We loaded onto a private plane, walking by a smiling flight attendant. He was a professional, maintaining a friendly smile even while his eyes tightened. I supposed his regular passengers didn't normally look so battered or include six children and one angry dog.

The doc was certain Dog had broken at least a few ribs. With Storri acting as interpreter, she concluded that there was no internal bleeding, but had wrapped his chest to keep his bones from jostling.

Alejandro and his niece, Maria, climbed in last. He'd carried Hallie down the driveway and onto the highway by the time Knox caught up with him. We couldn't be positive Thalasso had gotten a good look at him, but it wasn't safe for Alejandro or us to leave loose ends.

We were bruised, but at least most of us had stopped bleeding. Escaping with our lives from a demon king had been nothing but luck. We knew that as surely as we knew we hadn't seen the last of Thalasso.

If Claus—the same demon king currently flirting the sense out of the flight attendant—hadn't come when he did, we'd be dead.

Once the pack was loaded on, Knox jerked Claus into the main cabin and faced the attendant. "We don't need any service. If you need to come back here for a flight check, please knock first."

If the flight attendant was angry at being bossed around, he was at least equally pleased at the idea of having to do very little during our nonstop flight to Chicago. As the newest owner to a chain of hotels that stretched across the country, Jazz had been able to get us the entire penthouse in one of his most secure buildings. Faust wouldn't have a problem tapping into the hotel's existing security system, and we'd fill in any gaps in their setup.

We clumped together with the children in the center. All but Belle was sleeping. No one had gotten over seeing them in danger, their loud screams after the explosion. There were more than enough seats for everyone, but I pulled Quinlan into my lap anyway.

"I don't see why we had to send that perfectly fine gentleman away," Claus pouted. "I won't talk about you-know-what in a place like this. That is just asking for trouble."

I figured he meant stuck in a plane over thirty thousand feet in the air.

"We aren't. We'll do that at the location. But we need to rest. Everyone. Try and get some sleep."

He knew most of the pack wouldn't be able to fall asleep, but after what they'd just went through, they needed time to calm down.

"Well, I'm a spawn of hell and need no sleep, so I'm going to go continue my conversation." In case his meaning was lost on anyone, Claus thrust his hips lewdly, receiving several growls in reply.

Knox waved him away.

At the same moment, the doc stood. "I was able to grab much of the medication we had in stock. If anyone needs a sedative—"

Claus made a severe about-face away from the door. "On second thought, never mind. This just turned into my kind of party."

My sweet mate yanked his shoe off and launched it up the length of the plane where it bounced off Claus's shoulder. "Go on, get."

Claus's ridiculous lumberjack face went slack for a moment, his eyes on the shoe. He wasn't able to hide his smile quickly enough as he raised his head. "Fine," he sighed. "If you need me, I'll be nestled between—"

Quinlan covered his hands over his ears. "Go!"

———

THE PENTHOUSE WAS large enough for the pack to spread out, but mostly, they stayed in the large common area that overlooked the gleaming metropolis.

Quinlan warmed my thighs, wiggling the way he was. He warmed other body parts as well, but I wouldn't be able to do anything about that until after we found out what Claus had discovered.

It was only a tiny bit disconcerting when Claus pulled the grimoire and a knife wrapped in plastic out of his stomach.

More so for Maria, who fainted. She'd learned about the

existence of shifters, demons, and angels less than twenty-four hours ago, so her response was understandable.

"I'll get her some water." Doctor Tiff jumped up. "Just give her space to breathe."

Claus shrugged and set the *wet* items down on the long, dark, glass coffee table.

"Why didn't you wrap the grimoire?" Sitka asked with a single brow raised.

"Huh, that would've been good too. It's all itchy in there now." Claus scratched his red skin.

Jazz nodded toward the table. "What's with the knife?"

"A bonus that I'll just go ahead and call my finder's fee." Claus sounded absolutely delighted. He unwrapped the knife, a gaudy thing with more gems in its handle than anything capable of taking a life should have. "This is Abaddon's blade. It's been missing for over five hundred years. No idea how long it's been in a vault with this ole gal." He bumped the grimoire with his knuckles.

"What does it do?" Storri asked.

Claus's expression was one of outrage. "Do? What does any sharp pointy thing do? It cuts. And it's pretty."

"Can it kill a demon?" I asked.

Quinlan elbowed me in the stomach.

Claus rolled his eyes, unamused. "It can, but it's hardly unique in that regard. A great many powerful weapons can kill or hurt a demon. And no, I won't be providing a list of what those items are. Sheesh."

Knox returned from his and Jazz's room. "The Walker County pack has been informed of the attack. They're sending council soldiers to search the area and make sure no one robs the hotel."

"And Badger?" Faust asked.

"Finished with the contracts we gave them."

Huntley whistled low. "That might help explain why Pierce is still sort of upright. At crunch time, probably easier to keep shitty employees than train new ones."

The lines on Knox's face, already heavy with worry, deepened. "Another group of nephilim is missing, presumed dead. Seven nephilim lived in the same home that they also operated as a daycare. Badger's guys have combed through the police reports. The attack happened at night, and when parents showed up the next morning to drop off their kids, they saw the ransacked state inside and called the cops."

Claus made a noise that sounded like a curse, but in a rumbling language that made the hairs on my nape stand up. "That's worse news than you know." He slapped the book open to a page in the middle and pointed at the top line. "As I rushed to return to you all, I found some time to flip through the book. Thalasso used the," he spoke again in that same unsettling language, "or, as you would call it, the Heretic Rites. Thalasso is insane to utilize them. Created to mock heaven and hell, a mage spurned by angel and demon alike created rites capable of opening a gate to heaven or hell that, once opened fully, can never be closed. Anything will be able to come from that gate, and will. All the creepy crawlies of the underworld will swarm to the gate like moths to a lamp. Basically, fuck off equality, let those scales tip." He picked the book up, holding it at the spine with one hand as he slid his clawed finger across the page. "The entry describes the location and ritual. This thing *wouldn't* have been hard to close. We happen to have just the thing available here. A partial opening requires only a partial sacrifice. It's always harder to open a thing than it is to close it."

"What sort of sacrifice?" Storri asked.

"A full blood offering, given from the vein, that is equal parts nephilim and demon blood. The entry is very clear—

the mixture must be exact." Claus's gaze settled on my mate, and I snarled.

"*My* blood?" Quinlan squeaked.

I stood, taking my mate with me. I didn't know if he wanted to stand on his own, but I couldn't put him down anyway. "No," I barked over Quinlan's head. "No fucking way."

"Diesel," Knox grunted, getting to his feet. He approached slowly, and it was only then that I realized I'd carried Quinlan to the door. "You're right. That isn't happening."

"If I don't, everyone in the world dies," Quinlan said in a soft, high-pitched voice. "The whole world, Diesel."

The words dripped from me like venom. "Then the world *fucking dies*."

Quinlan smiled, but it wasn't happy. That fast, he'd already started saying goodbye in his head. We couldn't let the world end if we knew a way to stop it. But *this* wasn't a way.

"We go now, bring the book, figure something out. You said the longer we wait, the harder it is, so let's stop waiting. We can do a transfusion." I reached for our jackets.

"Because you have a large supply of type AD blood?" Claus called out from the other side of the room.

The motherfucker was casually discussing his half-brother's death. I'd let his helpfulness eclipse the fact that Claus was, and would continue to be, just a demon.

"Even if you did," he said, the combative tone leeching from his voice, "it wouldn't matter. Once the third blood offering has been given, and we can likely assume it was given the day the nephilim went missing, the gate cannot be closed until the moment before it fully opens, when it will be at its weakest—for the last time." He consulted the page.

"And that will only happen after *the raven caws twice around the world*, which is an ancient measure of time. Roughly translated, about a week, give or take a few minutes."

"Fine." The only thing keeping me from shouting was Quinlan in my arms. "We have a week to figure out another way."

"I am telling you there is no new way," Claus snarled, raising the temperature in the room with his anger.

Knox reached for his knives the same moment the twins grabbed their swords, but Claus closed his eyes, visibly attempting to calm himself.

"No matter what you might think of what I am, Diesel, I am not apathetic at the prospect of losing my brother. I'm also not the one who will be dying shortly after the gates open completely. Let me be clear. The entry does not only say equal blood offered from the vein—it explicitly states a full sacrifice. No matter how you get the blood into the gate, someone must die to close it."

———

IT WASN'T SUPPOSED to be a last meal, but it sure as fuck resembled one. The pack sat in a loose circle around the coffee table that Sitka had scrubbed no less than one hundred times since we'd arrived. Pizza boxes covered the table. Greasy white paper was all that was left in some of them, while others went untouched.

Knox went overboard ordering the food, but we all knew what he was compensating for. Despite Claus saying it was a lost cause, we'd spent the days since devising an insane, last-ditch, Hail-Mary-type of plan—I despised it. It went against everything I was as an alpha, and the parts that

I didn't find outright repugnant required everything to go exactly as we needed. All the working parts had to line up to line up, or the whole thing would crash over our heads.

Quinlan ate his slice with a knife and fork. He was trying his hardest not to let his nerves show, and it broke my heart. There wasn't a fucking thing I could do. To get out of danger, we had to put what we held most dear in danger.

There'd been a time when all we'd had were questions. We had the answers now. We knew our former leader, Pierce, avoided the explosion we believed had killed him in Colombia and, using Thalasso's power, was transported immediately to pack lands, where he kidnapped Quinlan— double-crossing the demon king he served. Thalasso needed Quinlan dead if he was going to eliminate any chance of the gate closing once he began the process of opening it with the Heretic Rites.

Pierce set the hellfire bomb off to cover his tracks, at which time he was able to use the weapon he was promised when he sold his soul on Quinlan, to attempt to turn him from me. With an obsession fueled by Quinlan's nephilim gift, Pierce believed himself in love with Quinlan, until it came down to his life or Quin's. That should've been proof enough to Quinlan that his power wasn't at fault for anything. It was Pierce who'd warped everything to fit the narrative in his head.

"At some point, Thalasso must've grown impatient waiting in hell for his people to find enough nephilim outside of their protection years to begin the first sacrifice, prompting the blood experiments we'd discovered at the Christmas Valley Portal compound.

I leaned in, inhaling softly as Quinlan chewed. He smiled and moved into the motion. "You need to eat. Tomorrow's the big day."

He smelled so much like home I could almost convince myself we were at the hotel, no demons chasing after us, just my pregnant mate, glowing with contentedness and satisfaction.

In reality, my mate smelled like home but with enough stress souring his scent to make it clear something was wrong. I didn't have to ask what; I knew what. It was the same reason why the other alphas had their noses buried in their omega's necks as well. The same reason no one spoke above a whisper or smiled.

When the pack had finished eating, we pulled the blankets and pillows from the individual rooms and brought them to the shared space. Those who weren't holding babies wordlessly pushed the furniture back, lifted the table from the center, and laid down thick mats.

I claimed a spot on the ground and pulled Quinlan against my front. He grabbed blindly for my hand, and I gave it to him. In front of him, the twins and Sitka curled up in their wolf forms. To their right, Storri lay with Faust and the girls, babbling happily to one another.

I hoped the others got some sleep but knew I wouldn't be.

Quinlan pressed my palm against his round stomach. We hadn't felt the baby move yet. Doctor Tiff had said it should only take a few more days before we could.

Quinlan squeezed my fingers. "We're meeting this child." The whispered promise was loud enough for everyone in the room to hear, and I suspected that was the point. He hadn't only been talking to me.

My normal promises stuck in my teeth. I couldn't tell him I'd keep him safe or that I'd never let anyone hurt him. Soon, he would be in danger. All of the nephilim would.

And if we failed, it wouldn't matter that we left the others behind.

One way or another, all of this would end tomorrow.

———

"OUT OF ALL THE places I imagined the gate to hell would be, I never thought *Pennsylvania,*" Jazz whispered

We looked like idiots—or would have, if anyone could see us. Concealed under a gauze sheet, Jazz used his ability to make us blend in with the forest. After weeks of practice, he'd learned how to manipulate an illusion even after the object left his hands. The end result was a sheet that constantly changed to match the scenery. He wouldn't have been able to maintain an illusion like that on more than one object at a time. That meant one sheet and walking at an infuriatingly slow pace while huddled together.

"At least Hellam Township sounds suitably more ominous." Only Storri would sound pleased by that.

"What's the status of the decoys?" Knox asked.

Storri cleared his throat and stood straighter. "The crow said they're in position. Ready to leave on time."

Knox grunted.

Sitka rubbed his face against Jazz's shoulder. Stress changed everyone in different ways. With Sitka, it made him more affectionate. "How much farther?"

"Half a mile until there can be no more chatter," Faust told him. "At that point, we'll be two miles from the gate."

Storri stumbled over a root, and everyone around him caught him at once. "Thanks, sorry." He set the foot down, wincing.

Faust hooked his shoulder under Storri's armpit. "I'm

sorry, love. We can't slow even for a second. The decoys can't go before we get there."

"I *know*."

I smirked at the light irritation.

"It's okay," he continued, his irritation gone. "I don't need to anyway."

Storri wanted to be tough for his alpha. All the omegas did, and I fucking hated it. From the beginning, they hadn't complained once, not when the doctor had to run her tests, nor when they practiced.

At two and a half miles away, we went silent. The last two miles passed in a blink. As the sight of the gate came into view, I searched the woods around it. If Thalasso and his men were here, we should've been able to smell it, but none of us were taking the chance. We kept the sheet draped over our bodies and shuffled soundlessly forward.

We'd never gone into a mission with so many unknowns. Usually, they listened well to Storri, but there was a chance the animals wouldn't cooperate, and Claus would always be a wild card.

The front line of guards were just ahead, always in the same place every time we'd passed over while preparing. Behind them, there were enough Portal soldiers surrounding the gate. There was no chance of us fighting through them all.

The moment we reached the first defense, the north side of the forest exploded with sound and movement. The trees came alive, the branches shaking and breaking. Thousands of birds—crows, vultures, finches, and sparrows—all squawked frantically, beating their wings, adding their noises to the wall of sound. The piercing wail of a wolf's howl was soon joined by hundreds of others. All the howls, growls, and snarls came together, making it all sound like something you'd expect to hear in hell.

The soldiers looked at one another, clearly waiting for one of them to take charge. Someone did, running up the path before stopping and putting his back toward us as he addressed his men.

"Third and fourth squad, move in!"

The soldiers turned to obey, taking the place of the squads investigating the disturbance that grew louder by the second.

We weren't able to fight through an army of Portal soldiers, but half of an army?

That we could do.

We followed the men, taking out the stragglers silently. Knox retrieved one of his daggers as the twins grabbed their swords. With a gun in each hand, Faust nodded.

More than one heart pounded beneath the sheet. I met Quinlan's gaze, letting my eyes soften despite our surroundings. I'd never known I could be soft until Quin. He brought out the very best parts of me while somehow being able to ignore all the things that sent most people running.

He smiled, reaching up slowly to cup my face.

It took all that I had not to throw him over my shoulder and run. The others would follow suit. We'd find a new way. We needed a new way—

Quinlan patted my cheek and shook his head. He knew the look in my eyes, what it meant. He dropped his hand from my face to between my legs, where he cupped my balls, winking when my shocked expression met his. I had to bite back my laugh.

Cheeky boy.

The same moment Quinlan reached back for his whip, the soldiers who'd left began screaming, one after another, joining until the majority of the voices shouted in terror. A deafening crack shook the trees, followed by rapid gunfire.

The remaining Portal soldiers shifted uneasily on their feet, peering through the trees like they could see. More than one squeezed the handle of their gun nervously. That's what we needed—frightened soldiers with guns. They should have thought about the danger before they sold their souls.

Knox yanked the sheet off our heads.

The closest soldiers hadn't noticed us before I shifted and leaped on the nearest of them, ripping out his throat.

The twins shot forward, mowing through the men like bulldozers through a forest. They twirled and spun, as though both were exempt from gravity.

Faust had already reloaded once and did again before dropping an incoming line of soldiers like figures in a carnival game.

I looked over my shoulder to the omegas. Jazz, Storri, and Sitka were in their wolf forms standing in a similar circle, facing out. Quinlan already had his whip flying, bringing down men before they could see the whip coming. I wanted to watch my boy do his thing, but neither he nor the other nephilim were helpless. We'd taken them hunting enough times I was confident they at least knew how to use their teeth. Proving my point, Sitka lunged at a charging soldier, opening his shadow-wolf jaws before dropping the man, making it look easy. He fell back in position with blood dripping from his muzzle.

As more of their men fell, the remaining soldiers proved they weren't as stupid as I thought and dropped back, running in all directions just as long as it was away.

Some stayed, which only meant they were more afraid of Thalasso than they were of us.

In less than fifteen minutes, an army became a handful of frightened men, the only thing standing between us and our goal. The gate sat behind them, a circular stone opening that must've been an old well at some point. It emitted an orange, otherworldly glow that smelled strongly of sulfur and rotting meat.

Claus had shared what would happen if we failed to close the gate. The gate would erupt with hellfire, killing anyone standing within fifty feet who wasn't a demon. As the fire spread, the lesser demons would emerge, sniffing out the first thing they could find to kill and eat. I had a hard time believing any of these soldiers knew what was in store for them if their master was successful.

The omegas shifted again, quickly grabbing one another's hands before standing in a half circle facing the gate.

Behind them, Knox dropped his rucksack to the ground, pulling out two medical kits. While still bent over, Knox's shoulders tightened. At the same time, the hairs on my nape stood up, but I kept my face down, to Quinlan.

"I have to say, I'm disappointed." Thalasso had a voice like butter—mixed with arsenic.

We could barely hear him over the animals' sounds. His men slunk from the woods like ghosts, surrounding us and the gate. The relief of the men behind us who'd remained was palpable even while their fellow soldiers raised their guns.

Every one of them aimed at only one person. I yanked Quinlan behind me, while Knox hauled Jazz with one arm to the spot beside him.

Like his men, Thalasso had eyes for only one of us. His black eyes narrowed but with something that looked more like curiosity.

"I expected Pierce to fail, like he has every other time."

The man in question hobbled forward, looking somehow worse than the last time we'd seen him, and he'd looked like shit then. One eye was completely swollen shut. He had a cracked lip and cradled his injured arm at his chest like it was an infant. The dirty bandage smelled of infection.

"I don't like being lied to," Thalasso growled and lifted the back of his hand as though he would strike him again before he let it fall heavily on Pierce's shoulder. "But I am a fair master. I told you you would be rewarded if you were right, and you were, so you shall." Thalasso brought his wrist to his mouth and bit down. Dark blood poured from the self-inflicted wound. He smeared his wrist over Pierce's face. Our former leader yelped, clearly expecting another punishment. What he got was a face covered with demon blood.

He licked his face, tentatively, until that first swipe into his mouth. His tongue slid immediately back out, licking his face like a dog who'd recently been given peanut butter. Thalasso brought his wrist to Pierce's mouth, and his hands flew up, holding Thalasso's gift in place while he sucked greedily.

Thalasso ripped his arm away, and the effect was immediate. Pierce stood straight. His swollen eye opened, disappearing as it should've, had he been able to heal like he once had. The cut on his lip healed. He lifted his left arm from his chest, ripping off the filthy bandage to reveal a *hand* growing from the end.

Sitka made an angry noise.

Thalasso turned his back on Pierce's transformation, his eyes finding Quinlan once more. He arched his nonexistent brow. "Where's Claus?"

"He's on his way," Quinlan snapped.

The soldiers snickered.

"Always trying to be fashionably late, that one. Doesn't matter. You're all too late, unless you're here to sacrifice his brother," Thalasso sneered. He looked over our heads, to his remaining guards. "Do not let that one anywhere near the gate." He gestured toward Quinlan. "I didn't think you had it in you. Really. So much for true love. Thankfully, Pierce's knowledge of you has proved his most useful asset. He said there was no way you wouldn't try to close the gate. He said you'd try to use a distraction, just like he said you'd sneak in using the nephilim's illusion power. In fact, every single thing he said about you came to pass. Exactly as he described."

"Do you want us to clap?" Knox snarled.

Thalasso grinned and raised his hand, readying his men to fire. "No. I want you to die."

"*Pierce is gonna be there. You fucking know he will.*" *Huntley poked the map at the location of the gate. "Like it or not, he knows us, knows our process. He taught us most of the field strategies we know. Closing the gate like this..." His distaste was obvious. "...how do we get close enough to it?"*

Knox stared at the map. He tapped a pen against his chin, none of us bothering to tell him he was drawing lines on his face. "We use it. He's a narcissist who thinks he's a genius. We use that."

The doctor carried a plastic tub full of needles, tubing, and empty blood bags. "We measured Claus's blood three times. Using the measurements he gave me, we've got an accurate volume. Now we just need to figure out circulation time and how to add the exact amount of angel blood at the exact same time."

"And get enough of it so that it counts as a full sacrifice," *Faust added.*

The doctor's face darkened as her lips twisted with disdain. "It will take all of them." She sighed. "They'll need to practice. Many more times than once. We can't guess here. The size, depth, location, that will all change the flow, and they each need to be precise."

Knox's face had become stone the day we'd landed in Chicago, but at this, he paled. "We'll handle that part when it comes. For now, we'll practice. Faust, go with Storri and Claus to start gathering volunteers."

"That's an awful lot of faith we're putting in wild animals." Faust grimaced. To make it worse, he'd already told his best friend he wouldn't be coming with us. Dog's injuries caused him too much pain, and since we couldn't risk the wraiths—the link they had with Quinlan made bringing them ill-advisable—they'd stay behind too.

Knox growled and looked to me. "Do you think Claus can be trusted?"

"No. But I do believe whatever bit of soul he inherited from their father does allow him to care for Quin. If it's for Quin, he can be trusted."

My gaze drifted back down to the plan, laid out in easy steps on the table. "Is this really what will save the world?" Everything about the plan felt wrong, but we'd been pushed to the brink, standing at the literal end of everything we knew.

Quinlan settled his hands over my shoulder while the other omegas went to their alphas. "This will work," he said clearly. "It has to."

I hadn't had the heart at that moment to tell Quinlan that even if we did everything perfectly on our side, something could happen. Failure was always a possibility.

And as Thalasso's men prepared to fire, failure didn't feel too far off.

As quickly as it began, the wall of sound quieted into silence. The lack of noise was deafening.

Pierce snarled and wiggled the fingers of his new hand. Once he was sure he could move them, he yanked the walkie from the nearest soldier and barked into it. "Report."

"Sir," came the reply, "the animals are running away. They were attacking and just stopped."

"Say again?" A confused edge of panic crept into his question. He looked to his master.

"Sir, the animals have ceased and retreated. They're *running* away."

I was glad Pierce's eye had healed. Now he could stare into both of mine and clearly see my smile as I reached for the detonator. "Mas—"

For the second time, the forest exploded, but this time not with sound, but with fire.

I hunched over, shielding Quin and Storri with Faust as Knox and the twins covered Jazz and Sitka. Heat from the explosion singed my hair and clothes, while filling the space with the distinct scent of burning flesh. There hadn't been time for any of them to react before. Their screams came now, mixed with garbled moans of pain.

Thalasso pushed off the tree he'd stumbled into. The fire couldn't hurt him, but it had leveled the playing field. This was almost all worth it just to see the demon king's confusion followed quickly by his anger.

That's right, fucker. You'll choke on us.

Score one for Storri's mice. Keeping the explosive small enough to carry but advanced enough that I could detonate remotely had taken tweaking.

I couldn't be mad at the results.

With deadly efficiency, Faust shot the guards standing between us and the opening to hell.

A beam of bright red light shot from the gate. The heat pouring from it made the air wobble and shake.

The gate wasn't supposed to open for another three minutes. "It's early," Huntley cursed.

"He said give or take," Jagger replied.

"Go." I pushed Quinlan to the gate. He scrambled forward with the others, stumbling over the dead and dying to snag one of the medical kits.

The remaining soldiers who'd survived the blast didn't get to their feet quickly enough to avoid Knox's throwing daggers. His supply had to be near depleted by now, but we were near the end. Do or die time.

Pierce roared and surged toward Quinlan. His face contorted with anger, fear, but also *affection*. It was the last emotion that boiled my insides.

Faust fired, hitting Pierce at the bicep and through his right shoulder, but Pierce was too juiced up on demon blood for the bullets to stop him. Quinlan looked up from the medical kit, face covered in sweat as his eyes widened long enough for him to grab his whip and unfurl it by his side.

Storri dropped to the ground a second before Quinlan's whip flew through the air, slicing ribbons up Pierce's cheek. He pulled back, controlling the whip like an extension of his body. The end wrapped around Pierce's ankle, and Quinlan tugged, cutting through Pierce's pants and into his skin. As fast as he'd been moving, he fell like a meteor. "Stay," Quinlan ordered before turning his back to the shifter, showing Pierce just how much Quinlan feared him.

This wasn't in the plan. We knew Pierce would be here, but not what Thalasso would do to reward him. It was better this way, with him at full strength, I didn't have to feel anything but joy when I pounced, cracking his body beneath my fists. He fought back at first, but not even demon's blood could match how much I desired for him to be dead.

I couldn't lose myself, couldn't pound Pierce into an unrecognizable pulp like I wanted. The only reason Thalasso hadn't attacked himself was how close Quinlan stood to the gate. If Quinlan jumped now, it would close.

I fought the urge to watch him and make sure he didn't do anything stupidly heroic. Thalasso surged forward. He didn't have an ocean's worth of water to create an army again, but he was still a pissed-off demon king.

Pierce wheezed. Something rattling in his throat. He looked up, lifting his chin to see over his head, back to Quinlan. He *moaned.* "Take care of—"

My roar erupted from me like a physical being. All the pain and grief, losing years with my mate, haunting his dreams and trying to turn him from me. I wouldn't let my mate's name be this piece of shit's last words. I clenched my fist and dropped it like a hammer on his nose. He grunted once before dying on the ground surrounded by the very people who once would've given their lives to save his.

Thalasso snarled, cursing in the same rumbling language Claus spoke. He stood too close to Quinlan, who, despite the heat, edged closer and closer to the cement ridge of the gate. The beam of light was darker now, hotter too, as hellfire surged toward the gate out of hell.

"Great job, everyone," Thalasso shouted. "You've killed all the people who were going to die tonight anyway."

Of everyone, I didn't expect Storri to growl in reply. "Not quite."

"You think you can kill me, little angel?" Thalasso crooned. "With what?" His eyes dropped to their hands, and he laughed. "Razors?"

As realization dawned, Thalasso's mouth twisted. He *flew* forward but came to a sudden stop when Claus dropped from the sky, grabbing the other demon around the throat. I knew it killed him not to take a moment to gloat and banter, but he refrained. He squeezed the grip he had around Thalasso's throat and dragged his kicking body toward the blistering opening. "Now or not at all!" Claus shouted.

Thalasso thrashed in his grip, weakening Claus's hold.

I lunged for the demon's leg, lifting as Faust lifted the other. Knox and Huntley grabbed hold of his arms, the four of us stretching him out like drying leather. We maneuvered his head over the gate, forcing Claus to straddle the stone circle with Thalasso's head held firmly. Jagger swung his sword through the air, piercing through Thalasso's stomach with so much force, the tip lodged between the cracks in the stone circle.

I checked to make sure the omegas were in position. Each had a razor in hand, poised over different arteries on their bodies.

I met Quinlan's gaze, reminding myself if we did this now, it would all be over. "Now."

At the exact same moment, the nephilim put their razors to skin, and Claus slid his fancy new knife across Thalasso's throat.

"Hold him!" Knox growled while Thalasso thrashed wildly.

If he moved too much, he'd change the flow, and everything had to happen exactly as the doctor had instructed.

Jagger grabbed the same leg as Faust and pulled.

The scent of blood mixed with burnt flesh and sulfur. Quinlan held his arm over the hole, his skin red and blistering. His grimace matched the others, all with different body parts open and bleeding into the gate. The doctor had outdone herself, calculating and comparing blood volume and circulation rate between demon and nephilim. For every drop of demon blood, the nephilim poured out drops of their own. Apart, none of them could give enough blood to equal Thalasso's without dying, but together, they could share the load.

Storri whimpered, and Faust jerked back, like he was going to let go of the demon's leg.

"Stop!" Storri ordered, his eyes flashing black. I'd seen that happen once before and knew it was best to do as the nephilim said when it did.

"Almost," Claus shouted. His skin caught fire, and though it didn't seem to hurt him, the flames licked at the nephilim. "It has to be every drop. Lift!"

Faust, Jagger, and I lifted his legs, inclining his body and sending his remaining blood up to his head.

Tears streamed down Quin's face. His arm was already covered in blisters. The scent of the nephilim's pain was maddening. Everything in me screamed for me to drop the demon and pull my mate from danger, to stop him from hurting himself. Faust's face had gone gray, his nostrils flaring, filling his head with the same thoughts that flew through mine.

I'd just started doubting the doctor's math when Claus screamed, "Now!"

We dropped the demon's body at the same time the nephilim pulled their limbs away from the heat.

I didn't look to watch the gate close. I pulled Quinlan into my arms, careful not to jostle his burns or cut, feeling the heat at my backside dissipate. Knox threw a jug of water from his rucksack, and I ripped the lid off, pouring the tepid water over Quinlan's body. The worst of his burns were on his arm, but his entire front side was red and chapped. I wrapped his arm, wincing when I applied pressure to his cut and made him gasp.

"Fuck, baby boy, I'm sorry. I'm so sorry."

"It's okay," he panted. "Is it closed? Did we make it?"

Even his eyelashes were singed, but he still blinked the shriveled strands, searching for the gate.

"It's closed, demonling," Claus replied. "We did it."

He didn't sound like he knew exactly why or how we'd been successful, but I did.

"*We* didn't." I shook my head and nuzzled the side of Quinlan's face gently. "They did."

19

QUINLAN

"MORE BLANKETS?" Hallie dropped a second throw over my lap. I wiggled against Diesel's chest, snuggling deeper into the position I'd been kept in since the closing of the gate.

Fat drops slid down the penthouse windows, showing a rainy, windy Chicago.

"Yes please." I beamed up at Hallie, knowing she needed to help us more than we needed help.

We kept telling her to sit down, but Alejandro could only get her down for a few minutes at a time.

"I've got coffee," Maria announced, pulling cardboard cups from one of several drink trays.

Jamie and Siobhan had gone with her to get food.

Today marked day fourteen of my pregnancy, and as much as it irked Hallie, by tomorrow, I'd have a baby. I'd be passed out the three days following, but Hallie still had to grow hers the old-fashioned way.

"It's crazy being out there." Maria handed me my hot chocolate.

Diesel immediately grabbed it, popped the lid, and tested the temperature. He must've found it acceptable because he fit the lid back on and returned the cup to my hand as if he'd never snatched it away in the first place.

I rolled my eyes. I'd have to remember to elbow him for that some time.

I wouldn't now because since the moment we returned to the penthouse, bedraggled, burned, and bruised—but alive—the pack treated the four of us so carefully, they nearly put the alphas to shame.

Maria—who'd fit right in, especially with Siobhan and Jamie—grabbed her own coffee and plopped down on the large sofa. "All these people have no idea how close they came to hell on earth. It's like, I want to tell them, 'Do you know who this sandwich is for? Someone who saved your life, *pendejo.*'"

"Maria!" Al scolded.

Maria shrank from her uncle, sinking her head between her shoulders and hiding behind Siobhan's hair. "It's just, they should give them their food for free and make it like they would for a hero."

"Nah." Jazz waved his hand, or would've if he wasn't feeding Angus. He waved his shoulder, though, and I knew what that meant. "I've gotten tons of free food and drinks. It isn't difficult. I can teach you—"

"Maybe not," Hallie said, returning with a pillow no one had asked for. She absently stuffed it behind Sitka's shoulders. "I know how you get free drinks."

"Hallie! I am a claimed man," Jazz gasped. "I am sure you meant how I used to get free drinks."

Sitting in a chair beside his mate, Knox didn't look the slightest bit convinced. That just meant he knew his mate.

Jazz cupped his hand over his mouth like he was telling a secret. "But seriously, if we ever have a no-alphas-allowed night, none of us will have to pay for a single thing. I'll just give you all a few pointers before we go out."

I enjoyed listening to their banter and felt no need to contribute. For once, I wasn't walking around with a bullseye on my back. We were safe, and not just for the moment, but at least until the next big bad popped up in our lives. My alpha held me. The pack gathered around us, both to dote, but also because this had been how I wanted to spend my fourteenth day. Lazy, watching the rain fall, while we all just *breathed* for a while.

I made everyone turn off their alarms. I didn't want my labor to be a countdown; we'd had enough countdowns. I simply wanted to sit, listen, and enjoy my pack and mate, and when I started glowing and turned into a wolf, the conversation could simply continue—hopefully for the next three days. Then we'd pack up, go *home*, and begin to rebuild what was destroyed.

"Here we are, demonling." Claus swept inside the penthouse, coming from the elevator. He'd adopted the lumberjack look as his main persona, but at the moment, he paired that burly physique with a long, gray, wool peacoat, crisp black slacks, and charcoal leather loafers that looked like they'd feel like butter beneath your fingers. His hair was slicked back, along with his beard, which not only shone but smelled like sandalwood and citrus.

He set a thin rectangular box wrapped in black velvet on my lap.

Diesel's body tensed beneath mine. He looked over my shoulder, breathing softly on my neck.

"Well?" Claus pushed his hands forward like he was urging us along.

The velvet slid from the box like water. The box beneath was black with gold gilding. I lifted it open, revealing a folded blanket made from a caramel-colored fabric that looked most like wool.

Jazz's mouth dropped. "Is that...? You're giving a Vicuna wool blanket to *a baby?*"

I decided not to take offense, but I was too distracted to be offended anyway when Sitka blasted from his seat, shadow-hopping the few feet between us, to land nimbly on the balls of his feet between my calves. "May I touch it?" he whispered. His burns were nearly healed, as were the others'. Mine were taking a little longer since I was still without nephi-shifter powers. Diesel hoped they'd be healed by the time I woke up.

"What is it? What's Vicuna wool?"

"Only the most expensive fabric in the world." Sitka dropped his head, depressed at putting the blanket back in the box.

I looked to Claus. "*Is* this for the baby?"

His lips pouted as his eyebrows joined in a furrow. "Of course. I am the little hellraiser's uncle. Or am I not allowed to bring the child a gift? Is this a Sleeping Beauty thing? It's not cursed."

He looked so close to being sad—and Claus was never sad—that I would've fallen from Diesel's arms if he hadn't held me down in my haste to console him. "No, it's perfect. I love it. I will totally let my baby pee all over this really expensive blanket."

Sitka's face turned a shade of green, like he was going to be sick.

I obviously wouldn't say anything now, but when we got home, that expensive wool was his. I'd feel bad and would have to hide it from Claus so he didn't think I didn't appreciate his gift, but how could I do anything but give it to Sitka when just touching it made his cheeks pink like his crush had just sat down next to him at lunch?

Claus's eyes rolled to the back of his head. "Ugh. I thought of that, demonling."

He reached under his jacket and pulled out a second box, exactly the same as mine. He tossed it to Sitka, who caught it with gentle hands and wide eyes. "This is for me?" he breathed.

"All yours. This way, Quin will *keep his*."

Sitka sighed softly, staring down at the box. "I love you."

His declaration of love was followed by two deep growls.

Sitka's head popped up, searching for his alphas. I'd search for mine too if I heard him growl like that. He frowned when their eyes met, and it was as if I could see him putting the blocks together in his head.

"Not the demon! I was talking to the wool!"

———

"A LITTLE MORE GREEN. Okay, and just wipe it, yeah, like that." I reached down for the paintbrush and brought it to the new sign that sat outside the hotel. I would've liked to have restored the old sign and had Faust stow it in the garage just in case, but a new start and a new pack deserved a new sign.

I looked down to Sitka and grinned. Diesel had demanded he help because he thought Sitka's shadow-jumping would be useful if I fell from the three-foot step ladder. And he'd demanded he handle the paint because Diesel thought if I bent over one too many times, I might grow suddenly delirious and leap from the *three-foot step ladder*. "I'll pretend to fall, and you pretend to—"

"Not funny," Diesel hollered from his spot under his own canopy set up far enough away that the fumes didn't reach our daughter. She slept happily in her favorite spot, her daddy's arms.

Though Claus was upset that Rebecca did not pop out horns when she shifted the first time, she did have a head of soft, yellow curls, which—well, also upset him—but then she'd opened her eyes, and he'd been satisfied. She'd inherited my eyes, but only one of the colors. Looking into Rebecca's gaze was like looking into the blackness of space, limitless with possibility and power.

Claus was still boasting about how strong demon genes were.

"Just joking, alpha of mine!"

Sitka smirked, but the expression quickly faded, his lips flattening to a worried line. "What do you think will change, Quinlan? Now that we are a recognized pack within the shifter council?"

I handed him the brush, and he dipped it in the bucket of water, rinsing the green paint away.

"Nothing, really. I think there might be some dues involved, maybe? But Jazz is loaded, so that doesn't really matter. Mostly the council steps in when packs request them to. And even then, most issues are solved by mediation. That's why Diesel dislikes them so much."

"They need to be told about the problem and then ask me how to fix it? Skip the middle man." His face dropped to Rebecca, and even from where I stood, I could see the tension evaporate from Diesel's shoulders.

"Then why join?"

The decision to become recognized had been one the pack had voted on. Ultimately, it was for the Alphas to decide, but they didn't just *accept* our thoughts on the topic —they specifically *requested* them.

"They can be of some good. They're sending their soldiers to guard the forest while we're building the house. Oh! And, when you are recognized, other packs are more likely to help you. Like the Walkers coming to help us rebuild."

Sitka gathered his lips to one side. "They would've anyway."

Diesel laughed.

The council had offered to send a crew to do the work, but that had made the room very loud with growls, so we decided against it. In other words, Knox had refused the offer flat.

Since our bedrooms were fine after they'd aired out, no one was displaced, and the pack had a chance to go slow and renovate exactly as we wanted.

It was clear I hadn't convinced Sitka the council was useful, but he didn't dwell for long on his uncertainty. His eyes looked over my head, like they did when he was seeing someone who wasn't there. "Mr. Paynes says he'd chosen that exact shade, but they'd sent blue instead."

It may have been strange, but I was proud of that.

"When we're done with the house, then you're throwing us a party, yes?"

I'd begun the preparations. Jazz had already demanded to help, which I gladly accepted, and it was only a matter of time before the others followed. I was glad for it, especially when I thought about our lives and how similarly we'd all grown up, missing moments that other people took for granted. This party would give us a chance to remedy that, and I wanted them to feel like it belonged to them as well. "It isn't a party, Sitka." I beamed, my tummy fluttering with anticipation. "It's a ball."

20

QUINLAN

Sitka's sewing room was alive with movement. Fabric flew as Sitka bounced from pack member to pack member, leaving a trail of sparkles and sewing needles.

Thankfully, the alphas had taken all of fifteen minutes to get ready, leaving the rest of us to dress for the ball together.

When Sitka had finally asked to help—with a soft, hopeful voice that disappeared the moment I said yes—he'd immediately declared himself everyone's designer.

Which meant he was now—minutes before we were to be announced—racing around the room like a baby goat. He inspected each of us, making small changes to our outfits along the way.

He'd already declared Storri—dressed in a formal Prince Charming suit—perfect, so he stood in the hallway keeping Jamie company.

We'd intended to have him change with the rest of us, but the alphas had unanimously demanded he dress in the room next door. They might've thought they were dissuading the young man, but really, every time the

274

alphas treated him like a threat, his chest puffed out with pride.

Hallie sat on the daybed with Maria and Dr. Tiff wearing a red cocktail dress with room for a baby bump, a pink satin dress with a modest sweetheart neckline, and a royal purple pantsuit, respectively.

"I don't know what I'm more excited for," Jazz swooned, playing with the layers of tulle he twirled. The strapless corset ball gown fit him like a dream. The cobalt blue satin slip lent the perfect contrast to the layers of navy blue tulle. "Quinlan's surprise or for Knox to see me in this *fucking* dress. He's gonna go *feral.*"

"He better not tear my masterpiece," Sitka growled, dropping to add some kind of stitch to the hem of Jazz's slip.

"Oh no, I'll make him take this off *slowly.*"

Siobhan snorted, blushing when everyone looked her way as she worried the hem of her LBD.

"Thinking of ideas for you and Jamie?" Maria taunted.

Siobhan growled, her eyes flashing from human to wolf. The emotion quickly faded, and Siobhan dropped her face to the floor and sucked her bottom lip between her teeth. "Maybe."

The room erupted with cheers.

"Um, you guys remember we're right outside the door, don't you?" Storri called softly through.

The shade of red Siobhan turned indicated that she had not.

"One minute!" Isaiah yelled from the foyer, saving his daughter from having to think of a reply.

Sitka squeaked, whirling to look me over. I felt ready for the red carpet dressed in the three-piece suit Sitka made. He'd stitched a slimming gray vest and fitted it over a white dress shirt with pearl buttons. Matching gray slacks paired perfectly with my velvet maroon suit jacket. "What are your thoughts on a hat?"

Jazz spoke up before I could come up with an answer. "Don't you think that'll make him too newsboy?"

Sitka tapped the pointed end of his fabric scissors against his lips. "You're probably right."

"If we're talking accessories, Sitka, I have a suggestion for you."

Sitka froze, staring down at his sleek, panther-like pantsuit that would've been just as suitable in battle as it was on the runway. It hugged him like a dream, accentuating every curve. The deep V highlighted his smooth, tan pectorals, but Jazz was right—they *were* bare.

Everyone but Sitka grinned.

"Okay, okay, we all came together, and, with the power of my horrible dead father's incredibly useful money, we chose this to thank you for your hours of work putting all these amazing outfits together." Jazz revealed the maroon velvet jewelry box he'd been hiding behind his back.

Sitka stared at the box, frozen for long enough I began to worry we'd overstepped. Finally, he took it from Jazz, stretching the lid open to reveal the vintage silver choker with four black diamond teardrops dangling from short chains spaced evenly across the neck.

"This is...*perfect*," Sitka breathed, yanking the necklace from the black satin padding. He pulled his slick black hair aside while Jazz helped him hook it on. Sitka rushed to the mirror, posing again and again to enjoy the necklace from different angles. "This is—you didn't have to do this. I wanted to dress you all. But *this*. I don't think I could've imagined anything as beautiful as this in my cell. Thank you, all of you. Truly."

Before anyone could ruin hair, makeup, or clothing by

blubbering into a group hug, Isaiah hollered from down the hallway. "Time!"

After one last look at himself in the mirror, Sitka wrenched the door open, grabbing Storri's and Jamie's hands as he marched down the hallway.

Isaiah waited for our group to gather at the foyer before heading down the hallway and playing his part as escort as well as announcer.

The concept of being announced had been Storri's idea, but the others quickly jumped in to voice their agreement. For most of us, this ball was symbolic of all those moments we'd missed out on while running from murderous parents, locked up in a cell, or strapped to a table watching your friends and family be experimented on. Not one of us, save for Dr. Tiff and Maria, could say they'd grown up with a normal life. Hallie had devoted most of her high school years to her ex, doing what he wanted to do.

But not tonight. For this one night, we were princes and princesses.

The closer we got to the ballroom—using the regular entrance since the secret passage might get dust on our clothes—the louder the string music grew, pumped in from speakers installed in every corner.

The alphas—plus Alejandro—had been in charge of the decorations. Not in designing or planning them, but in putting them up. I still hadn't seen the room in its full glory. The last I'd seen it, the room had been mostly empty, except for the large metal frame against the wall that held the drop cloth covering the finished mural. My second surprise.

Isaiah pushed open the double doors at the top of the stairs, revealing the warm glow of candles and ambient overhead lighting. The floral scent of wildflowers and sharp pine drifted out to the hallway where we were gathered.

Maria, Jamie, and Siobhan were first, each introduced by Isaiah to the crowd of people who already knew our names. We'd asked the Walker omegas to join in, but they'd made the point that if everyone was announced, no one would be there to see it. Plus, more than one of them seemed eager to stay in the background, and I wasn't about to push any of them into anything that would make them nervous.

After the first three, the doc and Hallie were introduced. Doc received a loud round of applause from the Walker pack—she was technically their pack doctor, after all—and Alejandro hadn't been able to wait for Hallie to make it halfway down the stairs in her dress and heels before he rushed up to meet her.

"You look amazing," he grunted, flashing bright white teeth.

Hallie snorted and bumped her forehead into Al's shoulder. "So do you."

He and the other alphas all wore variations of a tux. I couldn't let myself look at Diesel yet, not without sprinting down the stairs to leap on top of him when it was my turn.

"I present to you," Isaiah continued once Hallie had cleared the stairs, "Omega Storri, mate of Faust and father of four."

Storri's cheeks burned red, but the smile stretching his mouth was proof that he loved every minute. With his head high, he took the first step down and promptly missed it, causing the room to gasp. Faust was there, at the ready for his endearingly clumsy mate. He caught Storri before he fell, spinning so it looked like he'd been unable to wait before dipping his mate and kissing him.

I peeked around the door while they made it the rest of the way down. Alejandro and the alphas had done exactly as we'd asked. At the far end, the white linen-covered tables sat grouped together, surrounded by white, wood folding chairs. The refreshments table sat along the wall to the left, laden with decadent desserts, fruits, veggies, and a meat tray for the purists. Jazz had gone above and beyond baking a variety of petit fours that easily surpassed the most beautiful thing he'd ever created in the kitchen.

Streams of white gauze and twinkle lights stretched like a many-pointed star from the center of the ceiling, while well-placed candles lit up the dark corners and crannies. The dance floor gleamed, having been polished to its original luster.

"I present to you Omega Jazz, mate of Knox and father of the cutest bundle of chunky legs..." Isaiah cleared his throat, getting back on track.

Jazz pranced forward, no less in his element than he would be in his personal heaven. Unlike the others who had raced, or stumbled, down the steps, Jazz lowered himself to the dance floor with the confidence of a king. The navy blue tulle swished with each step, and, sure enough, Knox had taken one look at his mate and crushed his beer can.

We needed to get on with this, or Knox would haul Jazz over his shoulder before the festivities began.

He danced directly into Knox's arms, reaching across his alpha to grip the hand of his friend, Hollister.

When it was Sitka's turn, he didn't so much walk down the stairs as he swam, shadow-hopping to the dark mark cast on the ground between his alphas. Both men enveloped him in borderline inappropriate embraces before Sitka pushed them away. "Mind the clothes."

The look the twins gave him were reminiscent of Knox's, and I didn't think Sitka would be wearing his outfit for much longer either.

Alone in the hallway, I waited behind Isaiah, losing the fight to not look for my alpha. When I searched the dance-floor, I spotted the others: the Walkers all dressed up in their formal finest; the babies playing happily with Nana Walker or, as the case was for Rebecca, sleeping. But no Diesel.

"I present to you Omega Quinlan, mate of Diesel, father of one, and resident half-demon."

I twisted my head back to look at Isaiah, who just grinned and shrugged before pointing to the back corner in explanation. Claus stood in the shadows, in full tails and a top hat, holding a silver cane with a devil's head carved on top that he said made him look distinguished.

Any brotherly annoyance I felt for Claus disappeared the moment I spotted Diesel. He stood at the bottom of the steps, peering up, ready and waiting for me to be in his arms.

His eyes dragged over my body, and as I took the next step down, I felt suddenly naked. My alpha always could see through all the glitz as easily as he could the grime to the man I was inside. His omega. Forever.

Meanwhile, he wore his tux like a second skin. Who knew my mountain man cleaned up so well? He'd shaved the edges of his head for the occasion, leaving a blunt mohawk and full beard that was trimmed instead of scrag-gly. Suddenly, I needed to count the seconds until I could tear his clothes off *him*.

The rest of my steps felt like a dream, like walking on a cloud, until Diesel pulled me into his warm embrace.

"So what do you say—one song and then we get naked in the passageway?" Diesel murmured against my ear.

I grinned, but pretended to try to push him away. "After all our hard work? No way. We're enjoying every moment."

I joined the others huddled around the hanging drop cloth. The rope to release the sheet hung on the left side. I hadn't asked to do the honors, but the others had demanded it. "I painted this mural because I wanted to show how perspective can change anything. Whether a storm is coming or going, is sometimes only up to your perspective."

I pulled the rope before I could lose my nerve. It was one thing painting something your pack would enjoy now and again and a whole different thing to reveal it with dramatic flourish.

The sheet fell heavily, folding on top of itself as the others gasped and rushed forward.

"Quinlan! This is amazing!" Jazz cheered.

Diesel beamed beside me, for once, not allowing me to hide behind him.

"Thank you." I'd stuck mostly with my original design, though I'd added some supernatural elements to the storm, and I painted the beachgoers running in both directions, making it up to the viewer to decide which way the wind was blowing. There'd been nothing I could do about how the beachgoers ended up looking like all of us, despite the fact I hadn't wanted to paint the pack.

It was futile, they were family and inspiration.

Everyone crowded around, ooing and ahing at different sections.

"It this one me?" Sitka asked, pointing to a man with long black hair running in the waves.

I brought my fingers to my lips, dragging them across the seam in a zipping motion. "I'm not telling."

The crowd cleared—at my urging—some of us headed for chairs, others food, and the rest the dancefloor.

Diesel tugged us away from the others, toward the edge

of the dancefloor, where we were free to shuffle slowly from side to side.

"Should we tell them about the last time we danced in here?" I murmured, resting my cheek on Diesel's chest.

"Don't bother. Knox could smell it the second he walked in. Why do you think there are so many extra flowers?"

He spun us around, showing off his smooth dance skills.

I smiled. "You still remember." One of my favorite memories from before was of the three of us—me, Diesel, and my pack mom—in our living room as Rebecca showed Diesel the basics of a waltz. He'd grumbled the whole time, quieting only once we switched partners. It had been one of the only times in my young life Diesel had hugged me as tightly as I wanted.

"I remember everything that helps me take care of my baby boy." Diesel lifted me off my feet, continuing to dance despite only one of us touching the ground.

We'd settled into a sultry sway while the others joined us, lost in their own conversations with their alphas. I'd just begun to think about trying out some of those small cakes Jazz made, when the twinkle lights began to glow brightly, like someone had turned up the power.

Diesel's embrace went from soothing to protective. He rushed to the children, along with everyone else. The Walker and Royal Paynes alphas, along with Isaiah, Jamie, and Alejandro circled around the rest of the pack, while Claus stood at the front, transforming from dapper bearded gentleman to hulking red demon king.

"I don't care who is causing this. I'll tear 'em apart for ruining the demonling's—"

The light turned blinding, the purest white light that was impossible to look at but also impossible to look away from.

A whooshing sound blew through the ballroom, and when the lights faded back to their normal intensity, three bodies stood in the middle of the room, dressed to the nines in outfits that looked similar to the ones Jazz, Storri, and Sitka wore. The three omegas gasped and surged forward, stopped by their alphas.

"That's my mom!" Jazz cried out to Knox. "That's Sorrows."

The ethereal woman smiled at her son, her Grecian gown a matching shade of navy blue.

"But I thought archangels could only see their kids in their heavens at a time when they truly needed it?" Jazz rushed into his mother's arms. The angel wrapped him in a hug, spending a couple of seconds embracing as she pressed her cheek to the top of his head.

"It's true." Her voice boomed, almost like it was piping in through the speakers. But it wasn't loud, just *important.* "But, as you've learned, heaven and hell are about balance. *Hell,*" her mouth twisted with distaste, "broke those rules, allowing a demon king to influence the outcome."

"But he helped us." I didn't care for the way her face had soured mentioning my brother.

Sorrows's smile was not unkind. "That may be, but it is beside the point. Hell tipped the scales. We get to even them. With dancing." Her eyes sparkled.

Storri and Sitka rushed to their archangel fathers. Storri's dad picked him up and twirled him in a circle, much to Storri's giggling glee, while Power and Sitka seemed to be sizing each other up, both staring the other's outfit up and down.

"You have a talent, son." Power's voice rumbled.

Sitka ducked his head, covering his blushing cheeks with sheets of glossy black hair. "Thank you."

The alphas reluctantly allowed their omegas out of their arms to dance with their parents while many of the Walkers attempted to not stare at the actual archangels they were seeing for the first time.

Holding on to Diesel's hand, I brought him to the group, figuring I'd at least get to know the other pack while the others danced with their parents. I wasn't bitter that my parents were dead, but it also had never been more apparent that they were until this moment.

Someone tapped on my shoulder.

Claus stood with his hand out, still wearing his demon skin but dressed in the same tuxedo. "Will a demon king half-brother do?"

I wouldn't cry. I wouldn't cry. I wouldn't—

Claus pulled me to where the others were dancing and brushed a tear from my cheek. "You can cry, demonling. Wouldn't be the first time I've seen a human leak." He spun us in a fast circle before settling into a slow, casual waltz. "I never met your mother, but do you want me to tell you about my sire? Your father?" At my watery nod, he continued. "He was feared throughout all kingdoms. Cutthroat and a master of torture. I learned everything I know about evisceration from—" Claus caught my troubled look and switched directions. "I can't say I loved him, but I will say he instilled in me the foundations that I stand on today. Being a demon king isn't about hatred or cruelty, but giving back to people that which they deserve. No more no less."

I thought that over as we followed the music, keeping to the side, a good distance from the archangel parents. "Are you upset you're stuck here now that the gate is closed? How will you ever return?"

Claus shrugged. "Like I've said, time moves differently

in hell. I doubt I'm missing all that much. I'll find a way back, when I'm bored."

"What will you do? You're free to stay here. If any of them have a problem with it..." I jerked my head to the rest of the pack. "Send 'em my way. I'm angelically enhanced to persuade them."

Claus flashed every one of his silver fangs in a loud laugh. "I'm glad you are coming to terms with your duality. But no, as fun as changing diapers and listening to *other* people *constantly* have sex is, I think I'll head out. Find out all the ways the earth has changed since my last visit. I've been preoccupied since coming through the gate. Think of it as my vacation."

It wasn't at all difficult for me to imagine Claus in board shorts and a Hawaiian shirt; it was one of his favorite outfits.

In a second my insides went from tightening at the thought of Claus being blocked from returning home to panic at the idea of my life without him in it. "But you will come back to say bye before you go, right?"

Claus paused, stopping us in front of the refreshment table. For the first time since I'd met him, his face was slack, devoid of emotion. No frustration or sarcasm. Just blank, dumbfounded, like he couldn't believe I'd care whether he came or went. He found his voice, clearing his throat before replying, "Of course I will, demonling. I'll need to check on Rebecca, after all, and make sure she's growing up to be as evil as she can be."

That was, of course, the moment that Diesel tapped on Claus's shoulder, finished with sharing my attention. Before Claus could hand me over, Sorrows approached slowly, her eyes narrowed toward Claus.

I stiffened. Would my wraiths be at all helpful against archangels? I hadn't seen them since they'd disappeared with Dog to some corner of the hotel to do whatever it was those two did when they disappeared.

"I come in peace." Sorrows lifted her hands and smiled at me. "And with a gift."

Diesel dropped his arm over my shoulders, grounding me enough to keep from trembling. "For who?" I barked.

"For the demon. It is a token of our thanks. A feather from the wing of Malak." She lifted a long, snow-white feather. "Since you are stuck on earth, to thank you for saving our children, we want you to have this. It will help you travel between the realms, for a bit. The feather will work until it grows black. You'll just have to make sure you are where you want to be when that happens."

The underlying meaning was clear: that Claus would be back in hell, ruling over the kingdom of missed opportunities.

He didn't seem to mind the archangels' questionable intentions and accepted the feather with a sharp nod that turned into a rakish grin when our eyes met. "See, demonling, when a demon closes a gate, god really does open a door."

The others gathered to see what it was Sorrows had for Claus. Jazz stood arm in arm with his old friend, Hollister, both looking on as Erudite and Power joined Sorrows.

Kansas *didn't* seem to be paying attention. He hummed along with the music, but his eyes hadn't strayed from the sweets on the table. I was pretty sure I saw some drool. He danced between the groups, oblivious of the eyes watching him walk in the space that separated the archangels from Claus, me, and Diesel. He licked his lips, reaching for a chocolate-covered eclair and taking a bite. The sounds he made were just this side of sexual, and it wasn't until he chewed and swallowed his treat that he looked up to see where he was standing. It didn't bother him so much seeing Claus standing so near. They'd been cohabitating in the hotel for the week or so that the new construction took.

But when he looked at the angels, he squeaked and dropped his eclair. "Holy crap, you're angels." His eyes widened like a deer caught in headlights. "Oh no, I just said crap in front of angels. Shit!" Kansas clapped both hands over his mouth, looking around miserably for his mate. "Wyatt?"

"I'm here, kitten." Wyatt appeared by his mate's side, allowing the smaller man to bury his face in his chest. Wyatt balanced his chin on his mate's head as he spoke. "That all meant *hello*."

With his head still pressed into Wyatt's suit, Kansas nodded enthusiastically.

Whether he'd meant to or not, Kansas had broken the building tension, allowing everyone to get back to the party.

Hours later, the food was gone, our legs were tired, and the majority of the children had gone to bed. Only Nana Walker and Sitka's dad, Power, remained dancing. When we'd walked by, Power had her in a tight hold, whispering in her ear, "I haven't heard from you on the prayer chain lately, Ms. Nana."

My mouth dropped open at the blatant desire in the angel's tone. I searched the room for a pair of commiserating eyes and found Riley, Branson's mate.

"Are they...?" I mouthed.

Riley smirked, nodded, and then shrugged. It looked like he was trying to say *you never know with Nana*.

EPILOGUE
DIESEL

"I MEAN IT." Phineas released Sitka from a long goodbye hug. "We're doing it soon too. None of this 'let's meet up' but never meeting business. We're doing it. All the Star Wars movies, cosplay optional."

Sitka beamed and shook his head. "Oh no, cosplay required! I'll make them—"

Sitka walked Phineas to the truck, discussing which characters each of them should dress up as.

The other Walkers were busy saying their own good-byes. Quinlan held Rebecca, standing in a small circle of him, Claus, Riley, Nash, and Branson.

"You're welcome to stay," Branson told Claus. "Not sure how much fun a demon king could have in Walker County, but our doors are open."

Apparently, Claus and Nash had hit it off. I hadn't decided if that said more about Claus or Nash. But Claus liked the alpha enough to travel with them when they left and check out his hometown.

Opposite to what the archangels were probably hoping for, Claus figured since he could go home anytime, why not stay a while?

Really, the archangels should've known he'd be contrary like that. I'd been to Walker County. The people were quality, but the surroundings were trees, water, trees, and more water. Though he managed to entertain himself well enough while he'd stayed here. But he'd had Quinlan and Rebecca to take up his time.

I held my hands out for Rebecca so Quinlan could hug his half-brother with both arms. I still despised it when he called Quinlan *demonling*, but couldn't ignore how integral Claus had been to our survival, nor the unwavering affection he held for Quinlan.

"Remember your promise," Quinlan whispered before sliding in his space under my arm. "And don't cause too much trouble."

It wasn't until Claus had piled into the vehicle with the other Walkers and driven down the driveway that Quinlan turned to me. "He didn't agree not to cause trouble, did he?"

I shook my head. But compared to the danger we'd just clawed out of, how much trouble could one demon king get into?

Storri, who'd lingered a longer time than Faust would've liked to say goodbye to Claus, ambled over, a daughter on each hip. "I'll miss him," he sighed.

"What's to miss? You have an alpha right here," Faust grunted. He kissed his mate as passionately as he was able while both had their arms full of children.

"I know." Storri smiled. The next second, his smile fell, and his eyes popped open. "Didn't Claus say something about *more* demon kings clawing through the gate?"

Sitka and Quinlan groaned tiredly as Faust used his body to herd Storri toward the hotel. "Let's not search for problems, sweet prince. They have a way of finding us eventually anyway."

———

I WATCHED Quinlan shift from wolf to man, looking over his shoulder to see if I was close.

Sweet mate, you were never out of my sight.

A secretive smile stretched his lips. My baby boy thought he'd gotten away with cheating. He'd been the one to lay out the rules for our hunt: he was to remain a human, and I had to give him a fifteen-minute head start.

At least now I didn't feel bad for never actually letting him get far enough away that I couldn't see him. I was more than eager to fulfill his fantasy, but old habits died hard. It would be a while before I was able to part from him and not worry. This time, my protectiveness unveiled his deception.

Now, I was smiling, observing my mate gain his bearings. He headed toward the coast for a few paces, turning sharply in the opposite direction, where he jumped to the lowest branch of the nearest tree. He easily pulled his body over the branch—impressing the fuck out of me with how well he could move while his pucker hugged the black butt plug he'd donned before we set out for the forest.

My dick throbbed watching him scramble up the branch toward the trunk, where the other branches acted like a ladder he could climb to the top.

I found my own tree directly in front of his and climbed, keeping to the backside of the tree, hiding behind the branches hanging in the front.

Quinlan had found a thick branch that he'd hung his legs off of, one on either side. He peered into the forest, looking down at the ground instead of directly in front of him. He frowned, surely thinking he should've heard me by now.

A snapping branch drew his attention and gave me an idea. I grabbed a pinecone, launching it in the air.

Quinlan jerked toward the sound, his body tense with anticipation. I threw another in the opposite direction, but it wasn't until the third time a pinecone made him gasp that he slid from the tree, bringing his hand to his waist. "Okay, I get it, you've found me," he called out.

The hairs on his arms stuck up when I didn't answer.

"Diesel?" His voice sharpened. "Is that...you?" He rubbed his goosebumps, looking so much like the lost boy he'd wanted to be, it called to my wolf.

Omega. Prey. Claim.

He stepped gingerly back the way he'd come. When he passed my tree, I dropped soundlessly to the floor, following in his footsteps until Quinlan gasped, whirling around with his arm raised.

I caught his wrist before he could strike and pulled him close with a growl. He bounced off my chest, but I strapped my other arm across his back before he could get far.

"Diesel," he gasped, but with less fear than the last time and more breathy desire.

"Diesel? I'm the lone alpha wolf." I puffed out my chest, playing up my part more than I would've if I hadn't been trying to clear some more of that fear stench from my boy.

I preferred him shaking with anticipation, not trembling with fear.

It worked, and Quinlan smiled but quickly dropped back into his part. "Please, sir, I'm lost, and I just need help finding the road."

"You're mine now." I hauled him over my shoulder, kicking and shouting.

"No! Please!"

When my steps faltered, Quinlan changed his tone, sounding less afraid and more like an actor from a B-movie. "I swear, I'll do *anything*."

I set him down. "Get on your knees."

Quinlan's mouth closed with an audible snap. He peered up at my face, as though seeing me for the first time. There'd been no teasing in my command, no hidden joke. It had been an order.

One my baby boy obeyed.

He sank slowly to the forest floor, clasping his hands in front of his body before peering up at me. His scent was sweet, ripe with need. If we'd been at home, I would've undressed him slowly, laying him out on the bed so I could lick over every part of him. But we were in a forest, playing out his naughty fantasy.

"Take me out."

His hands shook, so much smaller than my own. They grabbed the button of my pants and pulled it free, letting my pants drop. I wore nothing underneath, so there was nothing separating Quinlan's lips from my rigid length. I rolled my hips, rubbing the head over Quinlan's mouth, smearing my precum over his lips like lip balm.

He moaned and rubbed his lips together, savoring the taste of his alpha.

"Suck my dick and I'll give you a ride."

His lips twitched up in the flash of a smile before he regained his composure. "Really? All I have to do is suck your dick and you'll help me find my way?"

"That isn't what I said." I grabbed the back of his head, snagging a handful of hair I used to pull his face forward. He had enough time to pull away or say something if it wasn't what he wanted, but my sweet omega just parted his lips and waited for me to fill his mouth.

Who was I to deny him?

My cock jerked the same moment I was enveloped in Quin's warm, wet mouth. He strained forward, attempting to take as much of my length as he could. He couldn't reach the bottom, but not for lack of trying. "Yes, just like that. Take me deep. Show me how much you want me to help you."

Quinlan squeaked and closed his eyes, sucking me off like his life really did depend on it. His cheeks hollowed, creating more slick friction around my shaft. He groaned but never let me fall completely from his mouth. His eyes teared up, his cheeks turning red, as drool and precum leaked from his lips in the corners.

I didn't grip his hair anymore but let my fingers card through the glossy strands, scratching along his scalp every time he brought his tongue against my shaft. Every swipe was a shot of pure pleasure that had my chest rumbling with a deep, unending growl.

"Good boy, getting my dick all ready for that ass."

Quinlan's eyes flew open, desire shining in their depths.

"Do you want that, baby boy?" I cupped his face, rubbing my finger along his chin and neck. "Want to stretch those cheeks open and show me my reward for finding you?"

He nodded as exuberantly as possible while stuffing his face.

His earnest reply filled me and my wolf with pride. Our omega wanted us. He wanted us when we were silly and playing sexy roleplaying games in the forest and when we were ourselves, no games, just him, me, and everything we could achieve together.

I didn't warn him before pulling him off my dick.

Quinlan whined and chased my length with his mouth, eager to get another taste. His eyes—both colors—were glassy and unfocused.

I ripped his shirt from his chest, letting the back hang off him in tatters while I ripped his pants open.

Quinlan mewled, small needy sounds that drove me higher and higher.

Only Quinlan had the ability to tear my attention from everything that wasn't him. He allowed me to relax, to be just me, for as long as we were together. There wasn't a side of me he hadn't accepted, and that was sexier than any tongue trick or new position. Thankfully, we both fucked like we were *grateful*.

I worked my way down his back, letting his skin prickle as I journeyed to his ass. The black plug lay nestled between his cheeks, and I gripped the rim, rotating the toy slightly and making Quinlan gyrate and wail.

"What's this?" I cooed. "Did you try to get lost, baby boy? Were you hoping I'd find you, pull this plug out, and stuff you full of my cock?"

Quinlan tried to speak, but his words came out jumbled, so he nodded instead.

I pulled, slowly freeing the plug.

"Oh fuck! Oh that... Diesel. Oh my god, that feels so good. But empty. I'm so *empty*, alpha."

He had to know, with a voice that begged so sweetly, he wouldn't have to wait long. I pulled his cheeks apart, savoring his gaping hole, stretched open, closing only to clench as if trying to catch the plug and draw it back inside. I had something better.

He didn't need to be told. Quinlan pressed his knees into the dirt, resting the rest of his weight on his splayed hands. His spine arched, popping his ass up and back as if presenting himself to his alpha. That was an archaic shifter tradition, but one I understood the merits of in that moment.

Watching him ready himself *for me* was better foreplay than all the blowjobs put together.

Most of them, anyway.

"If I take you, baby boy, you're mine. I won't show you the road. I won't let you leave. Ever. You'll belong to me. Are you sure that's what you want?"

Quinlan keened and shoved back on my dick, accepting me in one single backward thrust of his hips. His mouth parted, screaming silently as he got used to a length longer and thicker than his plug. His ass muscles clenched, milking me from the beginning.

"Yes, Diesel! I'm yours!"

I drove my hips forward, holding onto his so he wouldn't slam into the ground.

"Fuck! Claim me, alpha!" Quinlan screamed.

His cry snapped the thin restraint I'd clung to. My fingers tightened, my ass flexing as I thrust in, drawing nearly all the way out before slamming back in again. "Mine," I snarled, biting down on his shoulder, my chest blanketing his back as my hips snapped, smacking our bodies together. Reaching around his waist, I found his hard length, stroking it all of twice before he spilled cum into my hand. "Mine!"

I came with his shoulder between my teeth, snarling like the beast I was. Quinlan's high-pitched cries pushed me to go harder, longer, faster, and I did, drawing my orgasm out until neither of us could take it.

When we lay back, panting with him on my chest and my shoulders to the ground, he used his spaghetti-limp arm to drag his palm to my heart.

"This was a good idea." He panted, attempting to catch his breath. "Next time, I want to do a Red Riding Hood thing. I can pretend to be visiting a sick friend..."

"And I get to find you and fuck you in the forest?"

He nodded.

"I'm in."

I kissed him softly, cupping his face with the kindness that I'd held back before. "Whatever you want, Quinlan, it's yours." I stared up through the canopy to the blue sky above.

Quinlan snored and I looked down to find him drooling on my shoulder. I wrapped my arms around him, wishing I'd thought to bring a blanket. Next time I would.

Next time.

These moments still felt like a dream. Like I'd wake up and find Quinlan really was gone, we'd never found a new home or pack family, and none of the nephilim had ever existed. I doubted those worries would ever fade completely, but in time, I'd grow accustomed to this new normal.

To being *happy*.

The End

THANK YOU!

Thank you so much for reading Outlaw! Before I do anything else, I must thank my spouse who went above and beyond to help me have the time to finish this book. He bent over backwards, taking on so much more than a single person should be asked to take. And when I was still having trouble, and needed to dig double down in my author cave, he stepped up again, and went even beyond-er. Thank you boo!

I'd like to give a big thank you to Kiki's Alphas. You all help me so much with your amazing insight but also, your company! Thank you to Leslie Copeland for all your assistance, you make my life easier while making it look effortless. And finally, it wouldn't be a thank you section if I didn't thank my cover designer, Adrien Rose for being so amazing, my editor MA Hinkle and my editor Lori Parks of Les Court Author Services!

About Me

Kiki Burrelli lives in the Pacific Northwest with the bears and raccoons. She dreams of owning a pack of goats that she can cuddle and dress in form-fitting sweaters. Kiki loves writing and reading and is always chasing that next character that will make her insides shiver. Consider getting to know Kiki at her website, kikiburrelli.net, on Facebook, in her Facebook fan group or send her an email to kiki@kikiburrelli.net

The Den Series

(Wolf/Coyote shifter Mpreg and MMMpreg)

Wolf's Mate Series

(Wolf/Lion Shifter Mpreg and MMF)

The Omega of His Dreams

(Non-shifter Omegaverse)

Bear Brothers

(Bear/Hybrid Shifter Mpreg and MMMpreg)

The Jeweled King's Curse

(Dragon Shifter Mpreg)

Hybrid Heat

(Hybrid/Bear Shifter Mpreg and MMMpreg)

Akar Chronicles

(Alien Mpreg)

The Kif Warriors

(Alien Mpreg)

Welcome to Morningwood

(Multi-Shifter Omegaverse)

Omega Assassins Club
(Wolf Shifter Omegaverse)

Wolves of Walker County
(Wolf Shifter Mpreg)

Wolves of Royal Paynes
(Wolf Shifter Mpreg)

KIKI
BURRELLI

Printed in Great Britain
by Amazon